Apple Orchard, Lemon Grove

Sue Johnson

First published in 2017 by Endeavour Media.

Table of Contents

CHAPTER ONE

"It wasn't what you think, Gemma." Mark looked a little too wide-eyed and innocent as she demanded to know who the blonde girl was.

Gemma, coming home early from her mother's birthday party, had seen the girl as she tottered along the frosty street on vertiginous heels towards a white VW Beetle. She'd clearly been inside their house and, from her appearance in a low cut black dress, it didn't look as if she'd come to read the gas meter.

The hastily cleared champagne bottle and two smeared glasses told their own story.

"It wasn't what you think, Gemma," Mark repeated. "We'd just been voted the most successful sales team and were given the bottle of bubbly. It made sense for Marie to come in and share it."

"Particularly as I was safely out at my mother's boring birthday party I suppose?"

"You knew I'd got my sales meeting today and wouldn't be able to get there."

"Obviously not." Gemma whisked around the small sitting room plumping up the red sofa cushions and flicking away specks of dust, wishing she could wipe away the thought of another woman being in here with Mark as easily.

"We didn't sleep together if that's what you're imagining." Mark stood, arms folded, crowding her space.

"The thought never crossed my mind."

"You're paranoid."

"Am I?"

"Gemma, sit down. You're getting yourself worked up over nothing. Let me make you a coffee."

"I'd like to know how you'd react if you saw a man coming out of here at ten o'clock at night."

Mark ignored her and went out to the kitchen, crashing around with mugs and spoons with as much gusto as if he was preparing a gourmet dinner.

Gemma went into the bedroom.

This had been her pride and joy when they'd chosen the décor and furnishings together. The colour scheme was black, white and grey with touches of red. Black roses were entwined in the wrought iron bed frame and the sheets were crisp white linen. Gemma twitched back the black duvet cover and a grim smile crossed her face.

She went out to the kitchen. Mark looked up from his coffee making. He'd clearly been at pains to make amends – he'd actually put biscuits on a plate.

"How do you explain these?" Gemma held the offending pink lace briefs out between finger and thumb before dropping them in the bin.

He gave her the same wide-eyed look that was beginning to get on her nerves. He must've been practising it in front of the mirror. "I saw those in the bed earlier Gems, I thought they were yours."

"Think again sunshine – you should know me better than that. I can't stand pink and I'd never buy from Primark."

She threw the coffee down the sink and went back into the bedroom, hauling her dark blue suitcase out from under the bed.

"What are you doing?"

"I should've thought that was obvious. I'm leaving you."

"But you can't. We're going to Brian and Francesca's tomorrow."

"Take Miss Pink Knickers with you." Gemma bundled undies and jewellery into her suitcase, the mood that had persisted since she woke up this morning that had led her to call time on a job in a boring sales office with an obnoxious boss was carrying her through. *'New Year, new start.'* She repeated the mantra she'd been practising with her friend Laura.

Mark stood in the doorway, a smug expression on his face. "You and your mother won't last more than a week in the same house together."

"Who said anything about living with my mother?"

"You'd have to – you couldn't afford to rent anything on your own and your friend Sarah said you'd left your job, so it looks like you're stuck here doesn't it?" He stood, arms folded, still looking unbelievably smug.

Gemma made a mental note to give Sarah a telling off for blabbing her news. She hoped she hadn't plastered it all over Facebook like she did every time she had a row with her current boyfriend. Thankfully, Sarah didn't know the rest of her news.

She took a deep breath. "I'm not stuck anywhere I don't want to be, Mark." She quaked inside, knowing how angry he could get – cold, quiet anger that dripped like poison.

"If you don't mind me saying, it was pretty stupid of you to leave your job if you hadn't got another one to go to."

Gemma paused with her folding of t-shirts. "If I remember correctly, Mark, you were the one who urged me to tell Veronica what to do with her job – I was worth more than that."

He didn't say anything.

"Anyway, I already have another job."

"Where?"

"As a matter of fact, I have another job as a result of an inheritance – so I don't need anyone's help or patronising comments, least of all yours." She zipped up the case and locked it.

"An inheritance?" Mark's face was like a stopped clock. "Who from?"

"My Great Aunt Anna."

"The barmy one with all the cats? That'll be good, you'll be clearing up cat shit all day."

"It's got nothing to do with cats." His attitude stung her into saying far more than she intended. "I've got a half share in a restaurant."

"Half share with whom? Where is this place?"

"I don't know who the other person is – and all you need to know is it's a long way from here. And as we're not an item any more, it's definitely no concern of yours."

"So let me get this straight – you're heading somewhere you've not been before, so you're bound to get lost. You're going to be in partnership with some woman you've never met before who may well be a weirdo and you've got a half share in a restaurant and you can't bloody cook."

"Did I say I was in partnership with a woman?" Gemma picked up her suitcase and wheeled it to the door. She put on her jacket, slung her handbag over her shoulder and slammed the door on the mocking laughter that ended abruptly with her last comment.

She hurried to her car and slung everything into the boot and locked it. She'd just got in and started the engine when he came out, yelling at her to stop, be reasonable. Well, she'd had enough of his cheating behaviour. Miss Pink Knickers was the last in a line of occasions when she'd suspected him of cheating.

It was only when she'd reached the first roundabout that she remembered she'd lent her Satnav to Mark and that she hadn't the faintest idea how to read a map. Well, there was no way she was going back into that house to ask him for it back. She'd either have to buy another one or get someone to help her.

At the first service station she found, she stopped for the loo and phoned her friend Laura. Laura wasn't a snitch like Sarah and she'd always come top at geography in school exams.

Laura had looked it up on her computer and read her a list of road numbers. Armed with the list, Gemma felt ready to go.

"Ring me in two hours to let me know where you are," said Laura.

"I'm not that bloody hopeless," said Gemma.

"No, I know, I'd just like to know you're safe, especially as they've forecast snow."

Terrific, thought Gemma, *I hate driving in snow.*

According to what the solicitor had told her just a few hours ago, she and her unknown partner could move into the property tomorrow. It was fully furnished, although from what Gemma remembered of a long-ago visits to her Great Aunt, that could mean anything. She had a collage of memories of visits to a bluebell wood spliced with picking apples, eating lemon cake and the clamour of a litter of black and white kittens when they smelled fish cooking. Above all, she remembered the stories about Italy – although she was never sure if her Great Aunt had ever been there.

Gemma stopped when she reached a Travel Lodge not far from her destination and took a few hours well-earned rest. The next morning, after a breakfast of tea and pain au chocolat, she set off on the last section of her journey. Despite her assurances to Laura that she was OK now, this proved to be the hardest part. She got lost several times, stopped to pick up supplies which took ages because she wasn't sure of the culinary tastes of her new business partner, and arrived outside the dilapidated building just as snow was beginning to spiral from a yellow sky.

A sense of unease churned inside her when she caught sight of the tall, dark haired man walking towards her.

Stefano sat in his make-shift den in the orchard watching as large snowflakes drifted past, blanketing everything, deadening sound. It was a relief to feel the biting cold as it took his mind off the ache in his heart when he thought of Sofia.

At least this English orchard was nothing like the sun-kissed lemon groves where he and Sofia had made their promises to each other. Promises, it turned out, that meant nothing to her. They had met in a bar in Marina Grande. She was wearing a red bikini and had looked at him over the top of her sunglasses when she thought he wasn't looking at her. They had gone walking through the olive groves near his grandfather's house and he'd told her about the family-run restaurant and how he was saving his money to buy a small lemon grove.

"Why lemons?" she asked.

"I love to cook with them, I love the smell of the lemon flowers and I like to drink limoncello."

"It is a good thing I am not so passionate about my father's business," she said, "or I would be permanently smelling of fish."

"What would you do if you could choose any job in the world?" he asked her one day when they were lying on rocks by the glittering blue sea.

"I'd be a model or a film star," she said flicking back her rippling dark hair.

She certainly took amazing care of her skin and figure and bought all the fashion magazines she could afford. She worked in a boutique in Sorrento and spent all her spare money on clothes. On several occasions, she caused Stefano to question whether he could afford to have a girlfriend. "A girl expects flowers," she'd say and then he worried that if he didn't treat her well enough, paid too much attention to his own dreams, that she'd go off with someone else.

Trattoria Andrea was run by his family, but since his grandfather's retirement and failing health, Stefano felt increasingly pushed out by his step-brothers. Theo and Luigi were pushier, had ambitions for bigger and better things, for a chain of restaurants and for themselves to be just managers, sitting in the sun and drinking all day. They mocked Stefano for his love of food and for his passion in making sure that things were right. What did it matter – particularly with the English holiday-makers who came to Sorrento? Most of them didn't know good food from bad.

Theo and Luigi had a theory that most English girls who came to Italy on holiday wanted a romance with an Italian waiter that they could boast to their friends about.

"You can buy any woman with flowers and chocolates," was Theo's frequent comment as he went off to meet yet another pale English rose, leaving Stefano to finish his work.

Stefano was pleased at first when Sofia began working at the Trattoria.

"It's the only way I can get to see you. You are always working," she said with a pout that he felt compelled to kiss away.

He was less than pleased when Theo and Sofia began to exchange flirty comments and when his step-brother brought her a taste of tiramisu or anything else they were preparing in the kitchen.

"It means nothing," Sofia said when he challenged her about it. "It's you that I love."

Stefano had held her in the velvet darkness under a crescent moon that hung like a blade over the Bay and breathed in her scent that was a combination of lemons and roses, wanting to believe her.

Stefano looked out at the inhospitable English orchard. The trees were no more than black skeletons. Lemon trees flowered and fruited all year round – 'The Tree of Life' his Nonna had called them. He thought of their glossy green leaves and of persimmons that looked like Christmas baubles and the smell of roasting chestnuts that reminded him of all that was lost to him.

Until a few days ago, his future felt settled. He was going to marry Sofia in the summer. Then a few days ago on a bleak Tuesday when one storm after another had rolled in over the Bay of Naples, he had found Sofia and his step-brother Theo in a storage shed at the back of the restaurant in a romantic clinch that told its own story.

"I had not meant for this to happen, Stefano. Please believe me." Tears poured down Sofia's face but he turned away from her.

"It is not the first time, I doubt it will be the last."

"Tell him, Sofia," urged Theo. "Tell him you have promised to marry me."

"Stefano, your grandfather wishes to speak with you." The nurse who came to attend to Riccardo Andrea morning and evening broke in on the dramatic scene. Stefano was glad of the distraction. His heart vibrated with pain. He had no idea how he would get through the next five minutes of knowing Sofia had broken her promise to him, let alone be here for the rest of his life, attend her wedding to Theo, stand on the side-lines as she lived her life, had children that were not his.

Stefano went from the heat of the restaurant courtyard to the house that had once been a monastery. It was cool inside the thick walls and he remembered how, as a child when he'd got too hot, he'd come inside and laid down on the marble floor. He went up the stairs to the third floor where his grandfather's sitting room overlooked the Bay.

Riccardo's dark eyes lit up at the sight of his favourite grandson. Recently he'd been lost in some private world and had said some strange things. Stefano wondered if this latest distraction was going to be one of them. "You look just like I did as a young man," said Riccardo. "Now it looks as if you too will go to England."

"England?" Stefano stared at his grandfather. He wondered if this was another facet of the dementia that seemed to be gripping Riccardo Andrea as he grew older. However, the cream coloured envelope with its spiky black writing and English postmark was real enough.

The old man was tearful as he handed over the letter. "It arrived today with a letter for me." He paused. "My Anna is gone. May you have more luck in love than I have done, Stefano."

"When did you go to England, Nonno?" Stefano was puzzled. He didn't know anyone called Anna. His grandmother's name was Maria and as far as Stefano knew, they had been perfectly happy until she died three years ago. None of it made any sense.

Riccardo lapsed into drowsiness as the evening light faded and the nurse came to put him to bed.

"Give my love to the bluebell woods," Riccardo whispered as he clasped Stefano's hand for the last time.

Stefano opened the envelope but could understand little of it. He wished he'd paid more attention in English lessons. It was a legal document - that much was clear.

He spent the night twisting and turning restlessly until the lawyer's office opened in the morning. When the information had been explained to him, he spent the day walking by the sea, looking at the patterns of turquoise and aquamarine, at Vesuvius gently smoking on the other side of the Bay and the beautiful island of Capri.

Without a word to anyone – he couldn't face Sofia again or hear any more explanations of her betrayal – he packed a rucksack and left for the airport.

He slept on the plane, waking only when his meal was put in front of him. He got off the plane to the biting cold of a January day in England where everything looked grey and drab, even the people. He was glad there was nothing that reminded him of Italy and glad that fate had put this new opportunity in front of him just when he most needed it.

It was only when he was on the crowded train to Worcester that he began to have doubts. Maybe he should've fought for Sofia more. Maybe he shouldn't just have come to England on a wild goose chase. What exactly was he letting himself in for?

He waited in the cold for a bus to Charworth. An icy wind blew around his legs and he wished he'd got a thick jacket like some of the Englishmen wore.

"Not from round here are you?" asked an old lady with not many teeth. "Well, you're lucky with one thing – this is the last bus today."

The village had one street with a church and a building called *The Green Man* that had flags tied to it and lots of cars in the car park.

Stefano found the solicitors office – 'Leitch and Simpson' – and walked into the old-fashioned interior. A woman in a high-necked blouse who looked like Queen Victoria sat behind a desk that was surrounded by beige files tied with red ribbon. A small fire burned in an old-fashioned grate and she looked at him over the top of half-moon glasses.

"Signor Andrea," she said. "Piacere."

It was the first Italian Stefano had heard since he left Naples and he felt like crying.

"Piacere, Signora," he said clasping her hand.

"Caffe?" she asked, holding up a cup and he nodded gratefully.

"Con zucchero?"

"Si, grazie Signora."

These few words of Italian had unsettled him enough to make him think of customers drinking their coffee on the terrace at Trattoria Andrea. He thought with a grim smile of satisfaction that Theo and Luigi would have to pull their weight now that he was no longer there.

Mr Simpson who looked like an English Father Christmas with his white beard called Stefano up to his office and it was only then that Stefano learned that he was to share this bequest with a young woman.

Despite the old-fashioned ambience of the solicitor's office, the computer system was state of the art. Mr Simpson had scanned and translated the document for him. Stefano and his partner had six months to make a success of the business. If they did so, then the money would be theirs. If they didn't then the money would go to the Anna Murray Cat's Home.

"A home for cats?"

"Miss Murray was a little – eccentric," said Mr Simpson.

"Come una pazza," said the secretary coming in with more coffee.

Stefano left the office with directions to the property.

"Miss Lawrence has the key, she should already be there. Good luck."

"In bocca al lupo!"

Stefano trudged along the street, aware of curious glances. His heart sank when he saw the building. It was filthy and looked as if it would take all the meagre amount that had been allowed for setting up just to clean the place and make it habitable. He tried the door but it was blocked by a blackened plant with thorns on it and firmly locked.

He wandered into the orchard next to the property – rows of leafless trees some that looked as if they had once been plums but now hung like withered bags of wedding favours.

Don't think about weddings, he told himself.

The sky had turned the faded yellow of a bruise and snow like white feathers drifted slowly down. Stefano headed for the shelter of a hut that looked like a storage place for flower pots. It had no door on it and the roof leaked. He was hungry and miserable and trapped here at least until tomorrow – as the old crone on the bus had told him, there were only two buses a day out of the village. Nine o'clock and three o'clock. His feet and hands were so cold they ached and he felt angry at this Miss Lawrence – whoever she was – for leaving him out in the cold. He didn't feel in the mood to trust any woman ever again.

His mood wasn't improved when he saw a woman emerge from a red car by the entrance to the orchard as if she had all the time in the world. She was irritating him already – and according to the solicitor she couldn't cook. It was going to be a difficult six months.

CHAPTER TWO

Gemma advanced nervously towards the door of the café hoping the man would go away. She wondered if he'd been engaged to keep the orchard tidy – not that much looked as if it had been done to it. It was overgrown and the hut that the man had just emerged from looked as if it was about to fall down. He had a covering of snow on his dark hair and his almost black eyes sparked with anger.

"Mees Lawrence?"

Gemma felt agitated. How did he know her name? He sounded foreign – Spanish she thought. He was dressed casually and didn't appear to have a car. She wondered who he was. It was growing dark and the last thing she wanted was to be alone here with a man she didn't know – a man who looked dangerous.

"Who are you? What are you doing here?" Gemma was aware she sounded abrupt.

"I am Stefano Andrea. Your business partner." His dark eyes swept her body defiantly. "Please can we go inside? It is very cold here."

Gemma hesitated. She didn't want to go inside the café and the accommodation beyond with a man she didn't know – with any man come to that, given what she'd just experienced with Mark.

"How do I know you are who you say you are?"

He looked at her questioningly. "Non ho capito. I don't understand."

"Do you have a letter?"

He rummaged in his rucksack and produced a crumpled letter. She could see it carried the heading of Leitch and Simpson, the local firm of solicitors her Great Aunt had used.

"You don't believe me?"

Gemma got out her mobile phone and punched in the number. "Let's just say I don't trust any man right now."

"And I don't like women right now," he said, slouching back to his make-shift den and huddling there.

Five minutes brief conversation with the solicitor was enough to confirm Gemma's worst fears that this was indeed her new business partner and that in order to stand any chance of fulfilling the terms of the inheritance, it was in her interests to let Stefano in and make all possible speed to set up their business and get it going.

The café had a large wooden door now silvered with age. The building had previously been an inn and dated back to the early 1800s. Her Great Aunt had been full of stories about how the Cockatoo Inn had been the refuge of a famous highwayman. It was also said to be haunted by the ghost of a little girl who had drowned in one of the vats of ale, and the orchard next door was reported to have been the scene of many romantic encounters. Not that it looked particularly inviting at the moment!

The café was at the end of the High Street, the last in the line of Georgian buildings boasting cellars that flooded at times of extreme rain and snow and attics with low ceilings where the servants had lived. Her Great Aunt had kept the original name and had even had a stuffed cockatoo in a gilded cage hanging in the café.

Opposite the café was a village green with a duck pond where the carters watered their horses in days gone by. In the fading light it looked like a giant white tablecloth surrounded by the silhouettes of trees. Here and there on the opposite side of the wide street beyond heading towards the church at the far end of the village, a faint yellow light glowed from some of the windows.

Gemma took the large wrought iron key from her handbag and put it into the lock and turned it. Nothing happened. She was aware of Stefano watching her from his hideout and tried to ignore him. She didn't want to be in a position of having to ask him for help and have him look all superior and 'I'm the boss' like most men did. She wondered what had possessed her Great Aunt to treat her like this. She'd always said she loved her. She regretted that they'd lost touch towards the end of her Great Aunt's life and that she wasn't there to comfort her when she lay dying in a hospital in Austria near the Italian border. Nobody knew why she'd taken it into her head to close the café and go travelling.

Gemma took the key out of the lock and tried again, pushing against the door as she turned it. Again nothing happened.

It was much darker now and she could see the sparkle of frost on the pavement and on her car. She thought about leaving Stefano to his own devices and going to stay in a hotel or B & B until the fact that she didn't have much money sank in – plus the solicitor's voice in her head telling her that she and her business partner had to live and work together for six months before the inheritance would be fully theirs to dispose of as they chose fit.

"The best advice I can give you is to stick together," he'd said when she'd gone to see him about the letter she'd found at her mother's. "If one of you goes away for any reason then this will automatically hand the full inheritance to the other party."

"But that's hardly fair," Gemma had argued. "What if one of us has to go into hospital for any reason?"

"You must keep in good health," he said with (for a solicitor) an impish grin. "I and my esteemed friends at Leitch and Simpson will be checking on you on a weekly basis. May the best man - or woman – win!" He'd shaken her hand and she'd left with a feeling of uncertainty wondering what the other person was going to be like.

The feeling of uncertainty had disappeared rapidly when she'd arrived home after a tedious evening making polite conversation at her mother's birthday party, to find proof of Mark's infidelity. On the journey here she'd consoled herself that, however bad the next six months were, she'd gain enough money to buy a small flat and go back to college to do a creative writing degree – something that had met with negative comments and derision when she'd tried to talk to Mark about it. She'd almost forgotten her numb fingers and toes as she realised how he'd gradually been stripping away her self-esteem. Well, from now on she'd manage perfectly well without a man – particularly if he was anything like the specimen next to her.

"You must let me help you. I cannot stand zis cold weather any longer." Stefano's voice cut into her thoughts, sounding sulky.

Gemma jumped away as if he'd bitten her. She'd been so focused on putting her weight against the door that she hadn't noticed him come along beside her. She moved and an icy drop of wet snow went down inside the collar of her jacket making her feel cold and miserable and longing to be somewhere, anywhere, away from here.

You have to stay here whatever happens, she told herself. *It's like being in the middle of one of Great Aunt Anna's fairy-tales – except that there you know you reach the edge of the forest by the end of the story. It's not so certain here.*

Stefano's fingers brushed hers, their touch an electric shock despite the cold as he snatched the key from her impatiently. He thrust it into the lock, turned it with much more force than she had and then shoulder-charged the door. It opened suddenly with a loud crack as if someone had flung it open from the inside and they both catapulted into the dark space inside where a faint smell of gas, stale onions and dust surrounded them. Gemma stumbled against Stefano, found herself steadied by a strong pair of hands. She pulled away from him quickly, dusting herself off as if his touch was infectious.

The interior of the building was pitch-dark. Gemma tried the light switch inside the door. Nothing.

"You 'ave not told ze electric company." Stefano sounded aggressive.

"Neither have you," retorted Gemma.

"I know nothing about such things in England."

"I didn't know my Great Aunt had contact with anyone in Spain."

"Sono italiano. I am Italian."

"Whatever." Gemma felt too tired and dispirited to be polite.

"You have candles?"

"We need light to find them."

"Ecco." Stefano held up his mobile phone. It provided enough light to carve a pathway through to the large square kitchen at the back of the building. In a cupboard under the sink was a crumpled box of white candles. He placed one on a cracked saucer, produced a lighter and the blue and gold candle flame danced, followed by several more set at intervals round the room, illuminating the space enough for them both to see that the task they'd been set looked impossible.

They'd be lucky to make the place habitable within six months, let alone create a profitable business of any kind.

Stefano was the first to break the hostile silence that crackled between them.

"What do we eat?"

Gemma felt a flash of irritation. That was typical. Faced with what seemed like a major catastrophe, all this arrogant male could do was think about his stomach. Anxiety usually had the opposite effect on her. Her friend Laura could eat a whole loaf of bread with butter and jam when she felt stressed whereas Gemma's appetite shrank to mouse-size. The last thing she'd eaten was the pain au chocolat this morning and it was now early evening. Her stomach churned with nerves and she remembered how Great Aunt Anna's cure for any sort of worry was a large pot of tea and some cake.

"Cake makes everything better," she used to say. "It gobbles up the worry gnomes inside you."

"Didn't you bring anything?" she snapped.

"I got you in here," he retorted. "Without me you would still have been waiting outside."

"I've got some things in the car," said Gemma looking out into the dark night and the swirling snow. At this rate they could be marooned here with no prospect of starting any sort of business.

She picked up her car keys and went towards the door, hoping that Stefano didn't take it into his head to slam the door and bolt it and then claim that she'd gone off somewhere. The snow chilled her feet and she thought of the boots she'd left back at the house she'd shared with Mark. No doubt Miss Pink Knickers was prancing about in them – if she happened to be a size six.

She opened the boot and got out the bag of groceries and the tartan rug she kept in the car for emergencies. Charworth used to have a general store, but even if it was still there, it would be closed by now and it wasn't the night to be wandering along a dark street. As she headed back towards the darkness of the open door, Gemma smelled something comforting and familiar. Fish and chips. She looked towards the source of the smell. Further along the High Street there were barley-sugar coloured street lights. Suddenly hungry, she dumped the bag of groceries and the rug inside the door and headed along the street.

The fish and chip shop was quiet. The young man behind the counter who looked like Leonardo diCaprio smiled at her. Gemma smiled back, feeling the tension in her jaw caused by her irritation with Stefano ease.

"Hello stranger," he said. "We've not met before, have we? I'd remember if we had."

Gemma ordered two portions of cod and chips, said yes to salt and vinegar and felt herself thawing out in the greasy warmth of the chippy.

The man behind the counter, whose name was Dan, had eyes that reminded Gemma of a sunlit sea.

"Who have we here?" asked an older version of Dan coming through to the counter from a door at the back with a bucket of freshly cut chips.

"I'm Gemma Lawrence. My Great Aunt Anna used to run the Cockatoo Café."

"Never had the pleasure," said the older man whose voice carried a hint of a Birmingham accent. "When I tried to buy the building I was told some half-baked tale about an inheritance and two people running a restaurant."

"That's right."

"Well I'll tell you this for nothing, you'll have a job getting anything going in a place like Charworth. The locals here don't like change. And if it hadn't crossed your mind, January's a crap time for starting a business. It's just after Christmas and there's no money for poncey restaurants."

Gemma felt the happy glow her introduction to Dan had given her fade away faster than morning mist. She'd been right in the first place. All men were a waste of space. She picked up her fish and chips and headed towards the door. The door slammed behind her and she headed towards the dark end of town with a sense of foreboding.

When she got back into the café, Stefano was sitting with his feet on the scarred pine dining table drinking a glass of wine. He was wrapped in Gemma's green tartan car rug and she felt a flash of irritation. She had memories of making biscuits and jam tarts at this table with her Great Aunt and of sitting under it, sheltered by the red chenille cloth on days when she had friends round for private afternoon tea parties. Gemma had sat under that table cuddling her rag doll and eavesdropping on the stories and conversation. This was her place – not Stefano's.

"Where did you get that wine?"

"In cellar," he said as if it was the obvious answer. "I pour you glass – maybe you be less cranky."

"I am not cranky," snapped Gemma.

Stefano raised his eyebrows. "All women get cranky."

He sniffed. "What is that?"

Gemma looked in the cupboard for plates then decided against them because even without strong light she could see they were dusty and covered in cobwebs. She remembered day trips to the seaside when they'd sat on the beach and eaten fish and chips out of newspaper. Well, they could do the same thing tonight. She pushed one of the packages across to Stefano.

He opened it, sniffed suspiciously as if she was trying to poison him.

Gemma took a mouthful of wine. It was light, fruity and very cold. She sat down on a chair, still huddled in her coat. The kitchen had a modern-looking liquorice black range and a large Belfast sink. The fridge had been left shut and would no doubt be full of mildew. There were plenty of cupboards with duck egg blue doors. The floor was covered in mottled grey tiles and she remembered how she used to roll her marbles across it. Then, the room was warm and full of the scent of baking – combined scents of chocolate, vanilla, lemon and coconut that would soon be carried through to the counter behind the café next door and disappear onto plates or fancy boxes to be taken away.

Her eyes misted with tears as she thought of those happy days, knowing that they were gone for ever. She swallowed down the lump in her throat and opened up her fish and chips. They were still hot, the chips were chunky and fragrant with salt and vinegar and the fish perfectly cooked. She licked the grease off her fingers as she ate, suddenly realising how hungry she was.

Even in the faded light she could see that Stefano had a face like a bulldog chewing a wasp as he picked at his portion as if it was a punishment. Gemma felt a flash of irritation. After all, he was the one who'd complained about being hungry. He may have been the one who'd used brute strength to open the door but she'd had the gumption to go out and find hot food for them. If it hadn't been for her, they'd have been going to bed on a supper of bread and marmalade. *And wine*, she reminded herself. *Don't forget the wine. Trust him to find that.* If she had to have a male business partner, why couldn't it have been someone like Dan? *Stop it*, she told herself. *Men are nothing but trouble. They ruin everything.*

"Is this what English people eat?" Stefano's voice cut across Gemma's thoughts.

Her first instinct was to snap at him. *Calm down*, she told herself, *it's a perfectly reasonable question.* So why did the superior look on his face annoy her so much?

"Yes," she said. "Especially on Friday nights and when we're by the seaside."

"It's disgusting – 'orrible." He pushed the food away like a fractious toddler and poured the rest of the wine into his glass.

"Don't eat it then – go hungry," snapped Gemma. He was thoroughly ungrateful, given that she'd paid for it. She wondered what he'd think of the tins of sausages and baked beans she'd bought. She gathered up the remains of his meal and bundled them into her empty paper, then put the package into the plastic bag that the groceries had been in and tied it up securely.

She stood up and put the groceries – bread, butter, marmalade, teabags, coffee and biscuits into a cupboard and closed the door. She was worried that there might be mice here, especially if the building had been empty for a while. The spiders had certainly had a field day so far. There were webs like ships' rigging and Gemma remembered how Great Aunt Anna used to go round with a feather duster. *"Start up, work down,"* she used to say when teaching Gemma things about cooking and cleaning.

There was a knock at the door.

Gemma looked at Stefano who was still sitting with his feet on the table sipping his wine.

"There is someone at the door," he said.

And it's traditional in England for men to answer it at night when it's dark, she was about to say until irritation with the male race in general made her snatch up a marble rolling pin from the kitchen surround and head along the short passageway to the door.

Dan stood there lit by the torch he was carrying. "I just came to see if you were OK," he said, his eyes crinkling at the corners as he smiled at her. "You left before I had a chance to ask if you needed anything."

Gemma took a deep breath as she changed from irritation to a repeat of the longing that Dan could've been her business partner.

"We'll be fine once we get the electricity connected," she said.

"Is it not working? It should be because the electricity people were around here a couple of days ago. That's why we knew something was going on." He paused. "Mind you, there was a power cut earlier when the snow storm started. Maybe it tripped your switch."

Gemma gazed at him helplessly. She had no idea about anything electrical. She'd always left stuff like that to Mark.

"Want me to have a look? Your fuse box is under the stairs."

Gemma watched as he opened the door of the cupboard where Great Aunt Anna stored things like the vacuum cleaner and the bottles of cooking oil. She'd even grown mushrooms under here once.

"Yeah – just as I thought," he said. "Voila!" He pulled a lever and light flooded the hallway.

"You're a life-saver," said Gemma who felt like hugging him. "I'll be able to have a mug of tea before I go to bed now."

"You can't beat a mug of tea," Dan said. "Unless it's a pint of ale. Maybe we could go to The Green Man one night."

"Maybe we could," said Gemma.

Stefano appeared from the kitchen. He scowled at Dan. "If it was Italia I could have done zis."

"Sure you could, mate," said Dan edging towards the door. "See you, Gemma. Let me know if you need anything."

"Thank you," she said, feeling gratitude to Dan and irritation with Stefano in equal measure.

She went back to the kitchen, rinsed out the kettle, refilled it and switched it on. She opened the fridge door. As she suspected it was full of mildew and it smelled bad.

"We get new one," said Stefano.

"We don't have much money," said Gemma, rubbing her finger and thumb together. "We clean this one."

She made tea – which Stefano declined, along with the instant coffee she'd bought, also dismissing that as "'orrible." If he carried on like that he'd lose a lot of weight in the six months. She drank her tea while Stefano prowled restlessly around the downstairs, relishing the power of making him wait.

Then they did a tour of the building. Gemma, notebook in hand, made a list of the things that needed doing. It covered several pages with everything from cleaning to repainting some of the furniture.

Gemma had carried her car rug up from the kitchen and had put that, together with her suitcase, in the room she used to occupy when she stayed here with her Great Aunt. It had a view of the orchard and the bluebell woods beyond.

She steered Stefano in the direction of the room at the front of the building that was the other guest room. She didn't feel ready to look into her Great Aunt's room yet. The memories were too raw. In the airing cupboard on the landing, she found some blankets and some hot water bottles which she went downstairs and filled with hot water.

"What are they?" Stefano asked but grunted appreciatively when she gave him two to air his sheets with.

They went back downstairs and surveyed the café – the place that would be the nerve-centre of their business. Gemma's heart sank.

"It is impossible," said Stefano.

"Go home then," snapped Gemma.

He glared at her then turned away and stamped up the wooden stairs raising a cloud of dust. She heard his bedroom door slam.

CHAPTER THREE

Gemma woke the next morning to the sound of the church clock striking eight and a feeling of not knowing where she was. She felt a mixture of familiarity and strangeness waking up in Great Aunt Anna's spare room (always called Gemma's Room) with its powder blue wallpaper and indigo carpet. The hot water bottles she'd filled had helped to settle her off to sleep. She'd been so tired from the events of the day before that she'd drifted straight off without worrying as she might have done about mice, moths or anything else lurking in the room. She settled into the bed with its tunnel-like centre and the blue paisley-patterned feather eiderdown that she'd always loved. It had taken several changes of hot water bottle before the bed felt aired but she'd slept almost as soon as her head touched the pillow.

She felt twitchy now that she noticed a spider's web in the corner of her room. She'd gone round with a feather duster that looked dustier than the walls she was trying to clean prior to going off to bed. She'd heard Stefano grumbling as he cleaned his teeth in the cold bathroom about the lack of showers.

"In Italia …" seemed to be the focus of the comments. Well he could jolly well push off back there. It would save her a lot of trouble.

She didn't feel inclined to get out of bed to explain to him that Great Aunt Anna had never liked showers, preferring a hot, deep bath fragrant with rose-scented bubbles. Gemma also preferred baths to showers although she had a passion for jasmine bubble bath. The bath was deep, cast-iron with clawed feet and as a child she used to imagine it coming to life and turning into a lion when they were all asleep and flying over the woods and fields. Sometimes she dreamed it carried her on his back and she soared over the bluebell wood hanging onto his shaggy mane.

Gemma's mobile beeped indicating that a message had come through. She felt guilty when she noticed it was from Laura.

Worried abt u. R u OK? Did u get lost? How is new business partner? Laura xx

Got here OK, she texted back. *Not good. New partner naff.*

Gemma got out of bed and gazed at the orchard and the woodland beyond it that led to the distant hills. It was a monochrome scene. A

Christmas card picture of snow and skeletal trees and a cottage tucked away at the edge of the woods with smoke drifting from its chimney and a red painted front door.

The window she was looking out of was single glazed and frost patterned with exotic leaves and strange flowers. Jack Frost patterns they used to call them and Gemma had loved them, wondering why her mother always complained when they visited Great Aunt Anna.

Her phone rang.

"Are you OK?" Laura sounded worried. "I expected to hear from you last night. What's it like there?"

"Snowy," said Gemma. "Snowy and I'm stuck in a house with a moody Italian."

"Oo ooh," said Laura. "Sounds promising."

"Wish it was. Six months seems a long time. If we ever get off the starting grid."

"You will," said Laura. "What happened to all that 'think positive' stuff we've been talking about? You've got to be better off from getting rid of that arsehole Mark."

"I thought you liked him."

"I did my best for your sake, Gemma, but I didn't like the way he was always putting you down over your writing. I couldn't believe it when he told you not to keep telling people about your poetry because they'd think you were weird!"

"Maybe he was right. It's not like I'm ever going to win the Booker Prize."

"You don't know what you might do – and what about him with his golf. He's not exactly on target for winning the Ryder Cup is he? Come on, Gemma, it's not like you to be so down-hearted."

"I'll do my best," said Gemma. "Anyway, I can hear laughing boy in the bathroom. It's probably time I got up and made a start on this business we're supposed to be running."

She said goodbye and sorted through her case to find a towel and her wash stuff.

Laura rang back. "I knew there was something I needed to tell you. There's a letter addressed to you from that magazine you sent your poems to – Still Waters – was that it?"

"What do they want?" Gemma snuggled into her blanket. It was cold out of bed and she tucked her feet back under the eiderdown.

She was glad she'd had the idea a few months ago of having Laura's address as a return one for any writing she sent off. Mark had not been averse to opening her post and ridiculing anything that had been returned. He usually claimed that he'd thought the letter was for him. Even if the response happened to be an acceptance of a poem or two, he always managed to make her feel stupid because she wasn't getting paid for publication.

There was the faint sound of Laura slitting the envelope and drawing out whatever was inside it.

"Oh – my – God, Gemma," she said. "You've won!"

"Won what?" Gemma had worked on the basis of sending out as much work as she could and couldn't remember where she had sent it.

"A competition with a week's writing course as a prize. Oh congratulations Gem – that's brilliant."

Gemma got a heavy feeling in the pit of her stomach. "When is it?"

"When's what?"

"The writing course."

There was the sound of Laura riffling through pages. "A month from today."

"Bugger."

"What?"

"Bugger, damn and blast."

"What do you mean?"

"I can't go."

"Of course you can – Mark's not around to stop you, is he?"

"No – but my so-called inheritance is. If I leave here even for something like that then I've forfeited my share of the money and there's no way I'm handing over my share of Great Aunt Anna's stuff to some moody Italian."

"They'll let you change it won't they? If you explain."

"I can try," said Gemma doubtfully as she took the number from Laura.

They said goodbye and Laura promised to come if Gemma needed her. "Never thought I'd see you running an Italian restaurant," she said. "It must be your least favourite food. You don't even like pizza for goodness sake."

"I can't stand Italian food," said Gemma, "but I think it'll be down to what we can do between us. Stefano or whatever his name is must be able to cook, being Italian."

"If he can't then you're both in deep shit where the business is concerned," said Laura. "Do you remember how you drove Miss Morgan crazy at school because you always managed to burn everything? You really couldn't boil an egg without burning the saucepan!"

"Don't remind me!" Gemma finished the call with a feeling of frustration. It was her first serious breakthrough with her writing and she may not be able to take advantage of it because of the stupid rules imposed by Great Aunt Anna's bequest.

She gathered up her clothes and headed to the bathroom. Stefano had obviously washed and shaved and whatever else he did and had managed to soak the tiled floor of the bathroom. She pulled the cord that switched on the ancient electric heater that hung from the ceiling, remembering how a visitor of Great Aunt Anna's had been terrified of the fixings coming loose and the heater falling into the bath while she was in it.

Gemma and her Great Aunt had giggled together in the kitchen as they hatched a pretend plan to do just that because the visitor had been such a pain. Gemma noticed how the dust and fluff that had gathered on it had started to smell. She switched it off quickly in case the fluff caught fire – after all, a fire was caused on the London Underground many years ago when someone threw down a cigarette end.

Gemma dressed in jeans and sweatshirt, thinking that she ought to find a way of getting the rest of her clothes from the house she'd shared with Mark – if he hadn't taken them to the tip by now. He'd once said that if she ever left him he'd never forgive her. The intensity on his face had scared her but then it had changed to his usual expression and she tried to pretend that she'd not witnessed that other picture.

She went downstairs. Stefano was already down there. He'd switched on the cooker and it was putting out a comfortable amount of heat. He'd made coffee for himself and was drinking it with that same 'bulldog chewing a wasp' look that he'd used last night when eating his fish and chips.

"Zis stuff is not coffee," he complained, swishing it around in his mug. "It is undrinkable. Non mi piace. In Italia ..."

Gemma didn't want to hear it. "If bloody Italy's that great then piss off back there then."

He obviously didn't understand all the words but he caught the tone of her voice and sank even deeper into a sulk.

Gemma ignored him and put the kettle on, put a teabag in a pink mug that said '*Smile, this is the first day of the rest of your life*' on it. She put some Bran Flakes into a bowl and offered the packet to Stefano. He shook his head.

"I do not eat breakfast." He paused. "Italians do not usually eat breakfast." He looked her up and down. "It is why the women are very slim."

That was unfair. Gemma wasn't fat but she did have a slight 'muffin top' – something that Mark had a sly dig about sometimes. No doubt miss Pink Knickers was perfect in every detail at the moment. She remembered when she could do no wrong – and how she'd gradually become aware that things had changed and he was becoming increasingly controlling and critical.

When she'd checked her phone earlier there had been ten missed calls from Mark – texts and voice mail. She didn't bother to listen to them but deleted them all, feeling a sense of power and freedom that she didn't have to jump to attention every time he said anything.

Gemma ate her breakfast, drank her first mug of tea and made a second one.

She heard Stefano prowling around the downstairs. The place was quiet apart from the tiny sound of a tortoiseshell butterfly, disturbed from hibernation, hitting its wings against the ice-cold kitchen window.

She picked up her notebook with the list of tasks in it and went to join him in the café.

Stefano felt restless. He'd thought from what he'd been told that the business was a going concern and that all he'd had to do was turn up, start cooking and keep going for six months. Looking at this disaster-area of a place with its faded walls and filthy appearance, it could be six months before anything got going.

He felt cold, miserable and he desperately missed Sorrento with its blue sea, friendly people and the scent of lemon trees. He hated this cold, inhospitable country with its snow, bare trees and the unfriendly woman with the hostile grey eyes that he was currently forced to share his life with.

He was sorely tempted to catch the next bus out of this God-forsaken place and head back home. *Except it isn't home anymore*, a voice reminded him. Sofia was lost to him and he wished he could put the clock back, carry her away with him and kiss her until she promised she was his and his alone.

Stefano remembered his promise to his grandfather, Riccardo that he would give his love to the bluebell wood – whatever that was. He'd have to ask Gemma. He sat calming his breathing. His only way forward was to make the best of this place for six months and then he could return to Sorrento with his share of the money, buy the lemon grove he had always wanted and start his own trattoria. Maybe when he was rich and successful Sofia would realise she'd made a mistake and return to him.

He looked at the space he was in – when the windows were cleaned the room would be full of light. At the moment they and the tables and chairs were grimy and full of cobwebs. He tried to imagine an English version of the trattoria. Once he started cooking again he'd feel better. The smell of garlic and herbs would restore his spirits. No wonder the English all looked so miserable if they ate stuff like fish and chips.

Stefano looked up as Gemma came into the room. Her fair hair was scraped back into a pony tail and she wasn't wearing any make up. She was wearing jeans and a black jumper and carrying that stupid feather duster – now festooned with cobwebs and dust.

He looked up and tried to smile. "Today we turn this place into a trattoria – yes?"

She glared at him. "I hate Italian food."

Stefano glared back.

"Lawyer man say you can't cook. I make good Italian food."

She glared at him for a few minutes and then started brushing furiously at some cobwebs on the ceiling.

By mid-morning, Gemma and Stefano had made a good attempt at cleaning the café. They'd sorted things in order of priority – clean first, then see what equipment they needed. Only a limited amount of money had been allocated for redecoration and new equipment so they couldn't afford to waste it.

"Coffee machine," said Stefano. "You have good coffee, people come back."

Dan had returned to see how they were getting on – despite the hostile reception he'd received from Stefano. He'd brought a friend of his who coaxed the ancient boiler into life so now they had hot water and heat pumping round the radiators. He told Gemma about a website where she might be able to get second-hand equipment at a fraction of the cost.

"It'd do you to start off with," he said. "What happens after six months?"

"We go our separate ways I suppose," said Gemma making instant coffee for him. She didn't bother making one for Stefano because of the reaction she'd received at breakfast time. He acted like a spoiled child and made himself one, using the red mug that said 'Boss' on it in black letters.

"Fancies himself doesn't he?" said Dan with a grin as he handed his empty mug back to Gemma. "Let me know if you need any more help."

He went, leaving her with a feeling that she wished he'd stay.

"Why does he keep coming round?" Stefano sounded annoyed. "This is our trattoria. Not his."

"He's only trying to help – and this is a café not a trattoria."

"If I am cooking then it is a trattoria." Stefano looked defiant.

"Look," said Gemma, "if we keep bickering like this we'll just get nowhere fast."

He looked puzzled.

"We need to make a start," she said.

Leaving Stefano in the café cleaning the wooden tables and chairs with some soapy wood cleaner she'd found in the cupboard under the stairs, she headed upstairs and plugged in her laptop. She Googled the site that Dan had told her about and was pleased to find several items on their list that were a fraction of what she expected to pay. Two of the items – a coffee machine and a food mixer – were at the same place, not far from Charworth.

Gemma looked out of the window. It had stopped snowing and the road through the village looked clear. She rang the number and a posh but grumpy female voice answered.

"It's bloody Sunday morning. What's the matter with people? Bloody typical – I've been trying to sell that stuff for months and then the first phone call I get drags me out of the first decent sleep I've had since the Millennium."

"It is nearly midday," said Gemma. "I can call back at another time if you like."

"Call and collect the wretched stuff. If you're not here by three I'll take it to the local tip."

Gemma took down the directions, hoping she wouldn't get lost. She couldn't read a map, had been the worst in her class at geography and hated driving in snow or fog. With a sinking feeling she realised she'd have to take Stefano with her. She wasn't good with a man in the passenger seat either. Mark had always been hypercritical of her driving and on one occasion had even snatched the wheel from her.

She put on her jacket. Best to do it now before she had time to think about it.

Stefano put down his bucket and cleaning cloth eagerly enough. The tables and chairs did look better but there was a long way to go before they were ready to open. Last night they'd set themselves a goal of two weeks. That now seemed wildly optimistic.

Gemma's little red Fiat felt smaller than ever with Stefano sitting beside her. He smelled of a spicy aftershave – sandalwood – and toothpaste.

"Where are we going?"

"Dalesbury – about five miles from here."

Gemma started the engine and put the car in gear with a crunch that made Stefano wince.

"You want me to drive? I have licence," he said.

"I'm quite capable thank you," Gemma bristled.

He sank back into his seat.

After only one wrong turn they pulled up outside an immaculate-looking cottage with a holly tree in the front garden and an excited-looking black and white springer spaniel running around in the snowy front garden.

"I don't like dogs," said Stefano.

"He looks OK," said Gemma, but even so, she approached the front gate cautiously.

A woman with wild silvery hair and red glasses who looked to be wearing an assortment of purple layers opened the front door. "Barnaby, you daft creature, let them get inside before you try to eat them."

Stefano paled visibly.

"She's joking," whispered Gemma.

"Oh."

They went in. The inside of the cottage was a riot of colour. A table was piled high with fabric samples and sections of patchwork quilt. There was a strong smell of lavender which reminded Gemma poignantly of her Great Aunt's airing cupboard – another place she liked to hide when she was visiting.

"Diana Goldsworthy," said the woman holding out her hand. "Do you want a drink or anything?"

Gemma glanced through a door towards a kitchen that didn't look as if it had been cleaned in a long time. The floor was patterned with muddy paw prints and flies buzzed around a salmon she'd obviously been in the middle of preparing when they arrived. There was a faint smell of sour milk.

"We don't want to hold you up," said Gemma.

"This way then."

Diana led them out through the back door, past what looked like the herb garden judging by the faded lavender and rosemary spikes sticking out of the mini snow drifts, to a wooden garage that was sinking lopsidedly to the ground. She picked up a torch and shone it round the inside.

"It's like the Black Hole of Calcutta in here. I can never remember where I put the stuff. It all seems so long ago."

Stefano shot a questioning look at Gemma.

"She means: 'it's dark in here.'"

"Is he deaf or simple?" asked Diana.

"He's Italian."

"I see. It must be difficult having a relationship with someone if they don't speak the language."

Gemma felt hot and bothered. "We're not an item. It's a business partnership."

"That's how these things start," said Diana archly. "My ex had the idea of starting a tea garden here. Then he complained about the place smelling of cake all the time and took to spending more time at the pub. Before long I was left with all the work and he'd buggered off to France with one of the barmaids."

"It's an inheritance," said Gemma, wondering why she was bothering to explain anything to this woman who seemed so prickly. "We only have to do it for six months."

She took the torch that Diana offered her and headed towards the precarious stack of stuff she indicated.

"The bastard said he'd be back for it but he never did. That was three years ago. I wish I'd stuck to dogs in the first place. You know where you are with them."

Gemma found the food mixer and the coffee machine that hadn't even been taken out of its box.

Stefano looked at them and gave an appreciative nod. Then he leapt forward and picked up a box that still had its price label on. It was a pasta maker.

"We must have this."

"That was one of Silly Bugger's impulse buys! Gadget mad he was," said Diana. "There may be more stuff that could be useful to you. I'll get the wheelbarrow."

Gemma was about to retort that they weren't doing Italian food but at that moment she spotted something that almost stopped her heart. It was a chandelier made of crystal glass and tarnished silver. She'd always loved chandeliers, had always wanted one. Last night as she'd gone to sleep she'd imagined their café with something like this – an almost Victorian feel to it. She hoped it wouldn't be too expensive.

"We don't need that," said Stefano.

"If you have the pasta maker, I'm having this," said Gemma, determined to buy it with her own money if she had to.

Diana had poured small glasses of wine for them as they sorted the bill and had charged far less than Gemma had expected.

"It's not my stuff," she said. "I'm just glad to get rid of it. When that hell-hole of what used to be a garage is empty I'm going to replace it with a beautiful summerhouse to do my craft work in."

They loaded the stuff into Gemma's car, padding the chandelier so that the glass didn't break.

"Let me know how you get on," said Diana as she waved them off. "I'm interested."

On the way back they spotted a sign for Sainsbury's.

"We need supplies so we can try out menus," said Gemma, "but we can't get anything else in the car now. We'll have to come out again."

They unpacked the car and then headed out for food. Stefano took charge of the trolley and insisted on buying some pots of fresh herbs from the fruit and veg section.

"Dried ones would be cheaper," said Gemma.

Stefano wrinkled his nose. "They are –"

"I know," said Gemma, "disgusting."

They bickered their way up and down the aisles.

By the wines and spirits section Gemma saw someone she recognised. It was Dan's father from the fish and chip shop. He swept her a cold glance. "You look like an old married couple for all that my Dan's been saying you don't get on."

Gemma bristled and felt her face flush. She felt Stefano go tense beside her.

"Look," he said, "I'll make no bones about it. I want that place of yours and I'm prepared to move heaven and earth to get it. Name your price. You know you're never going to make a success of what you're doing so why not give up now and save yourselves the aggravation?

"No – we're not giving up." Gemma's voice cracked like a whip. "We're going to make a success of this. You wait and see."

The man's hollow laughter followed her all the way to the checkout. She wished she felt as confident as she'd sounded.

CHAPTER FOUR

"The nerve of the man," said Laura when Gemma phoned her later. "Fancy saying that to you. I wonder why he wants your place so badly – particularly when he was virtually running down Charworth and saying it was a naff place to run a business."

"Something there doesn't add up," said Gemma, tapping her pen against her teeth. "I just hope he's not going to prove himself right."

"Don't you even think it," said Laura. "Now I've got a few days off – how about if I gather a few of my cousins together and we come and give you a hand. The place will look totally different with a good clean and a coat of paint."

"But – we can't pay you," said Gemma. "I've been looking at how much it would cost to hire somebody – you know what I'm like up ladders and judging by what Stefano was like earlier when he was trying to clean the ceiling I don't think he's much better."

"We'll treat it like a holiday," said Laura. "We'll bring airbeds and sleeping bags and do some indoor camping. All you need to do is get some food in. And beer. Not to mention wine and chocolate."

"I bet you could do it, you know."

"What?"

"Eat your own weight in chocolate. And probably, knowing you, not put on an ounce. I only have to look at a slice of cake and I've put on half a stone."

"You look fabulous, Gemma. Don't talk yourself down. You get the stuff in, I'll round the lads up and we'll be there to give you a hand."

"Maybe we should take what that man offers," said Stefano as he and Gemma ate cheese on toast in the kitchen that now felt much warmer now that the heating was on.

He'd bought Italian ground coffee and was now inhaling the fragrance. The only problem was that doing so made him think of Italy and the way the sunlight made the sea look as if it was splashed with gold. It was a short step then to thinking of Sofia and the softness of her hair, and the way she'd felt in his arms, slim and fragile like a precious ornament, so different from the woman sitting opposite him with her scruffy clothes, plump body and severely scraped back hair. Sofia would never have dreamed of letting him see her like that.

Sofia is lost to you. She no longer wants you, he reminded himself. He felt a pain in his heart as the reality sank in.

If he went home, what would he go back to? He'd have no money, no girl and no job. He'd be further away than ever from his dream of owning a lemon grove and the best he could hope for would be a job in someone else's restaurant.

He looked at Gemma. "Forget I said that. We need to stay here – right?"

She nodded and he noticed how her eyes were the colour of a dove's feathers.

She's not your type of girl, he told himself. *The best you can hope is that Sofia misses you and realises she has made a mistake.*

He had sent Sofia a text with his address in England but she'd not bothered to reply.

Stefano watched as Gemma cleared the plates away, dumped them in the sink, squirted washing up liquid and washed them up. At least she was tidy. He couldn't bear working with people who were messy and unmethodical in the kitchen. His step-brother Theo was frustratingly untidy and never put kitchen knives or other utensils back in their proper place – something that slowed them down when the Trattoria was busy.

Stefano followed Gemma as she went into the café with its long windows overlooking the village green on one side and the orchard at the back. In one corner of the café to the left of the curved wooden counter was a door. He was surprised to see that it led to some toilets (obviously a café would have some) and that there was another room beyond.

"What is in here?"

He noticed that Gemma's eyes looked watery as if she was about to cry. He hoped not. He didn't cope well with crying women.

Stefano was relieved when she swallowed and seemed to recover herself.

"It's where the knitting group and the book reading group used to meet when Great Aunt Anna was here. She called it the Club Room."

"So what are you doing in here? We must make this trattoria work."

Gemma winced at the word 'trattoria' but couldn't be bothered to argue this time. She explained to Stefano about her friend Laura and her tribe of male cousins.

"They're going to come and help us. Many hands make light work and all that."

"But how do we pay them?"

"We pay them in food and beer."

"So what are you doing in here?"

"They need somewhere to sleep."

Laura could share with her. There was a large sofa in her room and it would be fun – like it was when they shared a flat together after they left college.

Gemma hadn't yet sorted Great Aunt Anna's room. It felt like going into a shrine somehow and she wasn't ready to disturb anything. She'd still done no more than peep round the door but just the sight of the dressing table with its triptych mirror, familiar violet patterned china dishes and the silver hat pin holder made her shut the door again quietly as if afraid of disturbing someone who was asleep.

Gemma swept the floor of the Club Room and beat the dust from the dark green velvet chairs that had been in that room ever since she was a small child. Great Aunt Anna bought them from an auction somewhere – she could never resist old furniture or antique jewellery.

Laura and three of her cousins arrived in a battered 4 x 4 that was so covered in mud you couldn't tell what the original colour was.

"Matt took it off-roading last week and just hasn't got round to cleaning it," said Laura as she hugged Gemma.

The six of them gathered round the kitchen table and made short work of mugs of tea and slices of fruit cake that Gemma had bought during a second visit to the supermarket. They'd found a kitchen shop in Dalesbury and Stefano had bought a fearsome looking collection of kitchen knives and a marble slab that weighed a ton.

"They are not as good as the ones I had in Italy, but they will do," he'd said.

Dan called round to see what was going on just as they were all looking at the café and deciding what the best use of their time would be.

Stefano glared at Dan. "Your father is very rude man. We are not leaving here."

Dan looked at Gemma. "What's he on about?"

Something about his wide-eyed innocent look sparked a memory of Mark. Gemma felt irritated with herself for being taken in by him. What if he was just here to see what he could find out and then report back to his father?

"Your father approached us in Sainsbury's and was very clear about wanting us out of here. Really strange since he wasted no time in telling me that Charworth was a crap place to run a business when I got our fish and chips the other night." She was aware that her tone of voice was cold but she didn't care.

"I'm really sorry," said Dan. "I don't want you to think that I feel the same way. My Dad and I don't always see eye to eye. I'm glad you've come to Charworth."

"Thought I might find you in here." A harsh voice with a trace of Birmingham accent intruded. The clump of heavy boots sounded along the hallway.

Dan's father swung the door back with no concern for anyone who might be behind it.

"I was looking for Dan," he said.

"I believe it's customary for people to knock rather than just barge in," said Gemma with more than a touch of Great Aunt Anna's grand duchess attitude.

"Get you!" Mike Bridges' ice blue eyes swept the room. "You've got a long way to go here haven't you – and no experience by the look of it. My offer still stands. Think about it. Come on Dan – time we were gone."

With an apologetic smile at Gemma that failed to have its previous effect on her, Dan followed his father out of the café.

"He treats him like a dog," said Laura. "What an objectionable man! You've got to get the better of him, Gemma. And bloody cheek to assume we've got no experience. What does he know?"

The group resumed their appraisal of what needed to be done. Matt and Kenny offered to find the local DIY store and bring back some paint.

"And come straight back," said Laura with mock severity. "No going via the pub."

"We paint it white," said Stefano.

"No – too cold," said Laura miming being cold.

"Si – capito," he said smiling at her.

He looked totally different when he smiled, Gemma thought. His eyes lit up like a jar of dark honey with the sun behind it.

"White looks clean, though," she said, wanting to show him a bit of support now he was being nice to her friend. "What about apricot white?"

Stefano's dark eyes looked confused, so Gemma looked at one of the paint charts Matt had brought with him and pointed to the suggested colour.

"Capito."

"Apricot white it is then – and then we could get some curtains in a terracotta colour. The tables and chairs look good as they are. No point making work," said Laura.

"Agreed," said Gemma.

"You'll get away with just a coat of varnish on the floor too," said Matt.

Stefano had gone back to the kitchen. It looked much lighter since Paul – Laura's other cousin – had started work on the windows. He apparently did a window cleaning round as his day job.

"Bit of a busman's holiday," he said as he got the ladder out of the cellar.

Stefano had no idea what he meant but he could see an immediate improvement. He arranged the pots of herbs – basil, thyme, rosemary and mint – along the windowsill. The leaves shone in the afternoon sunlight and he felt comforted by this link with home. At the Trattoria there had been a kitchen garden with pots of rosemary and sage. The washing smelled of lavender and fresh air when it was hung out there to dry.

His knives in their wooden block made him feel as if he knew where he was. He was also happy to have found a collection of good-quality saucepans and mixing bowls in one of the cupboards. In the kitchen shop in Dalesbury he'd bought some wooden spoons and a dark blue striped apron.

He felt an outsider amongst this group of English people even if they were all here to help him and Gemma against what he now saw as the hostile locals.

Stefano gathered tomatoes, oil, onions, garlic and cooking wine and began making a tomato sauce.

In the supermarket earlier Gemma had pointed out the jars of pasta sauce. She'd laughed when he'd wrinkled his nose.

"I know – 'orrible," she'd said.

Again, her dove grey eyes had lit up reminding Stefano poignantly that she wasn't Sofia.

He switched on the cooker and began chopping herbs and garlic, happier now he was working properly than he'd felt since he'd arrived in England.

Gemma felt a sense of relief as the café began to look loved again. Thanks to Paul, the windows were now gleaming. Inside the café, Kenny and Matt were preparing the walls ready to paint them tomorrow. Paul had unfastened the swinging sign that used to have a picture of a cockatoo on it and had brought it in so it could be repainted with the new name.

"What are you calling it?" asked Laura.

"No idea. Stefano wants trattoria something or other – and you know how I feel about Italian food!"

"You can't have a business without a name, Gemma. Come on – let's start thinking. Then we can set up a website and a Facebook page and start advertising."

"That sounds scary. Must we do that yet?"

"You've only got six months to show a profit. You need to get moving. You don't want to prove Mr Chips right do you?" Laura pulled a mock-severe face at her.

"Definitely not," said Gemma, "but we've not thought about menus or anything yet."

"Let's get going then. And you need to get that landline reconnected. Fast."

"I've always managed OK with a mobile."

"You're a business-woman now. You need a landline."

Laura made a scary-looking list of the people they needed to contact about the new business.

The smell of paint drifted from the café mingling with the fragrant aroma of garlic and herbs. The lads had demolished a large packet of chocolate Hobnobs, half a tin of Roses chocolates and copious amounts of tea and the café ceiling gleamed white. Paul had cleaned the chandelier and hung it and it flashed rainbows in the late afternoon sunlight.

It had gone colder and the pavement outside was sparkling with frost again.

Kenny had set his MP3 player on one of the tables and was jigging around to a loud fiddle tune as he transformed one of the walls from grimy grey to apricot white with his paint roller. All of a sudden, he stopped.

"Blimey – did you see that?"

"What?"

"Some bloke in a BMW took the bend a bit fast and just spun off the road. I hope he hasn't damaged his Beamer."

Kenny didn't have a very high opinion of BMW drivers, considering them all a bit reckless.

"Let's hope he hasn't damaged himself more like," said Paul heading for the door.

Stefano had already come from the kitchen – he'd heard the squeal of brakes – and was shedding his apron as he did so and following the lads out of the door.

They returned within a few minutes with a man and a woman, both dressed for a special occasion, he in a charcoal grey suit and she in dark blue silk, and both looking shaken.

The man looked annoyed. "Stupid young cyclist with no lights on – in this weather and at this time of day!"

"Are you both OK? Do you need an ambulance?" asked Gemma.

"Good lord, no," he said, "but a cup of tea would go down well."

Laura hurried out to the kitchen to make tea for them and Gemma settled them in two of the dark green velvet chairs in the Club Room surrounded by the three lads' mattresses and sleeping bags. The man had several conversations on his mobile – one about his car, another to the place they were going that evening and a third to someone who could have been his boss. He looked a bit despondent when he finished this call.

His lady friend was auburn haired with china blue eyes. "It's lucky for us you were here," she said to Laura and Gemma. Her voice carried a trace of an American accent. "I hope we're not putting you out. It seems the breakdown people can't get here for another two hours. The world and its dog appears to have had an accident of some sort this evening."

"It's OK," said Gemma, "we weren't going anywhere."

"It looks like you've got quite a party going on here," said the man. He had dark hair with distinguished looking flashes of silver at the temples and hazel eyes.

"It's not a party," said Laura. "Myself and the lads are here to help Gemma and Stefano. They're opening this as a restaurant next week."

"Really – how interesting." The man's face brightened up. "Molly and I were just on our way to Birmingham to visit friends and to interview a couple who first met when they worked in a fish and chip shop together. I'm Allan Sheppard, I'm a restaurant critic for The Telegraph." He turned to Molly. "What do you think, Molls? We've put the Spraggs off till next month when hopefully the weather will be better. Why don't I see if my editor would be happy with a piece about the … what's it called by the way … instead?"

"It's called *The Inheritance*," said Gemma with a confidence she didn't really feel.

She could hear Laura out in the kitchen squeaking with excitement as she told the news to Stefano.

"Great name," Allan said. "I look forward to hearing the story. Is there somewhere near here that we can get a meal? I can let the breakdown people know where we are."

Stefano came in. "I have food nearly ready for you. You eat lasagne al forno and salad? On the 'ouse. You are first customers."

"We both love Italian food," said Allan, his face brightening.

"Gee, this is so exciting," said Molly. She got up and headed towards the half-decorated café where Stefano had set a table complete with large white napkins and a posy of fresh herbs in a small glass vase. "Is it OK to take some photographs before I've had too much of that excellent looking red wine?"

She got a camera out of her black leather bag and started clicking away, trying out interesting angles, getting close ups of the table and shots of Stefano working in the kitchen and then of him and Gemma together.

"Look as if you like each other," she said.

"So – tell me about *The Inheritance*," said Allan when all the food had been disposed of. "It's an original name for a restaurant."

Gemma noticed how Stefano's jaw tightened. He obviously wasn't pleased about the name, neither did he want to say much about his home life in Italy – other than about his grandfather Riccardo Andrea having happy memories of England and telling him to give his love to the bluebell wood. His eyes looked sad when he talked about his grandfather and Gemma wondered once again what connected him to her Great Aunt.

Allan and Molly's breakdown truck arrived shortly after they'd finished their coffee. The food had been thoroughly praised, making Stefano glow with pleasure. Gemma noticed how his eyes had that look of sunlit honey again.

"Two satisfied customers," said Laura as she helped Stefano serve up lasagne for the rest of them. "Well done."

Gemma's only previous experience of lasagne had been a ready meal her mother had bought her from a supermarket. (Gemma couldn't remember her mother ever cooking anything from scratch). She remembered it as tasting bland and about as interesting as blotting paper soaked in tomato ketchup. That experience – and her mother's attempt to cook spaghetti Bolognese – had totally put her off Italian food. However, she didn't want to spoil the party atmosphere by making a fuss about preparing something else for herself.

She poked at her portion with a fork, lifted it to her mouth and swallowed it. She was unprepared for the explosion of tastes. It was quite possible that she was dog-tired again and that anything would've tasted brilliant with or without full-bodied red wine. Much to her surprise (and Laura's), she cleared her plate.

"Here's to *The Inheritance*," said Laura raising her glass.

"Why is it called that? I don't like it," said Stefano.

"It's what it is," said Gemma, "because we've both inherited it so it can be what we want it to be – café, trattoria or a mixture of the two."

"It's really exciting – the thought of you being in *The Telegraph*," said Laura when she and Gemma were settling down to sleep.

"What if he wasn't from *The Telegraph* at all and was just a posh bloke and his girlfriend trying to blag a free meal?"

"Gemma Lawrence – you really must get back to some positive thinking, right now," said Laura throwing her pillow at her. "How lucky is it that someone like Allan Sheppard crunches his car outside your soon-to-be restaurant and you get an interview without having to wait like everyone else? You wait and see – your business will take off like a Harrier Jump Jet and it'll be plain sailing all the way."

Gemma laughed at the mixed metaphors as she threw the pillow back at Laura. *Perhaps my luck is changing*, she said to herself as she settled down to sleep.

However, she was soon to find that it wasn't.

CHAPTER FIVE

In three days, the Inheritance Team, as they called themselves, had transformed the café into something that looked as if it would do what it said on the freshly painted black and gold sign that until now had a faded picture of a cockatoo on it.

The front door was repainted gleaming white, the brass knob gleamed from the polish Paul had given it. The windows were clean and free from cobwebs and the walls in the café glowed warm apricot and danced with light from the elegant chandelier. The tables all had small vases of fresh flowers and soft music played creating a peaceful atmosphere.

Laura had bought them an A-frame style chalk board that they could stand outside. 'BOOKINGS NOW BEING TAKEN,' it said in large letters.

Laura and the lads had departed at the end of the third day with promises to return later to see how things were going and to sample some more of Stefano's food.

"Maybe we'll get to taste some of yours next time too, Gemma," they said.

"Not if you value your future existence," she said.

"You're fine so long as you don't panic," said Laura. "As soon as old Ma Morgan started shouting at you at school you used to go to pieces and do something daft like the time you dropped that lemon meringue pie on the floor."

She hugged Gemma. "Good luck, love. You deserve it. Don't forget to phone if you need help with anything. We'll be here like a shot – won't we lads?"

Stefano gave Laura the traditional Italian farewell of a kiss on each cheek when she thanked him for all the lovely food. "It ees pleasure," he said with a smile that lit up his eyes.

Gemma watched the battered 4 x 4 disappear down the road towards the M5 with a feeling of panic. The place was unnaturally quiet without the four of them even though they'd only been there for three days. She felt that she and Stefano were now truly on their own and it was a weird feeling now that their business was being advertised and coming under scrutiny.

Mike Bridges had kept his distance since his last intrusion. Now he was making his presence felt – making snide comments about falling over their A-board when he walked along the pavement (although where he was going was anyone's guess as the café was the last port of call along the street) and staring at Gemma in a hostile way when he saw her in the Post Office queue.

The following day, the article was in *The Telegraph* complete with photos of *The Inheritance* and of Gemma and Stefano standing under the beautiful chandelier toasting each other with glasses of wine. Allan Sheppard had done a good job with the article and for several days the new landline didn't stop ringing. The local paper and several magazines rang to ask if they could come and do an interview.

"You should hold a Grand Opening and invite people to it," said Laura.

Diana, who had called in to see how they were getting on, had suggested the same thing. "I was also going to ask if I could hold a weekly patchwork class in that Club Room of yours," she said. "Maybe with afternoon tea – scones and so on."

They agreed on a Tuesday afternoon and Gemma wrote the details down in the black leather diary that she'd bought from the posh stationer's in Dalesbury.

"I'll let you have some names of people to invite," Diana said. "Bye for now."

Stefano didn't understand English people's fascination with afternoon tea. He'd tried a scone that Gemma had bought him when they went on one of their shopping trips but pronounced it ''orrible' as he did most English food. He also didn't understand why so many of them felt the need to eat as they walked along the street. In Italy, people met their friends for coffee and pastries in a bar or cafe. They only thing they might eat in the street was a gelato. Here people waddled about carrying far too much excess weight and they couldn't possibly taste the food they rammed down their throats.

Also, he'd noticed that the women particularly didn't dress well. In Italy there was emphasis on fare la bella figura – making an effort to look good when you went out. He'd only ever seen Gemma in jeans or jogging bottoms and a grey or black sweatshirt as if she was trying to fade into the background.

Stefano missed some of the clothes he'd left behind in Sorrento. No doubt by now Theo, who was about his size, was borrowing them.

There was a scullery just off the kitchen that housed a washer-drier and a dish-washer. It had a door that led to the garden and then into the orchard via a lop-sided wooden gate. From the doorway he could see the ramshackle den he'd sheltered in on the day he arrived.

He noticed Gemma come into the kitchen and felt a twinge of irritation. She looked awkward as she took the lid off the flour bin and started measuring the fine white powder into a bowl. A dusting went on the work surface and he suppressed the urge to go and wipe it up. He watched as she measured and weighed margarine and sugar and crumbled it into the flour. She started to look flustered as she fussed with the oven, getting the dial to the right temperature and then greasing and dusting baking trays with flour. She hunted in a drawer for a round cutter with curly edges before mixing the dough to a soft consistency with milk and beaten egg.

She flattened the dough to about two knuckles' width and then started cutting round shapes and placing them on the baking tray.

"That doesn't look right," he said. "It is too thick for pastry."

She jumped and her dove grey eyes darkened with – what? Fear? Stefano hoped she wasn't scared of him.

"I'm making scones," she said, "not pastry. To see if I still can."

Stefano shrugged and went off to his room. He'd need all the energy he could summon to cope with the evening's customers.

Gemma was relieved when Stefano left the room and let her get on with being in a world of her own. Laura's comment about the torture of being in Miss Morgan's food technology class had reminded her that it was around the time her father died and her concentration was poor. Then their nice food tech teacher had left to have a baby and Miss Morgan – small, dark and Welsh – had replaced her and from day one had taken a dislike to the dreamy Gemma.

"Waken up, Gemma," or "Pay attention Miss Lawrence," were amongst the more polite comments. Usually she just screamed 'No, no, no," at her – usually at the point when Gemma was getting something in or out of the oven – which was how she came to drop the lemon meringue pie on the floor, thus earning a detention on top of having the clean the floor. This in turn meant she missed the school bus and had to walk home and was then too late to get the things her mother wanted from the supermarket because it was closed.

Gemma remembered how it had been so different when she was staying with her Great Aunt. She'd let Gemma decide which cakes and biscuits would feature on the café's counter that day – and she'd be able to help make them.

Under her Great Aunt's gentle tutelage, she'd created a whole range of flavours from white chocolate chip to lemon and ginger. She'd made scones and she'd created bite-sized fairy cakes that looked so lovely on the large ribbon plates standing at different levels on the counter.

She'd been confident here – as if being at the café with Great Aunt Anna surrounded her with a special kind of magic.

Mark been partly responsible for killing that magic. He'd said he liked her cooking at first but then there'd been that terrible day when he'd invited his hyper-critical mother for Sunday lunch and everything had gone wrong. They hadn't been together very long and the original plan had been to go out for lunch – at least that's what he'd told her. Gemma was relieved because on the occasions she'd met his mother they hadn't really got on. She'd planned her outfit carefully and focused on the fact that it was unlikely to go on for more than a few hours.

Then the day before they'd met his mother while they were out shopping and he'd said: "We can meet at the Blue Boar and have something to eat or if you preferred, you could come to us."

Jane Cooper couldn't fail to have noticed Gemma's look of shock. There was a brief pause and then, her eyes gleaming with malice she said: "Ooh Sunday lunch at yours would be lovely. Thank you, Mark." She acted as if Gemma wasn't there.

"Why did you say that?" asked Gemma as they walked away. Her legs were shaky and she felt sick. "We've got nothing in and I don't even know what she likes."

"Oh Mum's no problem," said Mark. "She eats most things. I'm sure you'll manage to rustle something up."

He'd gone to football that afternoon, leaving Gemma to clean the flat and make a return trip to the supermarket.

"Chicken," advised Laura. "You can never go wrong with roast chicken. And stuffing, roast potatoes and veg, Aunt Bessie's Yorkshire puddings, gravy. That's the first course sorted out. Then you can do one of your lovely apple crumbles for pudding. Nobody could resist that."

Gemma put down the phone feeling more confident. By the time Jane's arrival was imminent, the house looked tidy, the chicken was in the oven and she'd made the apple crumble, adding chocolate chips and organic oats to the flour mixture.

There was just time to lay the table and then go upstairs and get changed. She'd pulled on jogging bottoms and a faded blue fleece to do the cooking in.

Then disaster struck. Mark had been out in the garage tinkering with the car. He walked back in through the back door bringing a trail of damp grass cuttings on his trainers that he'd promised to clear up three days ago when he cut the lawn. Gemma's immaculate floor was covered. Mark tried to help her clear up the mess but all he succeeded in doing was getting her more wound up.

Gemma got changed but her hair and makeup didn't go right.

Mark had told his mother to arrive at midday so Gemma had timed the lunch for twelve thirty. By one o'clock she still hadn't arrived and Gemma was going frantic.

"Are you sure you told her midday?"

"You heard me," he said.

"Well where is she then?"

She arrived at one thirty. The chicken was dry and tasteless, the vegetables overcooked.

"Oh dear, disaster in the kitchen is it?" she said as she surveyed what was on her plate.

"You were late," said Gemma through gritted teeth.

"We never used to have Sunday lunch before one thirty did we Mark?" she said.

"No," said Mark, not meeting Gemma's furious glare.

Since then, Gemma had never attempted anything like a Sunday lunch again – particularly as Jane Cooper always introduced her as "My son's girlfriend who can't cook."

Laura had told her at the time that the whole thing was totally unfair. Mark should've backed her up – or they should at least have eaten theirs and left the old bat's on a plate to be reheated when she deigned to turn up.

Great Aunt Anna would've restored Gemma's confidence in a flash but by the time of that incident she'd closed up the café and gone travelling.

"Gone a bit 'bats in the belfry' in her old age," was Gemma's mother's view.

The scones came out of the oven filling the kitchen with the smell of fresh baking. She put them on a wire rack to cool, made a pot of coffee and then called Stefano.

"Would you like to try one?"

He looked suspicious. "OK."

Gemma got two plates, split two scones, got clotted cream from the fridge and strawberry jam from the cupboard.

"This is a cream tea," she said. "Except we're having coffee. It depends on whether you're in Devon or Cornwall as to whether you put the jam or the cream on first."

Stefano smiled. "You English are very strange."

He bit into his scone. "Is good. Much better than the other ones."

"Not 'orrible then?"

"No."

There was a knock on the door and Diana arrived bringing with her a young girl who looked like her except that her hair was blonde not silver.

Gemma led them through to the kitchen, poured coffee for them and offered scones, jam and cream.

"This is my niece, Francine," said Diana. "She's at college in Worcester during the week but could waitress for you some evenings and weekends. I thought you could do with some help for your Grand Opening."

Leaving the kitchen table covered in sticky crumbs, they wiped their hands and went into the café.

"Very impressive," said Diana. "That chandelier deserves to be shown off." She looked thoughtful. "There is one thing though, if you don't mind me saying."

"No – what?" asked Gemma.

"It's a bit plain isn't it? Those walls could do with some pictures on them."

"I did think about that," said Gemma, but money's a bit tight until we get going and it needs to be the right sort of thing."

"I'm doing an art degree," said Francine who only looked about fifteen, "and I've got friends who could also show you some work. We could put price tags on them and if they sold we could give you some of the money."

"You paint pictures?" asked Stefano.

"Si, certo." Francine's Italian was hesitant.

"I used to paint pictures too," he said. "Once upon a time in Italy."

Gemma shot a surprised look at him. This was the first she'd heard of this. He'd not even attempted to pick up a paint brush and help when Laura and the lads were here. She noticed the glitter of tears in his eyes as he turned on his heel and went up the stairs to his room. She heard the door slam and then silence.

There was an awkward silence downstairs. Diana, Francine and Gemma stood under the chandelier.

"That's what you call a temperamental Italian," said Diana, "is he always like that?"

"Not always," said Gemma. Something had clearly upset Stefano and her heart ached for him.

Up in his room, Stefano leaned on the windowsill looking out at the street below and the remains of the snow that looked the colour of soft brown sugar where it gathered at the edges of the road and pavement.

He knew he was being over-sensitive but the mention of painting made him think of his childhood dream to be an artist. His mother had encouraged his dream, but she had died when he was in his early teens and his father married again barely a year later to a woman with cold eyes and two older sons. His Nonno Riccardo had been full of praise for Stefano's paintings but had sounded a note of caution. "Sono importante i soldi. Money is important."

When Stefano had followed his step-brothers into the restaurant he'd tried to put his artistic talent to use with every plate of food he served. He had a theory that if food was prepared and served with love then it tasted better.

Theo and Luigi merely chided him for taking too long to do things. "Customers want full bellies not works of art," they said.

He wondered if Theo was similarly impatient when making love to Sofia. Stefano had liked to make each occasion special. He'd planned each time they were together with care, paying attention to colour and scent, taking things slowly so that they unwrapped each other like a gift. He thought she was happy with him. What did he know? Maybe it was true what he'd read in magazines that women liked the 'treat them mean, keep them keen' approach.

He remembered how his step-brothers had ridiculed his attempts at painting- much as he expected they would. However, when he'd shown a painting of a lemon grove with sunlight lighting one of the lemons like a light bulb to Sofia she'd laughed too.

"I hope you have grown out of doing this," she'd said.

Stefano didn't want to grow out of it but he'd lost the confidence to try any more. He didn't know if it would ever come back.

Gemma knocked on Stefano's bedroom door. She didn't know if she was poking her nose in where it wasn't wanted, but the look on his face had struck a chord with her. She wasn't sure why – but something about the mention of artwork had made him look sad. She knew he'd recently lost his grandfather – maybe he'd been an artist?

The door opened and Stefano stood there. His hair was standing on end as if he'd been running his fingers through it. "I brought you some coffee," she said, holding out the red mug with 'Boss' on it.

"Thank you," he said. He took the mug from her, his warm fingers brushing hers causing an electric shock against her skin.

"You looked upset downstairs," she said, then faltered.

"Yes," he said.

He looked as if he might say something else but Gemma heard the phone ringing and hurried to answer it. The moment was lost and she didn't know if she'd ever find out what had affected him so much.

Gemma finally remembered to contact the organisers of the poetry competition to see if she could change her prize week to another time. Having read the rules again, she didn't hold out much hope.

"I'm terribly sorry," said the snooty woman at the other end of the phone, "but I'm afraid our rules clearly state that the prize has to be taken on the course running from 8th – 15th April. I'm sure if you explain this to your boss they'll let you take annual holiday so that you can attend. You can also bring a non-writing partner for £150 if that's part of the problem. I know some men don't like being left to their own devices."

"I have to stay here because it's part of an inheritance deal," said Gemma. "If I go away even for a night then the other person will have won." She paused. "I don't suppose it's possible to have the money instead?"

"No – definitely not. I am sorry."

She didn't sound it.

"Bugger, damn and blast," said Gemma as she put the phone down. It felt as if she'd almost reached the gates of the castle and now the drawbridge had been pulled up and there was no way of getting in.

CHAPTER SIX

The date for the Grand Opening was set for Valentine's Day and bookings were flooding in. Gemma and Stefano had been interviewed by the local paper and were now frantically trying to sort out menus, extra waitresses and other ideas to make the evening memorable.

The walls of *The Inheritance* were now hung with paintings – many of them had sold within days of being put there – and the Club Room (renamed the Cockatoo Room in memory of the original name of the building) now had three groups meeting there – Diana and her patchworkers, an art group and a book review group. In addition, a man called Guy with long grey hair who said he was a local poet called in to ask if he could book the café for a storytelling and poetry evening. Gemma agreed and also found herself promising to read some of her own poems.

Gemma had noticed how Stefano hung around the Cockatoo Room on Wednesdays when the art group was in residence. There were five of them, four women and a man and they clearly had great fun.

"Is that something you'd like to do?" Gemma asked Stefano.

"Yes," he said. "But I'm not good enough. It is long time since I do any."

Something in his face reminded Gemma of how she felt about her writing. "Listen," she said as an idea occurred to her, "if I can be brave enough to read my poems at Guy's poetry evening then you can go to the group the next day and paint a picture. Deal?" She held out her hand and after a moment's hesitation, Stefano shook it.

"Deal!"

"We'll have done the Grand Opening by then and if we can survive that we can do anything." Gemma sounded positive but her insides churned with uncertainty at the thought of having her own work under public scrutiny.

Gemma went into Dalesbury to visit the charity shops to find something to wear for the Grand Opening. The café was showing a small profit – and both solicitors had congratulated them when they'd phoned to check up on progress. The café had been signed over to them on 6th January so by the official opening they would be into their second month of trading. Gemma had been too busy to check messages on her mobile and when she did so, there were more missed calls from Mark. She didn't care.

She hurried round the charity shops looking to see what she could find that would create the right impression for their café. Up till now she hadn't bothered about her appearance. She couldn't remember the last time she'd worn make up and she didn't bother dressing in anything more than jeans and sweatshirts during the day. She had one black skirt that she'd worn with one of her two floaty tops when they'd been photographed or when she'd shown customers to their seats in the evening.

Allan Sheppard had phoned to see how they were getting on and he promised to try and get to the Grand Opening with Molly.

"You should start a Blog," he said. "All the best businesses have them. Tell everyone what you're up to and what your next ventures are going to be."

In the Acorns Charity Shop in Dalesbury High Street, Gemma found an indigo blue velvet dress. It was knee-length, close-fitting with long sleeves and a scooped neck. It looked stunning on her.

"I think the lady who brought that in also donated a bag and shoes," said the shop assistant. "I don't think they've been priced up yet, but we can soon sort that out if they're any good to you."

The bag was beautiful with a decoration made of peacock feathers. The shoes were the same blue as the dress but with heels so high that Gemma knew she'd never last ten minutes in them, let alone all evening. She bought the bag and regretfully left the shoes in their box.

She and Stefano had decided on a simple menu for the Opening Night. They'd also (at Laura's suggestion) set up a raffle and had printed a newsletter to give to each couple together with a loyalty card. Each of the ladies would receive a present of a hand-made truffle in a little gift box. This had been Stefano's idea and while he was making them the kitchen was full of the exotic smell of melted chocolate and brandy.

"You try?" he said offering one to Gemma.

She took it and bit into it.

"Good?"

"'orrible," she said and they both laughed.

With regard to the menu, there would be a choice of starter of melon and ginger or tomato and basil soup. The main course was either chicken in white wine sauce or vegetarian pizza with a choice of dessert of zuppa inglese (trifle) or tiramisu.

"*Tiramisu* means 'pick me up'," said Stefano as he showed Gemma how to make it. "My *Nonna* Maria used to make the best tiramisu in the world. She always said it was important to use the best coffee you could afford."

"It smells divine," said Gemma. "I didn't know Italian food came with such great puddings."

The Grand Opening passed in a blur of sensory images – seductive music, the combined scents of garlic and herbs, chocolate and brandy, the ruby glow of red wine under the chandelier and the cocktail of perfumes and the colours of the dresses the women wore. Cameras clicked, memories were made, proposals made and accepted.

At the end of the evening, Francine and the two other waitresses who'd happily taken part stacked the plates and glasses in the dishwasher and, together with a few others who'd been invited to stay – Allan and Molly, Diana among them - kicked off their shoes and accepted the glasses of Prosecco that Stefano poured for them.

Francine and her friends and Diana were getting a taxi home together. Allan and Molly were staying the night at The Green Man so there was no excuse not to celebrate. However, by the time the glasses of Prosecco were drunk and the remains of the cheese straws and truffles eaten, the taxi arrived and the three girls and Diana left, letting in a blast of cold air as they did so.

"Brrr," said Allan, "time for bed I think, Molls."

Gemma saw them to the door, noticing the crunch of their footsteps on the frosty pavement as they made their unsteady way up the street.

She headed back indoors, feeling a mixture of regret and relief. Regret that the evening had gone so quickly and relief that it had gone so well. Allan had promised to do a follow-up article for *The Telegraph* and she'd collected a notebook full of great suggestions to help boost the business. It was just a shame that it was only meant to last six months. She didn't know if it was just the Prosecco talking but she was enjoying this far more than her previous job - even if she did have Stefano to contend with.

Gemma stood in the café amid the lingering aromas of garlic and herbs. The flowers on the tables – little posies of snowdrops and rosemary that she'd picked in the garden complemented the décor perfectly. The paintings round the wall, many of them featuring hearts and flowers, chosen specifically for Valentine's Day created a feeling of romance. Several bore red dots, indicating that they'd been sold.

The music was still playing – a mixture of classical and slow dance tunes compiled by Francine's boyfriend Jed especially for the evening.

Stefano came into the café. He'd discarded his apron and looked pale with exhaustion. He was carrying two glasses of Prosecco. "You forgot your drink," he said.

Gemma was sure she'd finished hers, but she took one of the glasses and clinked it with his.

"Cheers," she said. "It was a good night."

"Cincin."

Gemma drank some of her Prosecco and then put her glass down on the nearest table. A song was playing – the theme tune to *Titanic* and she remembered how this had always inspired her to be brave. She remembered a comment that Leonardo diCaprio made during the film when he was making a toast: "*To making it count.*"

She raised her glass again. "To making it count." She took a sip of her drink so he couldn't see how emotional she was feeling.

Stefano felt a sense of relief that the evening had gone so well. He'd enjoyed being master of his own kitchen – at least that's how he saw it. He knew that Gemma had done more than her fair share of the work as she spoke to the customers and showed them to their tables, took their orders. Up till now, he'd felt a sense of anxiety that the business would never get off the ground and that the money would go to a home for cats. Now he felt confident that this would work for the six months that he had to be here and that – just maybe – he'd achieve his aim of buying his own trattoria and lemon grove and getting his own back on the family who'd let him down.

He took a sip of Prosecco feeling too fidgety to sit down. Gemma was swaying to the music a dreamy look on her face. He recognised the tune – the theme music to *Titanic*. He'd seen the film with subtitles and had felt a sense of horror at the loss of life. He'd been around boats and the sea all his life, but he had a healthy respect for it and its capricious moods.

He didn't know how it happened – maybe it was the euphoria of the night or maybe Gemma's perfume reminded him of the one Sofia used to wear – but suddenly she was in his arms and they drifted slowly on the tide of music. Her head rested at the level of his collar bone and he could smell the coconut scent of her shampoo.

The music finished and she looked up at him. Their lips met in a soft kiss that made his stomach feel as if he'd gone down too fast in an elevator.

She broke away first and the realisation of what he'd done struck Stefano. He didn't know why he'd done that. This was a business arrangement and should stay that way. Whatever the reasons from the past that had brought them both here it was nothing to do with them. Stefano had no intention of getting involved with an English girl – with any girl. He'd put his ambitions first from now on.

CHAPTER SEVEN

Gemma woke the next morning with a bad headache, gritty eyes and a dry mouth. She'd peeled off her dress and shoes and fallen into bed without even taking her make up off. There were mascara stains on the pillow and she had memories of a dream when she was in Stefano's arms and dancing with him, kissing him …

With a sense of shock she tried to remember what happened last night after she'd said goodbye to Allan and Molly. She remembered being in the café and dancing to the music and drinking a glass of Prosecco. Had he spiked her drink? She didn't think so. Had anything more serious happened between them? Had he come upstairs with her? No. It was just a kiss.

She definitely remembered breaking away before anything more serious happened. The problem was how to behave now? Should she pretend it never happened? She decided that was the best thing. After all, he was probably feeling just as bad about it.

She couldn't hear any signs of movement from his room. He was either up already or still sleeping. Gemma headed for the bathroom and had a jasmine-scented bubble bath. She dressed in her familiar jeans and sweat shirt and went downstairs. The kitchen was quiet and still full of some of the dirty dishes from last night that they couldn't fit in the dishwasher. They'd been rinsed but needed a proper clean.

Gemma made tea and toast. She spread the toast with Marmite and left it on the plate while she went to answer the phone. It was Allan, inviting her and Stefano for lunch at The Green Man before they went home later today. She accepted on behalf of them both and went back to the kitchen.

Stefano was making coffee for himself. He hadn't shaved and his face was bluish with stubble. Gemma remembered her father's face in the morning and how she'd loved rubbing her face against it. *Stop it*, she told herself. *He's not the man for you. Stay away from them, they're all bad news*.

Stefano was eating a piece of her toast and pulling a face. "What is this, it's 'orrible?"

"Marmite."

"Che cosa?"

"Marmite – it's made of yeast extract."

"Its 'orrible." He pulled a face.

"That'll teach you to steal my toast," said Gemma picking up a slice and taking a bite.

He laughed and turned back to making his coffee.

Gemma was thankful that he hadn't made any reference to last night and 'that kiss.' In fact, she was beginning to wonder if she'd imagined the whole thing.

There was no time to waste thinking about what had happened. The phone hardly stopped ringing and in between calls they sorted out the kitchen ready for that evening. As they were leaving the café to walk along to The Green Man they met Dan.

"I was calling to find out how the Grand Opening went," he said, his eyes crinkling at the corners as he smiled at Gemma.

"Why do you want to know?" asked Stefano. "So you can go and tell your father?" His eyes blazed with anger and Gemma thought he was going to hit Dan.

"Take it easy mate," said Dan. "I was just trying to be friendly."

"I don't want to be friends with people like you."

Gemma felt bad as she watched Dan walk back along the street. It wasn't his fault that his father was so unpleasant.

She turned to Stefano who was striding along the road with his fists rammed into the pockets of the sheepskin lined jacket he'd found in a charity shop.

"You didn't have to be like that to him. He was only trying to be friendly."

"Si," he said. "If you say so."

The Green Man was lively for a Saturday lunchtime and had a roaring log fire and a 'good pub grub' menu featuring dishes like cottage pie, bangers and mash and faggots – all of which thoroughly bemused Stefano as they tried to explain what was in the food.

"You wait till we get to the puddings," laughed Allan. "Try explaining spotted dick, brown betty and Queen's pudding."

Gemma's laughter caught in her throat. She was looking towards the corner of the bar where the specials board was and she was sure she saw Mark going up the stairs to where the bed and breakfast accommodation was.

"Are you OK?" asked Molly. "You look like you saw a ghost."

"Something like that," said Gemma.

She looked again. There was nobody there. It had been a busy few days with a lot of stress. Maybe she'd been overdoing it. One of the barmen had light brown hair like Mark – perhaps he'd just gone upstairs for something.

They decided on what they'd eat. Fish and chips for Molly and Allan, cottage pie for Gemma.

Stefano hesitated. He felt out of place in this English pub with its strange customs – he hadn't understood much of what Allan had said about what a green man was. It sounded more like something from a science fiction film but he gathered from the gestures Allan made that it was something to do with the seasons and fertility. The names of the food looked equally strange and didn't give much idea as to what was in each dish. As far as Stefano could remember a cottage was a type of small house and yet it was the name of the meal Gemma had ordered. An English girl he'd once gone out with had described a man on the tour she was on as a 'faggot.' It didn't sound as if it was a compliment. He gazed at the menu feeling totally out of his depth.

"How about steak and chips?" *said* Allan.

Stefano nodded gratefully. They couldn't do much wrong with that.

While they waited for their food to come, Molly and Allan were keen to hear more about their ideas for *The Inheritance*.

"It almost feels like my own special project," said Allan, since we met you right at the beginning. "Even my editor is getting really interested and nothing much usually excites her."

"You could go on past the six months if you wanted, couldn't you?" asked Molly.

"I suppose so," said Gemma, "but I don't think we will."

"You never know," said Molly with a smile.

"I forgot to mention – there's a competition you might be interested in," said Allan. "If you win it you'd be on the telly. I'll email you the details when we get back."

There were three stages to the competition which was called Dining Hotspots. Each stage was in three parts. Gemma read the instructions to Laura.

"If we get through the registration bit, then this is what they want. Part one – the café or restaurant needs to have an imaginative name. The building should have a history to it including three interesting characters from the past and there must be an interesting story as to how the partnership between the chefs started. Extra points will be awarded if there is a love story here! Well, no chance with that one."

"Couldn't you pretend?" asked Laura.

"Definitely not. I'm off men for life."

"Well – apart from the lovey-dovey bit you shouldn't have any trouble. What's the next stage about?"

Gemma scanned down the page.

"Stage two is about signature dishes – and they're not looking for ultra-exotic like crocodile burgers or wombat steaks. Apparently they awarded a prize last year for someone's extra-special cheese on toast. They want familiar dishes with a new twist."

"Stefano must have a fair number of dishes in his repertoire."

"Yes – but it can't be all the same thing. One Italian dish would be OK but you have to choose three times of day – like breakfast, lunch or afternoon tea. I've been experimenting with different scone recipes for afternoon tea – so maybe I could do one of those."

"So what happens with Stage Three? Dancing girls, bells and whistles?"

"Very funny. No – it's about added value. Getting the community involved. One example they give is putting on a play and giving the money to a local charity. You have to show proof that the event has been advertised in three unusual ways."

"Dead easy then," said Laura.

Gemma groaned. "I don't suppose we'll get anywhere – we're not really established yet and we're still fumbling round in the dark."

"Sounds a bit kinky to me!"

"Very funny."

"At least fill the forms in and register. If they like the sound of you then they'll be in touch for part one. If they don't then you can forget about it. Either way you've got nothing to lose."

"I don't exactly know why Great Aunt Anna left the café to us both," said

Gemma.

"Then make something up," said Laura. "You were always the best at creative writing at school. Lie through your teeth if you have to. Nobody's really going to care once the competition is under way."

Gemma down-loaded the competition entry form and filled it in. That afternoon while she and Stefano were drinking coffee in the kitchen she asked him about his connection to England. He started to talk about his grandfather and then his voice faltered.

"Before he died he told me to give his love to the bluebell wood," he said. "What is this? Can we go there?"

"The bluebells won't be out yet but when they are we'll go. They look just like an inland Mediterranean sea."

"Nothing could be as lovely as the Mediterranean," said Stefano with more than a touch of his usual arrogance, but his eyes looked dark with pain and he abandoned his coffee and went upstairs to his room. Gemma heard the door slam and then silence.

She looked at the closing date for the competition. It was the day after tomorrow so there was no time to waste. She didn't have the energy for any more verbal tussles with Stefano. She switched on her laptop and created what she hoped was an intriguing taster about a legacy left to two people who had connections with England and Italy. She hinted at a past romance between an English lady and an Italian man that ended with a stormy argument in a bluebell wood. She checked through it for spelling mistakes, wrote a brief covering email to the Dining Hotspots Team, attached the form and pressed send.

Gemma then sent a brief text to Allan and Laura saying she'd completed her entry.

Keep your fingers crossed – I think, she wrote.

Creating the brief story for the entry had reminded her how much she loved and missed her writing and renewed the disappointment of winning the competition but not being able to claim her prize. She thought again about the suggestion to create an *Inheritance Blog*.

"You could do give-aways and special promotions," Molly had said earlier, looking at Gemma over the rim of her wine glass, "and I know from what Allan has said loads of people have engaged with your story."

Right, thought Gemma, sitting alone in the kitchen as the February light faded, *I'll do it.*

She created a Blog post about the link between food and storytelling. Great Aunt Anna had always told stories as she worked and Gemma had always loved fairy-tales and legends – particularly the ones that related to The Cockatoo.

Her mother, who had been brought up on these stories, used to dismiss them as so much bunkum, but there were places in the building where Gemma had always felt a sense of people from the past still being around. There was a special cupboard upstairs, almost like a priest hole, where Black Marley the highwayman had hidden for hours while the local magistrate and his men searched the building.

There was a strange feeling in one of the attics where, years ago, a young servant girl had hanged herself when she'd discovered she was pregnant. Great Aunt Anna had once held a séance there and the girl's presence had been felt by the medium who claimed she needed to get out of the room because there was something tight round her neck. She'd also claimed she'd seen an old woman working downstairs at the kitchen table – and Gemma had noticed how a smile had lit up her Great Aunt's face.

Several of the poems Gemma had written were about her childhood visits here – hiding under the table and overhearing gossip and stories as her Great Aunt and friends drank tea or sherry and ate cakes and scones.

Great Aunt Anna used to recount the spookier local ghost stories gleefully, particularly to some of her friends who were of a nervous disposition. "I could make a fortune charging for tours," she used to say.

She was also a great one for practical jokes and had sent a story of a reported sighting of a ghost in a local telephone box. Within a week, fifty more sightings had been reported.

Gemma had included some of these memories in her Blog, together with a recipe of the week. *We need to get away from computers and get back to good old-fashioned story-telling*, she put at the end of her post. *Contact me for details of our storytelling and poetry evening being organised by local poet Guy Travers*.

Within hours what seemed like an army of storytellers, musicians and poets had contacted *The Inheritance* about the special evening.

Guy Travers was thrilled when Gemma got in touch to tell him about the response she'd had. He called round to see them bearing a bottle of wine and a notebook in which he scribbled down ideas and notes for the evening.

"What sort of food do you suggest?" asked Gemma.

Guy's blue eyes shone. "They'll make short work of most things," he said, "but I'd suggest keeping it simple – pizza maybe or chilli and rice. Charge a door price and include the food in it with a glass of wine or beer. Put some crisps or nuts on the tables – that way people think they're getting something for nothing. I'll sort out a microphone and speakers. OK if I come round the day before to set up?"

Gemma was relieved that the event seemed to be sorting itself. She contacted the local paper and they came round and did a story. The local radio station also promised to cover the event. She offered them a free meal if they turned up. The library in Charworth agreed to put up a poster, as did the doctor's surgery and the village hall. The only sour note was from Mike Bridges who was blocking their path as they returned from visiting the library.

"This 'special event' of yours better not be noisy," he said, arms folded belligerently. "Some of us need our beauty sleep."

"I hardly think we're going to trouble you. You're quite a way away from us," said Gemma with more than a touch of Great Aunt Anna's hauteur.

"You do bother me," he said. "You're taking my trade away."

He made no attempt to move out of the way. Gemma could see from the equally belligerent look on Stefano's face that he wasn't going to back down and walk in the road.

"Scusi," said Stefano. "I have work to do." He strode forward almost catapulting Mike Bridges into the hedge.

Mike glared at the pair of them. "Think you're really smart don't you – with your fancy ideas? Well you'll be laughing on the other side of your faces before too long."

"What a horrible man," said Laura. "Maybe you should report him to the police?"

"I doubt if they'd take any notice," said Gemma. "He's hardly committed the crime of the century has he? I'd just like to know why he's so hostile though. It's not as if we've done anything to him and we're not exactly cooking the same type of food."

"He's just jealous of your success."

"Don't speak too soon."

"I'm coming to hear you read your poems."

"Please don't," said Gemma – but Laura had already gone.

The bookings for Storytellers flooded in. Stefano decided to cook two varieties of pasta – lasagne al forno for those who ate meat and risotto primavera for vegetarians. There'd be a choice of dessert of pannacotta or torte di limone.

On the day before, Gemma and Stefano went to Dalesbury to the Cash & Carry. She still felt uneasy with him in the passenger seat but at least the snow had long gone, the spring was well and truly there and St David's Day daffodils were nodding in the gardens.

Gemma bought some bunches of daffodils to do some posies for the tables. Fresh flowers were so much nicer than artificial ones and she'd always loved daffodils.

On the way back into Charworth, she swerved and almost crashed into the car ahead of her when she saw a black Audi 3 that looked like Mark's.

"What are you doing?" Stefano was piled onto the dashboard.

"I thought I saw something – someone."

"You thought you saw him in The Green Man," said Laura when Gemma phoned her in a panic when they got back to *The Inheritance*. "Don't be daft – there must be thousands of black Audi 3s in circulation."

"But not with personalised number plates – I'm sure it was his."

"You're working too hard. Think about it logically. What would he be doing so far from home? He's probably got more than enough to do satisfying Miss Pink Knickers – if he's still with her."

Gemma had no time to worry about cars with personalised number plates. They'd no sooner put away the stuff from the Cash & Carry and had lunch than Guy arrived with his microphone, lighting rig and amplifiers. He created a little stage at one end of the café near the old fashioned fireplace with its dark green tiles.

"I've got fairy-lights too if you'd like them," he said.

Gemma nodded enthusiastically.

Guy and Stefano re-arranged the tables and chairs and the room looked sparkly and exciting.

"Read us one of your poems, Gemma, so I can check the sound levels," said Guy.

Gemma felt sick. A memory of Mark making a joke of one of her poems to his mate Pete surfaced. *I can't*, she thought.

Then she thought of the pact she'd made with Stefano. If she read her poems, then his task was to get back to painting. She couldn't be the one to falter at the first hurdle just because she was nervous.

"I'll go and get some," she said heading towards the stairs in the hope that she could gain a few minutes freedom, take some deep breaths and stop feeling panicky.

While she was upstairs, she collected a couple of poems and then quietly opened the door of Great Aunt Anna's room. Just being there, breathing in the combined scents of faded roses, face powder and polish steadied her and she headed downstairs with a renewed sense of confidence.

She walked up to the microphone, trying to remember what she'd read somewhere about facing an audience. *Smile. Don't be shy. Speak slowly. Don't gabble. Take time to do a short introduction. Look as if you want to be there – not as if you're visiting the dentist.*

Guy had worked on creating the right sort of ambience. He'd drawn the curtains, put up the fairy-lights and switched them on. A few of his mates were setting up amplifiers. They weren't taking any notice of her. Gemma tried to imagine the room full of people all focused on what she was saying. *They aren't going to eat you*, she said to herself.

She took a few deep breaths.

"My name is Gemma Lawrence and my poem is called 'Bluebells.'

She started to read, reminding herself to slow down ...

The shadows near the door shifted.

Mark was standing watching her. Gemma carried on reading, feeling like a rabbit caught in the headlights.

"That sounded great, Gemma. I look forward to hearing more of your work," said Guy.

Mark stepped forward proprietarily. "It's been a long time, Gemma. I've missed you."

CHAPTER EIGHT

"One drink, that's all," said Gemma, anxious to get Mark out of her life once and for all.

Mark's appearance and behaviour had upset the ambience of the café and Stefano had come from the kitchen and was now standing in the doorway from the kitchen, arms folded, causing Mark to ask: "Who's your friend?"

"He's not my friend, he's my business partner."

"What do you mean, he's your business partner? Where does he live?"

"Here. And before you jump to any conclusions there's nothing going on."

Guy and his friends had stopped fiddling with their screwdrivers and were now paying Gemma and Mark their fullest attention.

Gemma collected her bag and jacket from the kitchen and led the way from the café towards The Green Man. Mark ordered a pint and Gemma asked for a J2O.

He looked surprised. "I'd have thought you'd have a glass of wine."

"I've got work to do," she said.

"What work? Your café or whatever it is doesn't open tonight."

"There's still work to do on future events."

"Future events! Who do you think you are, Gemma?"

Gemma ignored him and went to sit at a table in the corner. She took a sip of her drink, wishing she'd not been so quick to leave the café. Mark had kept up a flood of one sided conversation on the way to the pub – about how he'd missed her and that his life wasn't the same without her. His body language didn't quite match the words.

When Gemma first caught sight of him, she'd felt a burst of longing to feel his arms round her, remembering how things were when they first met on a hot summer night on the Thames. A mutual friend was having a birthday disco and they'd found themselves standing next to each other on the deck watching the landmarks of London drift slowly past – the Houses of Parliament, St Paul's and the newer buildings like the Gherkin and the Shard. By the time they got off the boat, her legs felt unsteady from the Bucks Fizz she'd drunk and from being on the water. She'd gone with her friend Sarah who'd been really sneaky and given Mark her mobile number.

He'd phoned her the next day and asked her how her legs were. She'd laughed and agreed to meet him for a drink the following evening.

It had been a whirlwind romance. He'd swept her off her feet, promised her an engagement ring – which never materialised – and within a few weeks they'd moved in together.

Later, she wasn't sure whether he just wanted a 'mother' figure in the kitchen to cook his meals and iron his shirts and a permanent fixture in the bedroom if other options didn't work out.

Before long, she noticed the tell-tale signs that he was cheating on her – the smell of strange perfume on him, which he always tried to claim was hers, money spent and not properly accounted for and mysterious sightings of him with other women for which he always had a ready excuse.

He claimed that his previous long term relationship had broken up because Claire was paranoid – something he'd accused Gemma of being on previous occasions. Then she'd always given him the benefit of the doubt, overridden any suspicions and gone back to him. This time it wasn't going to happen.

"You didn't give me a chance to explain," he said, a whiny edge to his voice that she suspected had always been there but that she hadn't noticed until now. His face had that little boy lost look that at one time she'd found quite endearing but that now was just irritating.

"Explain what?" She couldn't afford for him to get the upper hand like he always used to.

In the past she always seemed to be the one apologising for doubting him like the time when she'd seen him going into an upmarket lingerie shop with a girl and had accused him of having an affair. With a martyred look he'd admitted to going shopping with another woman – but it was to buy just the right type of undies for her.

She'd gone back to him even though her friend Sarah had said there was every possibility that he'd bought two sets – one for her and one for the mystery woman.

"You saw the two champagne glasses and jumped to the wrong conclusion," he said.

"What conclusion would most people jump to if they came home to their house to find two glasses, an empty champagne bottle, a rumpled bed and a discarded pair of knickers?"

"I know it looks suspicious but Marie, my colleague, is well-known for playing practical jokes and causing trouble. She did the same to my mate John."

"Yeah, sure," said Gemma. "What was she doing in our house anyway?"

"Look – I told you. We'd won the champagne for being the best sales team. She couldn't take me to her house because her boyfriend wouldn't have understood …"

"Meaning I'm a soft touch I suppose?" Anger surged through Gemma like a tidal wave.

"You were out. If you hadn't have come back so early than you wouldn't have known anything about it."

"So that makes it right does it?"

"Gemma – you always were prickly. You're not giving me a chance to put things right. I've missed you so much. I've driven up here to try and make things up to you, so at least hear me out."

"I didn't ask you to come," said Gemma. "How did you find out where I was anyway?" She made a mental note to give whoever it was a telling off.

"My mate John saw you in *The Telegraph*. I thought he was winding me up."

"Why on earth would you think that?"

"Well, cooking isn't exactly your forte is it?"

"Perhaps I've changed."

"You're not going to suddenly morph into Nigella Lawson are you? Anyway if you're running a restaurant, what were you doing reading poems?"

"I was practising for our Storytellers Evening tomorrow. I'm reading some of my poems."

"So you're going to have a café full of gay blokes." He gave a hollow laugh. "I'm glad I came to see you today."

That was typical of him to make an assumption about people before he knew the facts.

"Why did you come?"

"We used to be good together, Gemma. We could be again. You could sell up here – I know there's someone local who would make you an offer straightaway."

"I'm not selling. Stefano and I are staying here for six months and then we're going to claim our inheritance."

"What's he got to do with you?"

"At this moment I don't know."

"I'm not happy about the two of you being alone in that place together."

"It's not something you need to worry about, Mark. I'm quite capable of looking after myself – and besides, what I do is none of your business anymore."

"Gemma, don't let's bicker. What I'm trying to say is, 'Will you marry me?' If you insist on sticking to the six months here, I could come and stay with you at weekends. It would be romantic – like it used to be."

"No, Mark."

"You haven't seen the ring I've got you yet."

"Watch my lips. N – O. I'm not going to marry anyone – ever."

"You might have to sell the café – and then what would you do?"

"Why do you suddenly know so much about it?"

"I've been talking to people."

"What people?"

"You never used to be so awkward."

"I can't stay here listening to any more of this, I've got work to do."

"I'm going to the Gents."

Gemma watched him walk away from her. This was Mark's stock behaviour when things got sticky. He'd go off to the loo or to the bar and leave her waiting around.

His mobile bleeped with an incoming message.

It wasn't the sort of thing Gemma usually did but curiosity got the better of her. She picked up the phone and read the message.

Hi babes, Missing you. Hope the conference is going well. See you soon. Love and kisses Marie. xxxx

Gemma put on her jacket and picked up her bag. As she did so, the barman came and spoke to her.

"Can you tell Mark that we've cancelled his room for tonight? I gather he's staying with you. Have a good evening."

The nerve of the man, thought Gemma as she walked back along the street, her footsteps echoing in the darkness.

Mark caught up with her.

"What's up – what's the tearing hurry?"

"Mark – just go away. Piss off. Leave me alone. I don't want to see you ever again."

"Why?"

She stopped and turned to face him. "You're at it again – in fact you've never stopped have you? While you were in the Gents you had a text from Miss Pink Knickers saying she hopes you're enjoying the conference. She must be every bit as gullible as I used to be."

"Gemma …" Mark put his hand on her arm. "She's tapped in the head. She can't accept that I don't want a relationship with her anymore."

"Get your hands off me – and while we're on that subject, fancy assuming that you could just move back into my life and my bed."

"What do you mean?"

"The barman came to tell me that he'd cancelled your room for tonight since you'd be staying with me. Nice of you to ask or is he tapped in the head too?"

"Come on, Gemma, don't be difficult." He pulled her into his arms and forced his lips against hers.

Gemma felt his teeth graze her lips and she fought back, tearing her jacket as she struggled free from his hands.

Mark soon regained his grip and pushed her down an alleyway between two houses. She struggled and screamed but the street was quiet and nobody was likely to come to her rescue. She felt rough brick graze her back as he fumbled with her top, feeling for her breasts.

Then, just as suddenly, she felt Mark's weight pulled away from her.

"You leave her alone, dirty bastard." Stefano dragged Mark to one side as if he weighed no more than a flea. "She does not want you."

"Mind your own business." Mark had a graze on his cheek from where Gemma's nails had caught him.

"You go – or we call police."

"You won't get away with this." Mark limped away down the alley back towards The Green Man.

"You have ten minutes to get in your car and drive away. If I see you here again, then I will set my brothers on you. They are Mafioso."

Stefano had put his arm round Gemma to steady her. Together they walked down the street following Mark who looked much less cocky now. He got in his car and Gemma noticed it was already loaded with his stuff, no doubt with the intention of coming straight back to her bed after the pub. Well, Miss Pink Knickers was welcome to him. He started the engine and drove off into the night. He didn't look back.

"What made you come looking for me?" asked Gemma as they turned back towards *The Inheritance*. Her legs felt shaky and she knew she'd had a lucky escape.

"I don't like him. He not right for you," said Stefano.

"I'm very glad you did," said Gemma as she stumbled against him. Everything went black and for the first time in her life she fainted.

Merda! thought Stefano. *Shit! What if someone comes along and thinks I've done something to her?* He'd managed to catch her in his arms as she fell and lower her gently to the pavement. Her face was pale, bringing back unwanted memories from childhood.

There was no sign of anyone and he didn't want to leave her alone on the pavement while he went to seek help. It was dark there, because of the lack of street lighting at their end of the village. There was nothing else for it. He would have to carry her. He bent down and scooped her into his arms. She stirred and her eyes opened.

"What are you doing? What happened?" She glared at him, her grey eyes like flints.

They were back at *The Inheritance* now. The creak of what used to be the inn sign could be heard swinging in the breeze.

Stefano put her down gently, leaning her against him while he unlocked the door.

"You … faint," he said, miming her eyes going weird and her falling down.

"I don't do things like that," she said, her eyes closing again.

Stefano watched her go slowly upstairs, wondering if he should call an ambulance or a doctor. She hadn't said. He hoped she didn't think he'd done anything improper when he picked her up. He wouldn't want her to get the wrong impression – whatever the TV people were aiming for.

Gemma woke in the early hours of the morning. She'd been dreaming about being carried somewhere in someone's arms. She heard Mark's voice say: "Marry me and everything will be different."

She shot up to a sitting position, aware that she'd yelled out loud. The dream image was so vivid it was as if he was in the room with her. She held her eiderdown round her, realising that she was still in her undies. She'd not had the energy last night to do more than take her make up off, clean her teeth and take off her jeans and the purple sweater she'd worn to the pub. She noticed she had grazes on her back and bruises on her arms and she remembered how Mark had dragged her into the alleyway intending to do as he wished with her and how Stefano had come to her rescue.

It was still dark – a fragment of moonlight shone through a gap in the curtains.

She heard footsteps along the landing, followed by a knock on her door.

"Gemma – you are OK?"

"I'm fine," she said, trying to stop the tears pouring down her face.

"Open this door," he said.

Gemma wrapped herself in her dressing gown and went to the door. Stefano stood there, his face dark with stubble and his hair on end.

"I heard you shout," he said. "You are not OK."

"I am," she said and promptly burst into tears.

Stefano was faced with his worst nightmare – a weeping woman at three o'clock in the morning.

It is your own fault, he said to himself. *You should've stayed in bed. Pretended you didn't hear.*

"I fetch limoncello," he said, heading downstairs to find small liqueur glasses from the glass-fronted cabinet in the kitchen.

Gemma sat on her bed, her feet under the eiderdown, wondering how fetching a musical instrument – if that's what a limoncello was – would help her at this precise moment. She was surprised when he came back with two small glasses of yellow liquid.

"Salute," he said. "Good health." He downed his glass in a couple of mouthfuls.

Gemma sipped at hers. "It tastes like medicine," she said.

"It is like a kiss from the sun," he said. "Each family makes it differently."

He was pleased to see that her tears had dried and that the colour had returned to her face.

"You make it?" she asked. "As medicine?"

"Si. From lemons. No – not as medicine. In Italy we drink it after meals, usually in a cold glass."

"Tell me about it," she said. "I've got an idea for the competition."

He rolled his eyes. "In the morning," he said. "You have had enough excitement for one night. Sleep now."

Gemma slept and this time her dream was about walking through the orchard next door except that lemons hung on the trees instead of apples and the woodland ahead of her had changed into a deep blue sea.

It was only when she woke up with sunlight instead of moonlight streaming through the curtains that she remembered that today was when the Storytellers event happened and she had promised to read her poems. It was part of the pledge she'd made with Stefano – but she felt terrified because she knew it would bring back memories of Mark standing and watching her from a shadowy corner.

CHAPTER NINE

The smell of frying meat and garlic drifted up the stairs as Gemma dived out of bed, the bad dreams of the previous night temporarily forgotten. She had a hundred and one things to do on her list and she was worried she wouldn't finish everything by the time the musicians and storytellers arrived.

She had a wash, bundled her hair into a ponytail and pulled on jeans and a black sweater. As soon as she got down to the kitchen, the phone rang. It was the local paper wanting to know if they could come and interview them.

"Better still – come for the evening," she said. "There's nothing like seeing something first hand."

She noticed Stefano shooting her a questioning look. He was busy adding fresh tomato sauce to an appetising concoction of mince, onions, garlic and herbs for the lasagne al forno. He'd gathered the ingredients for the risotto primavera and she noticed a basket full of lemons bright as light bulbs where the sun caught them.

She picked up the cafetiere that always seemed to be full these days. "Coffee?"

"Si – grazie."

He looked hot and the kitchen was already full of the steamy warmth of the bread he'd baked. He offered some to Gemma with a pot of honey. She sat at the table enjoying the contrast of the dark bitter coffee and the fresh ciabatta bread with salty butter and amber-coloured honey soaking into it.

"What is happening?" he asked. "I do not understand some of the things you say. What does 'first hand' mean?"

"The local newspaper want to do a special article on us and I said it is better for them to come and see for themselves – not just for me to tell them about it."

"Ah! Capito! I understand."

Guy came to help move the tables and set up the craft stalls in the Club Room.

"This evening really seems to have captured people's imaginations and got them off their backsides," he said. "Well done."

"Don't speak too soon," said Gemma. She was worried that Mark might take it into his head to come back – and she was even more worried about reading her poems.

"Don't be daft – he won't come back," said Laura when she rang to wish them luck. "He's not to know whether you've contacted the police or not. Personally, I think you should've done. Serve him right for the way he's treated you. And don't worry about reading your poems. You'll be great I know you will. I've got everything crossed for you."

Stefano watched Gemma as she set tables, dealt with phone calls and directed an assortment of people to the room beyond the café. She worked hard, he'd give her that. He'd always believed – from what his step-brothers said – that English people were fat and lazy. Gemma certainly wasn't fat, although she was bigger than Sofia (something he'd noticed when he'd carried her back to the café last night). She didn't cook much, apart from scones (why did the English have such a fascination for them?) but she was good at talking to people and they needed plenty of customers to make their business work.

He was glad to be left to do what he did best. Cooking comforted him, reminded him of home and gave him hope that things could change and that Sofia might get back in touch with him.

Gemma was talking to a strange looking woman. She looked about ninety, Stefano thought, with a face like an apple left at the bottom of the barrel, criss-crossed with dozens of wrinkles. She had long grey plaits and wore a patchwork dress with hooped red and blue tights underneath it.

She was like a character from a fairy-tale with her green eyes shining behind round glasses. Gemma was laughing and Stefano wondered what they were talking about. He didn't have time to wonder for long as there was work to do in the kitchen and Francine and the other waitresses were eager to carry in the baskets of bread and olives. He'd done most of the preparation for the evening and was now feeling uncharacteristically anxious about not wanting to be the one who let the partnership down.

Gemma had felt immediately drawn to the woman with the green eyes and the hooped tights. The idea she'd had last night after she and Stefano had drunk glasses of limoncello surfaced. He'd told her to go back to sleep, they'd talk about it in the morning, but they hadn't and she didn't know if he was worried about reminding her about what had led up to the nightmares or whether he wasn't interested in what she had to say.

The idea she'd had was to use something about the landscape they'd each grown up in to create a signature dish or series of – but that was as far as the idea had got. Now, it seemed, the universe was supporting her. This woman called Hilda Bradford who'd arrived with her wicker baskets full of brightly coloured crochet work, jars of apple puree and bottles of apple juice was the answer to her prayers.

Gemma told Hilda about her idea.

"We can sort a price out for the apple puree," she said.

Hilda rocked with laughter, her hands on her hips. "Bless you love, they're your own apples I'd be selling back to you."

Gemma looked at her. "What do you mean?"

"I can't stand waste," said Hilda, "and every year since Anna left, nobody has bothered to pick the apples. They've either rotted on the trees or dropped off and been eaten by rats. So a couple of years ago I started my own conservation campaign. I picked the apples, got a friend of mine to press some of them into juice and made chutney or apple puree with the rest. I've been selling the stuff for charity and I'm quite happy to show you the accounts."

"Don't worry about that," said Gemma. "I know that Great Aunt Anna would just be happy that someone was using the apples. She hated waste too."

"So what's your idea?" asked Hilda.

"I need to talk it over with Stefano but basically, we've entered a competition and if – if – we get through to the next round we'll need a few interesting but unusual dishes that reflect the business we're running. Stefano's got the Italian side sown up with the pasta dishes and the like – but I need something that shows my side and what better than English apples?

"So what would you want me to do?"

"Supply me – us – with some apple juice and apple puree and I'll try to come up with an idea for a different type of cake or pie. We'll give your charity a mention of course."

"Gemma, we'll be ready to start in about half an hour," said Guy.

Gemma was amazed to see that the café was filling up. It had felt cool in there earlier and she'd been worried about people being too cold. Now there was condensation running down the windows and tables were filling up. People were chattering excitedly as they looked at the objects on the tables and helped themselves to bread and olives.

Gemma hurried up the stairs to change. She'd decided she couldn't wear the same dress that she'd worn to the Grand Opening so a few days ago she'd raided the charity shops in Dalesbury again. She'd found a full length long-sleeved red velvet dress and had bought it with no hesitation. She did her make-up, sprayed on Chanel perfume, took a deep breath and headed downstairs.

The haunting sound of a tune played on the fiddle drew her towards the café and she was amazed to see how crowded it was. Guy, dressed in dark jeans and a red jacket was doing a great job as Master of Ceremonies, outlining to the sea of eager faces what was going to happen that evening. Fairy lights glittered and the food smelled delicious, although Gemma didn't think she'd be able to eat anything until after she'd read her poems – she was too nervous.

She put her poems in a safe place in the kitchen and went to help Francine and the other waitresses. The plates were filled and cleared. The kitchen grew hotter and Stefano looked as if he was about to melt in his white t-shirt and chef's trousers.

Guy got everyone's attention. "Now, ladies and gentlemen, this is the second part of the evening that you've all been looking forward to. There will be a short break for you to recharge your glasses and go into the next room to see the wonderful array of items for sale, then we'll begin our storytelling and poetry open mic.

Gemma's insides twisted with anxiety. She wasn't sure if she could do this. She'd put herself at number three on the list so as to get it over with. Also three felt like a lucky number in the context of the competition they were waiting to hear about. *They may not even accept your registration,* said one part of her brain. *Don't think like that,*" said the other part. "*Of course they'll like you.*

When Gemma's turn came, she walked slowly up to the microphone, trying not to think of last night and Mark looming out of the shadows. She was thankful to see that Guy had moved a table there so that it at least looked different.

"Hello everyone, I'm Gemma Lawrence and I'm one half of *The Inheritance* partnership. These are my poems."

She almost faltered as she said this but then she saw Stefano watching her from the doorway. He smiled and gave her a thumbs up sign. She smiled back and began to read, gaining a huge round of applause when she finished.

She walked away from the microphone, her legs feeling shaky, and headed towards the kitchen.

"Here," said Stefano. "You eat this. I do not wish you to faint again." He pushed a plate of risotto and a glass of white wine in front of her. Gemma ate and drank gratefully.

"You know what this means, don't you?" said Gemma.

"What?" Stefano looked wary.

"You have to paint a picture."

He shrugged. "Maybe."

"We shook on it."

"I don't know how anymore."

Gemma felt sad when Stefano said that. She experienced a great sense of freedom and release once she'd read her poems. Several people had come up to her and asked where they could buy her book and her confidence felt thoroughly boosted. It made up for all the times that Mark and his mother had belittled her. *It was your own fault*, she said to herself. *You allowed them to do it.*

She wondered what had happened in Stefano's background to make him so definite that he couldn't re-start doing something he clearly loved so much.

After some careful questioning, she'd discovered that his birthday was at the end of March. Maybe she could buy him something that would at least give him a start with creating something and restore his faith in himself. He'd supported her in his own way – now she needed to do the same for him.

Gemma finished her food, stacked some of the plates into the dishwasher, hand-washed some glasses and then headed back into the café to listen to some of the music and stories. There was a real buzz of excitement about the place. Some people were dancing to the music, their shoes kicked off under the table.

She stood at the door when the evening ended, thanking everyone for attending and promising to sort another date soon. She wondered where Stefano was. He should certainly be here to share their moment of triumph, but he was nowhere to be seen. Guy had wanted to thank his friends for their help with setting the place up yesterday but they'd also disappeared.

"They're probably in the pub, knowing them," he said.

Gemma laughed and then let out a startled cry as Stefano came back in followed by Guy's friends. Stefano had a black eye and a cut on his cheek and the two friends looked as if they'd been rolling on the ground.

"I think we need coffee," said Guy, "or something stronger".

"What happened?" asked Gemma. "Was it Mark?"

"Your friend from the chip shop turned up and decided to cause trouble," said one of the men. "He was trying to get in through the kitchen window – not a good idea with the amount of whisky he'd drunk – but Stefano spotted him and called us. We got the police."

"You don't mean Dan?" asked Gemma.

"No – I think his name's Mike. Anyway, he's been taken away by the police. They may want to interview Stefano tomorrow."

Gemma got out her mobile phone and took a photo of Stefano's injuries.

"What are you doing?" Stefano was sipping at his coffee as if he was in pain.

"I saw it on a police programme once. You may need photos with the date on if this gets to court."

"Looks like he needs a bit of steak on that eye," said Guy.

"That cut needs bathing," said Gemma. "I'll get some water."

"We'll leave you to do your Florence Nightingale bit," said Guy, "and I'll be in touch about another date." He shook Stefano's hand. "It's been a great night. The food was wonderful. You two are good together. Sorry about what happened."

Stefano sat while Gemma bathed his eye and the cut on his face. It reminded him of when he was a child and he'd come home injured from some game or another and his mother had tended to his cuts and bruises. The thought made him sad.

He sipped the brandy Gemma poured for him.

"It will help you sleep," she said.

Stefano went up to bed feeling stiff and sore. He hoped they'd seen the last of Mike Bridges but he wouldn't put money on it.

He lay down and closed his eyes.

Just as he was drifting off to sleep his mobile bleeped with an incoming message.

It was from Sofia. *Missing you. Wish you were here. Sofia. x*

CHAPTER TEN

A week later Dining Hotspots emailed to say they wanted *The Inheritance* to complete the first part of the competition challenge. Gemma didn't know whether to be glad or sorry – but Laura was fizzing with excitement when she got Gemma's text.

"See – I knew you could do it. Is Stefano pleased?"

"I don't know," said Gemma. "He's been really moody this week. He'll probably bite my head off if I so much as mention it."

"Do you think that Mike character really hurt him when he tried to break in last week? Maybe he should've seen the doctor."

"You know what blokes are like if you suggest anything like that. No – I think he got some news that upset him and again, like most blokes, you can't get him to talk about it."

"I thought you got on OK."

"If he was more like Dan this six months would be so much easier."

"Yeah – but just think who you'd have as a father-in-law."

"They let him go with just a caution you know! It was so maddening. We saw him in the Cash & Carry and he spoke to us all smarmy-like and said Stefano should be grateful to him because he didn't make a claim against him for personal injury. The bloody cheek of it when he was the one trying to break into our place."

Stefano couldn't believe it when he saw Mike Bridges in the Cash & Carry. It took all Gemma's strength to grab his arm and pull him in the opposite direction.

"But he should not be out of prison," he said. "In Italy the police take such things very seriously. Here – they treat it as a joke."

"You must not do anything to him," said Gemma pulling Stefano round to face her. "If you do then you may be the one the police take away. Then you will lose your share of the business."

Gemma didn't know why she was saying this to him. If he did fly off the handle and get taken into police custody then it would make her life easier. She'd have money and she could go where she liked. Being able to sign up for a proper course for her writing was a severe temptation but Gemma always liked to finish what she'd started and if Great Aunt Anna had challenged them to six months then she would do her best to honour that request, however grumpy Stefano was.

Stefano sat in the kitchen toying with his coffee. Gemma had gone out slamming the door behind her. Golden sunlight spilled through the window onto the vase of daffodils. The colour made him think of lemons – and Sofia.

She'd sent him several texts saying she missed him. His first instinct was to get on the next plane and go and see her. He'd been so desperate to see her and hold her in his arms that he'd almost been on the point of booking a plane ticket to Napoli.

He'd phoned her instead and she'd answered, sounding wary, as if there was someone in the background. This had made him feel even more confused and desperate. He just needed one sign, one loving word, that showed she was his again and intended to wait until he came home.

Gemma came into the kitchen sparkling with the news about the competition just as he was dithering with the airline's number. It brought him back to earth with a crash as he realised his only chance of having the money to assure a secure future with Sofia was to stay here.

"So what do you think?" Gemma asked, looking as if she was about to explode with happiness. "I was a bit shocked when I got the email but Laura was so excited it's infectious."

"So you tell your friend before you tell me," he said sourly.

"You were busy talking to someone. Shall I draft some answers to the questions and then we can talk about it over lunch?

"Do what you like. It's what most women do."

"OK, I will," said Gemma, feeling irritated. She hadn't got away from someone like Mark to let herself be treated badly again.

She picked up her jacket and bag and headed out to her car.

Within twenty minutes she was parking in the riverside car park at Dalesbury. It was a beautiful spring day. The gardens she passed were full of raspberry pink flowering currant and sherbet lemon forsythia. There were daffodils and tulips in window boxes and small white clouds raced like lambs across a blue sky.

She stopped outside the charity shop where she'd bought her dress with a gasp of surprise. There was a sign that read 'Bargain Basement – all items £1.00.' Most of the items were soft toys, costume jewellery and china ornaments but standing at the back were two pictures in solid pine frames. One was of a branch bearing rosy red apples and the other was a lemon on a branch with white blossom.

Gemma bought the pictures, imagining them side by side above the old fireplace in the café. It felt like a good omen for their success.

She passed an art shop and, remembering it was Stefano's birthday next week and also the pledge they'd made that if she read her poems, he'd start painting again, she went in and bought him what was described as a 'starter kit' in a wooden case. Then she remembered the bad mood he'd been in earlier and wondered why she had bothered buying as much as a card for someone who was so grouchy.

She found a café with seats outside, ordered a pot of tea and some cinnamon toast, got her notebook out and sat doodling pictures of hearts and flowers as she tried to think of some good answers to the competition questions.

She jotted down the tasks.

1. What is the name of your business or the building it is in?

2. Name three interesting characters who once lived there.

3. How did your partnership start?

A sneaky optional extra question was 'Give us a 'taster' of your business. Tell us about one of the special dishes you offer that links both partners. What time of day would you serve it? How?

Gemma sipped her tea and ate her toast, feeling her earlier irritation with Stefano melting away.

"Hello, mind if I join you?" Hilda Bradford was wearing a pink and purple crocheted waistcoat and a long blue dress. She carried one of her familiar baskets over her arm. It was full of jars of mint jelly that reminded Gemma of sunlight on the sea when they caught the light.

"You could sell some of those at the café if you wanted to," said Gemma.

Hilda looked pleased. "Are you sure it wouldn't tread on Stefano's toes. Italians can be a bit temperamental can't they?"

"They certainly can."

Hilda ordered a coffee and shared the last slice of Gemma's toast. "So what are you up to? The Storyteller evening was wonderful – but I gather you had a bit of a problem at the end of it."

"It's not the first run-in we've had with Mike Bridges and it probably won't be the last," said Gemma. "It's a shame because I really like his son Dan." She felt herself blush under Hilda's scrutiny.

"Dan's a nice lad," said Hilda. "He's done his best to stay and help his Dad – but I think it's time he branched out on his own now. The trouble is, he feels responsible for what happened?"

"What do you mean?"

"You mean you don't know? Well it was a few years ago now, but there was an argument between Mike and his wife over something Dan wanted to do. Mike's always liked a few drinks too many and when he does its best to stay away from him. Anyway, his wife stuck to her guns that time and he lashed out and killed her. Young Dan saw it all and has felt responsible ever since."

"But that's terrible. Poor Dan."

"Be a good friend to him Gemma. He needs that more than anything." She lowered her voice and looked around. "Between you and me, Dan's got a strong spiritual side to him and he's convinced that his mother's ghost is in the chippy."

"I wonder if Mike knows he's got a haunted chip shop," said Gemma.

"Probably. I suspect that's why his drinking and his behaviour have got out of control."

There was a pause as they drank their tea and Hilda greeted a couple of passers-by. One of them had a border collie that came and snuffled round Hilda's basket.

"He knows I keep a special biscuit for him," she said.

Gemma smiled. She'd known Hilda only a short time but it seemed she had an emergency kit about her person for just about everybody. On the Storyteller night she'd produced a sewing kit to repair a drooping hem, rescue remedy for Gemma before she did her reading and headache tablets for one of Guy's friends who suffered from migraines. Looking at the capacious bag that Hilda carried in addition to the basket, Gemma was willing to bet that she had a crystal ball and a book of spells in there as well.

"I've sorted some jars of apple puree and some apple juice for you," said Hilda. "A friend of mine will drop them round later. Now, looking at your aura this morning, I'd say you've had some news."

With a gasp of surprise, Gemma told her about the competition and how she'd not noticed the 'taster' question when she'd last looked at the rules.

"They have a habit of changing things just to keep people on their toes – and I think it's their way of finding out who's really keen and who thinks anything will do."

"I was thinking of doing some poems about how the building used to be called The Cockatoo and about Black Marley the highwayman and Great Aunt Anna of course."

"If you're writing about interesting characters and spooky happenings, then you have to mention the Grey Lady," said Hilda.

"Tell me more – who is she?" Gemma picked up her pen.

"She's thought to be the ghost of a lady called Dorothy Beacham who once lived there. Several groups have held séances – I went to one there once. You'll smell bread baking if she's about."

"I remember Great Aunt Anna holding a séance once. The lady who conducted it did mention seeing a lady in the kitchen."

There was so much for them to talk about that they ended up having more tea and toasted cheese and onion sandwiches.

Gemma showed Hilda the pictures she'd bought.

"Definitely a good omen," Hilda said. "Besides, it would've been rude not to buy them." Her green eyes shone behind her round glasses.

"So all I need now is a recipe that uses something English and something Italian," said Gemma.

"The pictures have given you the answer," said Hilda getting to her feet and picking up her basket. "You can't go wrong with apples and lemons."

Gemma headed back to her car. On the drive home, an idea came to her. Great Aunt Anna used to make apple cake flavoured with cinnamon. She wondered how it would work with lemon instead of cinnamon. She stopped at the supermarket and bought some ingredients. She'd experiment later. There were plenty of recipes available on the internet. Surely she could adapt one of them? She'd get up early tomorrow and experiment.

Gemma parked her car in its space near the gate to the orchard. She was surprised to see Dan walking down the street towards *The Inheritance* from the direction of the road that ran past the orchard and towards the woodland and the ridge of hills that looked down on the village. He was wearing walking boots and a jacket and his face flushed with embarrassment when he saw her.

"Gemma – I'm so sorry about what happened the other night. My Dad can be – a bit difficult sometimes."

Gemma could see Stefano staring at them from the doorway of the café where he was just saying goodbye to a man who looked like Hilda's partner – judging by the iron-grey hair and the patchwork trousers. Stefano still looked as hostile as he had this morning. Gemma ignored him. She'd had enough of his moods.

"I'm sorry Stefano got hurt," Dan went on.

"He'll get over it," said Gemma. "Look, Dan, it wasn't your fault. You're not responsible for your father's behaviour. You need to look after yourself."

His eyes looked sad. "I really like you Gemma and I didn't want anything to spoil it."

"I like you too," said Gemma, despite the fact that a warning voice inside her head was screaming: "You don't need another man right now."

"Would you come for a drink with me sometime?"

"Yes," she said, a feeling of anxiety filling her when she remembered what had happened when she'd gone to the pub with Mark.

Dan's not like that, she said to herself.

She was rewarded with Dan's lovely smile and the light returning to his sea green eyes.

She paused outside the kitchen. Stefano was talking to someone on his mobile.

"Si chiama Gemma," he was saying, followed by a torrent of Italian that she didn't understand.

The call ended abruptly and he tossed his mobile onto the table in a gesture of frustration.

His face was like a thundercloud as she hung up her jacket and put her bag in the cupboard.

"Why were you talking to *him*?"

"If you mean Dan, he's a friend. I like him. He can't help who his father is."

"Don't expect me to rescue you again."

"I didn't expect you to do anything last time."

"Women – you're all the same," he said, getting a knife from his butcher's block and dicing an onion.

Soon the air in the kitchen was full of the aroma of onion and garlic, tomatoes and fresh basil. Stefano's face was like a mask of anger and Gemma wondered what had upset him so much. There was so much tension in the kitchen that the atmosphere crackled like an approaching storm.

"I feel sorry for the people eating with us tonight," she said. "It's supposed to be better to eat food that's created in love rather than anger."

She made herself a cup of tea and headed for the stairs. If he wanted coffee he could make it himself.

He followed her, blocking her path. "Who told you that?"

"What?"

"About creating food with love?"

"My Great Aunt." Gemma pushed past him, narrowly avoiding slopping her tea on the wooden stairs. She went up to her room, shut the door and lay on her bed sipping her tea trying to recapture the happy light in Dan's eyes when she said she'd go for a drink with him.

Stefano went back to the kitchen. It had not been a good day. He knew that Sofia was going through a bad patch with Theo. He hated to think she was unhappy and wanted nothing more than to go to Sorrento, walk into Trattoria Andrea and take her in his arms.

What then? asked the voice inside his head, you've *got nothing to offer her until you've finished here.*

He had a feeling she was playing with him like a cat does with a mouse to see how serious he really was. Then this afternoon she was in a bad mood with him. She'd seen a photo on the internet – a friend had told her about it. It was the photo of Stefano and Gemma on the Opening Night, the one that went in *The Telegraph*. Molly had taken the photo and had urged them 'squeeze up together real close' and they had done.

Now Sofia had seen it and was clearly jealous, wanting to know what this woman was to him.

"Her name is Gemma. She is a business partner nothing more. Yes we live in the same place but we don't sleep together. No, Sofia I swear I've never kissed her."

The questions went on until someone came into the room and she finished the call abruptly. Since then she'd not replied to any of his texts.

Stefano made himself a coffee.

"*Things look better when you eat and drink something,*" his mother always said.

He ate a slice of torta di limone that he found in the fridge. This made him think of the big dream he'd had since he was young of having a lemon grove in Sorrento with a view of the sea. He closed his eyes and imagined the sight and smell of lemon blossom. He thought of the big 'bread lemons' they had at home that they ate sliced and sprinkled with a little sugar.

Once, when he and Sofia were lying on the beach together he told her about his dream. She thought he was mad.

"If I had a choice, I'd live in a city," she said. "Rome or maybe London."

"Girls change when they get married," he'd said. Now he wondered if that was true.

CHAPTER ELEVEN

Gemma got up early the next day and began her idea for the new recipe that would link England and Italy. Happy memories came flooding back as she set the oven, assembled the ingredients and put on an apron she'd found upstairs in the airing cupboard. The apron was one of Great Aunt Anna's. It was bright scarlet and in big white letters it said 'Eat, Love and Dance on the Table.'

The air in the kitchen was full of the combined scents of lemon, apples and fresh baking as 'Torta Inheritance' came to life. It was a combination of the usual cake mixture she used to make with Great Aunt Anna - butter, sugar and eggs and flour – but with the addition of lemon zest and a touch of ginger. As she mixed, Gemma felt her Great Aunt's presence so strongly that she turned around expecting to see her. She whispered a little prayer as she combined grated apple and lemon juice and continued to mix. When she judged the consistency to be right, she put it in the greased tin, smoothed the top and put the cake in the oven.

While she waited for it to cook, she fetched her laptop from upstairs, brought it down to the kitchen and plugged it in. There'd been no sound from Stefano's room for which she was grateful. He'd made her angry yesterday and she wondered why she'd gone to the trouble of buying him a birthday present. *So he doesn't make any excuses for not fulfilling his part of the bargain*, she said to herself.

She checked through the answers she'd written for the next round of the competition. Now all she needed to do was to check that the recipe worked and then she could send it.

She knew she should test the recipe on Stefano, but judging by the mood he was in yesterday she felt he would take one bite and tell her it was "'orrible."

The kitchen timer reminded her to check on the cake. She got it out of the oven and pressed the top lightly as her Great Aunt had taught her and it felt just right. She placed it on a cooling rack and waited a few minutes before turning it out of the tin. It came out perfectly - the delicious smell of it reminded her of how hungry she was.

She heard the postman's cheerful whistle and went to the door to collect the post. As she looked out she saw Dan coming back down the hill from the direction of the woods. He was dressed in walking boots and sweatshirt and his skin glowed with fresh air and exercise.

Gemma waved to him.

"I wasn't trespassing," he said. "I was in the fields behind where the old house was. You get a great view from up there – it helps to put things in perspective."

"I wouldn't care if you did walk in the woods," said Gemma. "I feel bad that I've been here all this time and I've not been to see them. I do remember the ruins of the house, I found an old necklace there once, but for some reason Great Aunt Anna was never keen on that end of the woods."

"There's a lot to see around there. It's a great place to watch badgers."

Gemma blushed as she thought of being in close proximity to Dan under the moonlight. Again she wished it could've been Dan not Stefano that her Great Aunt had partnered her with.

"I wondered if you'd like to give me your opinion on a cake I've just made," she said.

"Now you're talking," said Dan. "It's just what I could do with after my walk."

He followed her through the front door and out into the kitchen. She made coffee and cut him a generous slice, watching his face as he ate it.

"Great," he said. "Will this be featuring on the menu soon?"

"I hope so."

Gemma suddenly felt wary. No matter how much she liked Dan there was still his father to content with and she didn't want to give too many secrets away in case it harmed the business.

Stefano felt like a caged animal skulking in his room. He'd intended to get up earlier and try and put yesterday behind him. Then from his window he'd seen Gemma talking to that boy with hair the colour of straw. Dan. The son of the man who had tried to break in.

He stood watching, noticing the way Gemma fidgeted with her hair the way girls did when they wanted men to notice them. *Why*? he wondered. What did she see in him? He expected her to say goodbye and come back inside but instead he seemed to be following her indoors. He heard their voices interspersed with laughter in the kitchen. He stayed in his room.

Stefano came down when he heard them leave the building. There was the sound of the front door closing and then he saw them walking along the road – too close for his liking – along the road towards the pub. Well, she needn't think he'd come to her rescue this time. If this other English boy turned crazy she could sort it out for herself.

He went into the café noticing that the pictures she'd brought back from Dalesbury yesterday and that he'd merely grunted at because of the mood he was in were now hanging above the fireplace. He guessed that Dan must have put them there and felt annoyed that she'd asked him to do that.

He felt another surge of irritation when he realised Gemma had been busy baking. He looked around but could not find fault with the way she'd left the kitchen. She'd tidied away everything she'd used and the surfaces were clean. He could smell coffee and it immediately made him realise that it was exactly what he could do with.

On the table was a cake – three quarters of a cake to be precise. Stefano looked at it critically. He didn't understand the English obsession with cake, particularly those sickly looking little cupcakes that were in every bakery he'd passed. The English were welcome to them – although he did concede that their cheeses were something to be reckoned with, particularly Cheddar and Red Leicester which he gathered were place names.

He looked at the cake as he sipped his espresso. That was another thing about the English. In Trattoria Andrea they used to laugh when yet another holidaymaker asked for a cappuccino after their evening meal. In Italy it was a breakfast drink and no self-respecting Italian would have one after midday.

He cut a thin slice of the cake and ate it slowly, savouring the blending of the various flavours. It needed something to go with it. Ordinary cream would be OK or that clotted cream that Gemma gave him with the scones. Something was missing and he couldn't think what it was.

Gemma had fun at the pub with Dan. They drank glasses of cider and ate ploughmans lunches with crusty bread, cheese and pickles. He told her about his love of walking and how it had started as a result of an injury.

"I used to love running," he said. "I competed for the school and was really happy when I got through to the County Sports." He looked sad. "Those were good days. It was before Dad started drinking too heavily and he and Mum used to come and cheer me on. Me and my little sister, Sarah," he added.

"What happened to her?"

"She went to live with my Auntie Pat when Mum died. Dad said he'd never wanted a girl." He looked as if he was about to cry. "I do miss her."

"You can change things," said Gemma.

Dan chewed his lip. "I'd like a proper job – not just being Dad's partner in the chippy. He still only gives me pocket money. I can't afford to move out. I know it's only because he's shit scared of losing me, but I feel – trapped. That's why I go walking."

"What happened to your running?"

"I got injured – broke my ankle. It never healed properly. Dad used the excuse of his disappointment that I missed competing in the County Sports for his drinking."

"It wasn't your fault," said Gemma. "He should be proud of the person you are now."

"Thank you."

Gemma felt as if things were moving too fast. She'd found Dan easy to talk to and had told him about her own uneasy relationship with her mother. She realised from what he said about being trapped that she'd been lucky to escape when she did. She could see now that being with Mark for so long hadn't been good for her self-esteem but at least she'd learned from the experience and wouldn't be repeating it anytime soon.

She spotted a dart board in the corner of the room. "Fancy a game?" she asked in an attempt to lighten the atmosphere. She hadn't played for ages – not since she and Laura shared a flat and used to go down to their local, The Beehive, on a Friday night.

He agreed readily enough and stepped up to the board, pulling out the darts and handing them to her.

The next half hour had passed quickly as they drank more cider and played darts. Dan beat her easily and Gemma, who was competitive although she never liked games lessons at school, was all set to challenge him to a return match. Then she noticed the time and realised she should be back at *The Inheritance* to prepare for their opening time.

They'd just left The Green Man and were saying goodbye to each other when battered white van pulled up next to them. The passenger door was flung open.

"Get in." Mike Bridges' face was mottled red with anger. "You don't need to hang around with a tart like her."

Stand up to him, Dan, Gemma wanted to say, but he had to make that decision for himself.

"Thanks for a lovely lunchtime, Gemma," he said.

"See you soon, Dan."

Gemma walked back to the café wishing there was something she could do to help. She could offer him a place to stay but that would mean him camping out in the Club Room – which would be difficult now the room was being used so much.

If she sorted Great Aunt Anna's room then that would create another guest room – but she didn't feel ready to do that yet. There were too many memories and she didn't want to break the atmosphere that still hung around the room in case they disappeared.

She could hear a commotion going on long before she got anywhere near the café. A black taxi had pulled up outside and a harassed looking driver with thinning sandy hair was unloading a large assortment of suitcases and overflowing bags.

With a feeling of trepidation, Gemma stepped over the mound of baggage and into the café. Her mother was sitting at a table smoking a cigarette and flicking the ash onto the floor. Her face was perfectly made up as usual, the eye-shadow too bright a blue for someone her age and the foundation a shade too orange. Her artificially blonde hair was perfectly styled as always and so stiff with hairspray that it wouldn't have moved in a ten-force gale. Her red lipsticked mouth looked sulky and she was totally ignoring Stefano's entreaties to move outside with her cigarette.

"There you are, Gemma," she said. "I could do with a cup of tea and someone needs to bring my bags in." She looked pointedly at Stefano when she said this.

That was typical of her mother to turn up unannounced and then expect everything to revolve around her. Well she could think again. Gemma had had years of playing her mother's games. It was time to put a stop to it. She couldn't advise Dan to go against his father and then carry on dancing to her mother's tune.

Gemma stepped forward and snatched the cigarette off her mother. She took it outside and put it out, feeling irritated because she had to step over the mound of luggage again. She put the remains into the bin placed outside for those customers who needed it.

The taxi driver was still there. "Someone needs to pay me," he said. "I didn't drive her all the way from London out of the goodness of my heart."

Gemma went back into the café. "Your taxi driver needs paying," she said.

"Sort it out for me will you, Gemma? I can't find my purse at the moment."

"That's funny, neither can I," said Gemma keeping a firm hold of her bag. "Looks like he'll have to stay the night which will cost you even more."

Pamela's mouth set in a thin red line. She picked up her handbag and stalked outside, her dagger-like heels clicking on the wooden floor.

"She is your mother?" asked Stefano.

"Yes."

"She is staying here?"

"Not if I can help it."

Pamela returned looking pathetic. Her grey eyes were watery and she looked like she was going to cry. Gemma had had a lifetime of pandering to her mother's moods and it looked like she was about to fall into the same trap until her mother got out another cigarette and sat tapping it on the side of the box.

"Put that away." Gemma's voice cracked like a whip and even Stefano looked startled. "You'll get us closed down if you start smoking in here."

"I've got no money," said her mother. "I can't believe that Anna left nothing to me in her will. I always was her favourite."

"She was more than good to you and you abused it."

"Is he going to carry my bags in or is he just going to keep staring at us?"

"His name is Stefano and he's my business partner. He's not a servant. He's got food to prepare for tonight. There's nothing the matter with your arms and legs. You can carry your bags upstairs yourself. And you're only staying two nights."

"Two nights. I need at least three weeks, Gemma."

"And we're not here to wait on you."

Stefano returned to the kitchen and within minutes the smell of frying meat and garlic drifted towards the café.

"I don't eat stuff with garlic in it. It upsets my digestion." Pamela had made no attempt to get to her feet.

"It looks like we might have a shower," said Gemma pretending to look out of the window. Your stuff might get rather wet."

"You'll carry it in for me won't you, Gemma, if *he* won't?"

"We're both busy. The café will be opening in less than two hours. You can sleep in my room. I'll sleep on an airbed in the Club Room."

"You don't sleep with *him* then?"

"No, of course not. I told you, he's a business partner."

"Mark got the impression that you two were an item."

"He was wrong then – and how do you know what Mark thinks?"

Pamela looked shifty. "I'll go and get my stuff in. Like you say, it does look like rain."

Gemma felt a shaft of anger. Something was going on. It was most unlike her mother to travel any distance unless she had an ulterior motive.

She went up to her room and cleared away anything she didn't want her mother rifling through.

"Why can't I sleep in Anna's room? Then you wouldn't have to move."

"Nobody is going in there yet."

"It's not a shrine you know, Gemma. Most of the stuff in there could be chucked in a skip if you want my opinion."

"I don't."

"What time is dinner?"

"You'll have to fit in with us. Stefano will do you something in the kitchen."

Pamela pulled a face.

"If you prefer you can take yourself off to the fish and chip shop or the pub."

Gemma knew her mother wouldn't be seen dead in either place.

"I don't see why you finished with Mark. He seems really cut up about the whole thing. He said he came to see you but you got stroppy with him."

"He tried to rape me. I fought back. He's lucky I didn't press charges."

"You're not getting any younger Gemma. You can't afford to keep chopping and changing."

"I'm hardly chopping and changing. I'm just not prepared to put up with being treated badly – by anybody."

"How long is she staying here?" asked Stefano when Gemma stormed into the kitchen for a restorative cup of tea.

"Two days – no more. I've told her."

He nodded. "Family can be very difficult."

"Yes."

She noticed that the cake she made had a bit more missing from it. She pointed to it. "Did you try it?"

"Si. Ha un sapore molto buono. It tastes very good."

"Not 'orrible?"

"*No*. Not 'orrible." His eyes lit up like sunlit dark honey. "It needs – something. To go with it. Your clotted cream with amaretto added. A hint of almonds. England and Italy, yes?"

"Yes," said Gemma smiling back, all thoughts of her mother temporarily forgotten.

"That's a great idea."

"I hope I'm not intruding on anything," said Pamela coming into the room. She'd changed and was now wearing a gold-coloured dress that was so tight it made her look as if she'd been shrink-wrapped. Her perfume was sickly and overpowering and Gemma moved her as far away from the food as possible.

Gemma switched on her laptop and added Stefano's idea for the amaretto cream to go with the cake. They hadn't tested it, but she was sure it would be just perfect. She crossed her fingers and sent the entry.

"I thought we could go shopping in Worcester tomorrow," said Pamela. "I haven't been there for years."

"I thought you had no money."

"Well – you know." Pamela flapped her hands distractedly. "When an overdraft gets beyond a certain size a bit more doesn't make much difference."

"I don't know," said Gemma. "I've never had one – and I can't go shopping with you. I've got things to do here."

"You're boring – just like your father."

"There's a bus at eight o'clock from the end of the road."

"Can't I borrow your car?"

"I'm using it."

Pamela looked sulky and picked at the carbonara Stefano put in front of her.

"No garlic," he said.

Stefano had never met anyone like Gemma's mother. It didn't seem possible that they were the same family. In Italy older women still dressed in black and behaved quietly. This woman was the total opposite. He didn't like her and he didn't trust her.

Gemma wasn't surprised that her mother didn't get up and go for the eight o'clock bus. She felt a bit mean for being so hard on her and woke that morning after a night on one of the airbeds that had been left behind by

Laura and her cousins determined to be nicer to her however irritating she was.

Dan's story about losing his Mum had touched her heart and Pamela was the only mother she'd ever have.

Her new resolve began to crumble when Pamela proceeded to use all the hot water having a bath and hogged the bathroom for an hour and a half doing her make up.

"I'm going to Dalesbury to do a few things if you'd like to come," Gemma offered. "You'll need to be quick with your breakfast though. I'm going in ten minutes."

"I never eat breakfast," said Pamela. "We can have coffee when we get there." She got out a silver compact, opened it and looked in the mirror to touch up her already perfect scarlet lipstick. "You'll have to do something about the mirror in the bathroom," she said, her voice distorted because her mouth was half open. "It needs more light."

"It's not troubling me," said Gemma.

"You've certainly let yourself go since you split up with Mark."

Gemma decided to ignore the comment. She picked up her bag and car keys and headed for the door. The journey to Dalesbury was taken up with a monologue from Pamela about how there was nothing to do in the country and the best thing Gemma could do was accept a good offer on the café.

Over coffee, which Gemma paid for, Pamela started quizzing her about money and what happened when she and Stefano had completed the six months.

"We won't get anything unless we make a profit at the end of six months."

"Well, you could sell it anyway couldn't you? Mark said he'd spoken to someone who'd made you an offer."

Gemma's temper flared at this. They were sitting outside the café and several passers-by stared as she leapt to her feet and confronted her mother.

"This has got nothing to do with Mark or anyone else. It's none of his business. We – are – no – longer – an – item. I wouldn't have him back gift-wrapped. And it has nothing to do with you either, Mum. If you came here expecting to get something out of it then you've had a wasted journey. If the business doesn't succeed then the money will probably go to a cats' home."

Pamela's mouth was a round 'o' of shock. "I can't believe you'd accept a deal like that without contesting the will. Anna must've lost her marbles. We'll take this further Gemma. We'll finish our coffee and go and see the solicitor."

"No, we won't," said Gemma. "You will mind your own business and leave me to look after mine. Now if you've finished your coffee it's time we headed back. I've got stuff to do – and you need to sort somewhere else to stay."

"I can't believe a daughter of mine could be so hard." Pamela looked as if she was about to cry.

"Spare me the water-works," said Gemma. "We both know you're just play-acting."

Gemma went to the bank and the Cash & Carry. She took posters advertising the next Storytellers evening to the library and some of the local shops. Pamela trailed along behind making the occasional disparaging remark about the town and its inhabitants which Gemma chose to ignore.

It was a silent journey back to Charworth.

Stefano was sitting out in the cafe garden when they got back. He'd been drinking an ice cold beer and enjoying the peace and quiet. It was a small space surrounded by a brick wall accessed from the Club Room. The raised beds containing herbs and lavender were overgrown and choked with weeds. He noted that there was rosemary and fennel and several varieties of mint. The smell of rosemary reminded him of the shampoo Sofia used and he ached to hold her in his arms again. Looking at the blue sky he could imagine he was home again and that he'd see her later that day. Gemma arriving back with her dragon of a mother only reminded him of what he had lost and may never get back.

"You are early," he said.

"Yes," said Gemma. "I have things to do."

"There was a phone call," he said. "A lady from the television. I could not understand her. She will see you later."

"You mean she will call back?"

He shrugged. "Whatever." He finished his beer and got to his feet. There would be no more peace outside today with that woman in residence.

Gemma wondered what they wanted. She couldn't believe they'd have made a decision that quickly. She hoped she hadn't forgotten to answer one of the questions or something daft like that. It would be awful if they missed out on an important chance because she'd been careless.

She sat for a few minutes soaking up the spring sunshine. She remembered playing for hours out here when she was a child, making a den under one of the wooden tables by hanging a blanket over it. Now the tables looked as if they could do with replacing and the garden itself needed weeding and pruning. If she was staying for good she'd certainly want to sort this out and open up the garden so that customers could use it.

It was sad to think that, if she and Stefano succeeded, the café would be sold and the proceeds split between them, even though it meant she would be able to fulfil her dream of taking her writing more seriously. Her mother had been scathing about this when Gemma mentioned it this morning.

"You're full of airy-fairy ideas just like your father," she said.

"It's something I enjoy doing."

"I don't think I could bring myself to read anything you wrote," said her mother.

Since Gemma could never remember her reading anything anyway, this didn't mean a lot, but the barb still stung. She wished she could just be pleased for her for once. She couldn't remember her mother ever showing up for parents' evening – apart from the time just after her father left when Pamela fancied the maths teacher and had turned up at the school in a low-cut black dress that was more suited to a nightclub.

Gemma went out just after lunch and Stefano didn't much like being left alone with the woman he'd started calling la Strega – the witch - under his breath. He heard her on the phone, her false laugh rising and falling, as she talked to one person after another, oblivious to the fact that she was blocking callers who might want to book a table for the evening.

"Do you have a mobile?" he asked her when she came back into the kitchen to make herself tea.

She was messy and left a trail of liquid from the teabag across the surface he was about to use and down the front of the fridge.

She clearly did have a mobile – he could see it sticking out of the top of the expensive looking bead encrusted handbag she carried.

"A bit fussy for a bloke, aren't you?" she said. "But then I expect you're gay. Lots of chefs are aren't they?"

Stefano's command of English wasn't brilliant but he did understand the implied insult. He'd hung around with enough English tourists who'd visited the Trattoria to pick up most of the words and phrases he would never learn at school.

He glared at her. "I like my kitchen to be clean and tidy."

"Oh – so it's *your* kitchen is it? I thought this crazy idea involved both of you."

"Si, it does. Both of us."

Pamela looked at him and he was reminded of seeing a snake staring at a frog before it pounced when he was on holiday playing near a river. He wondered what she was going to say next. He wished Gemma would come back.

"Well see here Antonio or whatever your name is – how about if I make it worth your while to go back to wherever it is you came from? You could pack up and go now before Gemma comes back."

Stefano faced her squarely. "*No*," he said. "I stay."

"You'll be sorry," she hissed. "You'll both end up with nothing."

She stormed upstairs.

Stefano got a beer from the fridge, took the top off and took a long drink. He would be glad when la Strega had gone.

Gemma returned from a visit to Diana where she'd had another search through her aircraft hangar of a shed to see if there was anything else the café could make use of. Diana was keen to clear the final bits and pieces so she could pull the shed down and put up a summerhouse that she could use as a workroom.

Gemma had spent an interesting couple of hours exploring the mounds of boxes and shrouded items and helping Diana to sort them into sections labelled 'keep', 'sell' and 'chuck.' Barnaby the springer spaniel had run around yelping excitedly at first and had then laid down in a sunny patch keeping an eye on what they were doing. Gemma got covered in cobwebs and dust and hoped her mother hadn't done her usual trick of hogging all the hot water. She'd need a bath when she got home.

On the plus side, she'd acquired some beautiful glassware and some cake stands and a tea service that would be just perfect for the special afternoon teas they'd be offering at *The Inheritance*.

Diana had helped her wrap everything carefully in newspaper and bubble-wrap and Gemma put it in the boot of her car. She drove slowly back to Charworth hoping she didn't have to do an emergency stop.

The minute she pulled up in her space near the orchard she knew something was wrong.

She could hear raised voices and a lot of banging and crashing. Her first thought was that Mike Bridges had returned for another battle. She knew she should stay out and call the police but she knew they could be slow to respond or may not bother at all. Without hesitating she dashed in.

Stefano and her mother were facing each other on the stairs like two cats hissing and spitting at each other before the fur started flying.

"Ladra – thief! Put those things back. They do not belong to you."

Pamela's suitcases and bags were in an untidy heap near the door. She was holding a large bag close to her as if it contained the crown jewels.

"What's going on?" yelled Gemma.

Stefano turned to her. "Your mother is a thief."

Pamela's face grew mottled despite the thick make up she wore. "He's lying," she hissed.

"I am not a liar. You are a thief. Those things belong to Gemma." He lunged at her and the bag dropped spilling a shower of jewellery and silver down the stairs.

Pamela hurried after them, struggling in her high heels.

Gemma picked them up. She recognised some of the items as necklaces and rings that Great Aunt Anna had worn. There were silver ornaments and brass candlesticks and even the hat pins that had aroused so many memories for Gemma.

"How could you, mother?"

Pamela was defiant. "I'm her niece. I'm entitled to them."

"You are not. They were left to me."

"You'll only sit and look at them – treat them like the Holy Grail. Some of these things are worth a fortune."

"That's all you think about isn't it, mother? Money, money, money. Well you're not having any more of mine. That's exactly why Great Aunt Anna didn't leave you anything – because you wouldn't value it any more than anything else she's ever given you. Stefano, search the bags."

"I'll have the police on you," screeched Pamela.

"Go ahead, mother," said Gemma grimly. "We'll ask them to arrest you.
"

"Have we come at a bad time?" asked a man with an Irish accent. "My name's Seamus McGinty and this is Lucinda Stockton-Smith. We're part of the team from Dining Hotspots and we've come to interview you for the programme."

"E magnifico," said Stefano. "You come to kitchen and I make you coffee." He gestured towards Pamela. "She is just leaving."

"I'll get you a taxi," said Gemma.

"But where will I go?" wailed Pamela.

"I'm sure you'll think of somewhere, mother."

The atmosphere felt lighter once Pamela's baggage had been bundled into a taxi and she'd been driven away in the middle of a tearful apology that Gemma was sure would be forgotten as soon as she was allowed to stay. It meant about the same as Mark's promises to be faithful to her.

By the time Gemma got into the kitchen, Lucinda and Seamus were well under way with filming Stefano in action.

They were fascinated by *The Inheritance* and its history and the interesting characters who had once lived here.

"We love the fusion of Italian and English cultures," said Lucinda who had auburn hair gathered into an immaculate French plait, "and I can't wait to find out more about the reason for the challenge you've both been set. This is a truly atmospheric building and the stories you've given us are just wonderful."

They went from attic to cellar taking photos, making notes and asking questions.

"If you two aren't an item then you should be," said Seamus who was clearly gay. "I've never sensed such chemistry between two people before."

Gemma smiled, not wishing to be drawn into that line of questioning.

Fortunately at that moment, Stefano summoned them back to the kitchen where he'd prepared food for them and glasses of ruby red wine.

Out in the café, the first customers were just arriving, together with Francine who was doing some waitressing when she could in between college lectures.

"Sorry I'm late," Francine said. "I had to stop for an ambulance that was in a bit of a hurry."

"You're good to get here at all."

Gemma greeted the customers and showed them to their table and gave them menus.

She returned to the kitchen to carry on the conversation with Seamus and Lucinda who were really enthusiastic about their competition entry. "We'll be televising this interview later in the week," said Lucinda, "and then it's up to the viewers to vote and tell us who they'd like to see in the next round. We've got six contenders and only four can go through."

They were packing up their camera equipment and preparing to leave when there was a commotion at the door. Gemma rushed forward hoping it wasn't her mother making a return visit complete with an embarrassing display of emotion.

She was surprised to see Dan standing there, white faced and shaking.

"He's dead, Gemma," he said and burst into tears.

Gemma put her arms round him and pulled him into the kitchen out of the way of the curious stares of the diners.

"What's happened?" she asked, breathing in his scent of sun-dried cotton and coconut shampoo.

"It's like Paddy's Market here," she heard Seamus say to Stefano as he and Lucinda left. "I haven't had so much fun since the last time I was in Dublin."

"Che casino! What a mess," said Stefano as he headed back to the kitchen.

Gemma was sure this had blown their chances with the competition – if they had any to start with.

Gemma had made Dan a mug of hot sweet tea.

"What happened?" she asked.

"It's my sister," he said, rubbing the back of his hand across his face. "Sarah. She's sixteen. She rang earlier to say that Auntie Pat had thrown her out because she'd got pregnant and could she come home." He gulped down some tea. "Dad said no. It was her own fault – she should've kept her legs together. He said some terrible things about Mum too. I couldn't hack that, Gemma. I'd had enough. I told Dad I was going to fetch Sarah." He took a deep breath and his voice cracked.

"Then what did you do?"

"I opened the front door. Dad was at the top of the stairs at the back of the shop where we keep the cooking oil and the paper to wrap the chips in. He'd been drinking as usual. When I walked out he knew I meant it. He came after me but he tripped and came crashing down to the ground. There were three customers in the shop at the time. They witnessed everything."

"Was that the ambulance Francine was overtaken by?"

"They sent a second one. Someone said they thought I should go to hospital to be checked over, but I wouldn't go. I just want to find Sarah. She must be so frightened."

"Where is she?"

"Worcester. At the bus station, but she's got no money and I don't like the idea of her being there all night. Anything could happen. I've missed the last bus and the police say they're coming to interview me but that may not be till tomorrow."

"Where is … your father?" asked Gemma.

"They've taken him away to the hospital mortuary. They told me to follow them – they assume everyone's got a car. I'd have taken Dad's van but he smashed it up yesterday which was partly why he was in such a foul mood."

"Take my car," said Gemma without hesitating. "Find your sister and go and see your Dad."

She went into the kitchen and fetched her car keys.

"Thanks a million, Gemma," said Dan wrapping his arms around her.

Gemma was aware of Stefano glaring at them from the doorway but she didn't care. She'd dreamed of being in Dan's arms but now that it had happened she was surprised she didn't feel anything.

"You don't let me drive your car," said Stefano when she returned to the kitchen, "but you give him your keys like *that* when *he* asks." He snapped his fingers. Gemma wouldn't have been surprised to see sparks appear, he looked so angry.

"He didn't ask, I offered," she said. "There is a difference. I'd do the same if it was your sister stranded in the middle of Worcester at night."

"Si. I believe you," he said, proceeding to chop an onion savagely. "That family is a disaster."

"He can't help who his father is – was."

"You should stay away from him. He is not good for you."

It was late when Dan returned with the car bringing with him a plump girl with lank mousy hair. They both looked as if they'd been crying.

Stefano had gone to bed but Gemma had waited up after the café had closed and they'd cleaned the kitchen and done the cashing up. She fiddled about on her laptop, adding a post to the blog she'd started and was surprised at how many followers she'd had. There was an email from Allan congratulating her and saying he'd do another interview with them once the Dining Hotspots episode had gone live.

When she heard her car pull up outside, she went to the door and called them in.

"Come and have some hot chocolate."

She made hot chocolate and some toast which Dan and Sarah tucked into as if they'd not been fed for a week.

"We saw him." Dan's face was pale. "I've got to go back and collect the death certificate and we need to get Sarah's stuff from our aunt's."

"If I'm not using my car, you can borrow it again," said Gemma knowing how much this would annoy Stefano but not caring. It was the least she could do to help.

She was rewarded by one of Dan's smiles that lit up his eyes.

"Thanks, Gemma," he said. "Come on, Sarah, let's go home."

Gemma watched them walk up the dark street together, Dan carrying Sarah's bag in one hand and the other arm protectively round her shoulders with a feeling of envy. Sarah was lucky to have someone who cared about her so much.

She closed the door and went back to the kitchen, washed up the mugs and plates and left it tidy. She climbed the stairs feeling as if every step was an effort, thankful that at least her mother had gone and she could collapse into her bed and sleep.

When she opened her door, she gasped with shock. It was as if they'd been burgled and the room had been turned. The doors of her cupboard and wardrobe stood wide open. Clothes spilled out of drawers and a bottle of the sickly perfume her mother used lay smashed on the dressing table. The scent clogged her throat and she knew she wouldn't be able to sleep in here tonight. A silver perfume bottle was missing from the table by her bed.

Gemma hoped it would be one of the items in the bag that she'd snatched back from Pamela before she left and had hastily bundled into the Club Room to be sorted out later.

With a sense of dread, she went along the landing to her Great Aunt's room. The scene here was even worse. Gemma felt a shaft of hatred for her mother that she could cause so much damage. The tranquil, shrine-like atmosphere had gone and she didn't know how she'd begin to restore it.

"What is the matter?"

Stefano stood outside the door. He was wearing a t-shirt and jogging bottoms and his hair was standing on end. "What has happened?"

Gemma opened the door wider so he could see.

"Gesu bambino! That woman is an animal."

"You should see what she's done to my room."

"You cannot sleep in there," said Stefano. He went into the room, noting the disruption to the normal order. He'd glimpsed it through the door – the way she left the bed tidy and the perfume she wore that reminded him of Christmas.

Her mother had left the bed just as she'd got out of it. There was a scattering of face powder on the dressing table and the smell of her perfume where she'd broken the bottle was overpowering. He got some tissues from the box by the bed and picked up the fragments of glass. 'Poison,' the label read. Well, that was certainly true. He mopped up the obnoxious liquid and bundled it all into a plastic bag, wrapping it securely so that nobody would be cut by the glass.

He opened the window noticing how the crescent moon hung like a blade in the dark sky.

He could hear Gemma along the landing trying to sort the mess in her Great Aunt's room. She looked ill and he was reminded of how his grandmother had reacted when his grandfather was rushed to hospital. Everyone was so concerned about Riccardo that they didn't notice Maria until she collapsed with what was later said to be a shock reaction.

"You cannot do this tonight," he said. "You must sleep in my bed."

"No," she said. "I'll sleep on the airbed downstairs. She headed along the landing but Stefano took her gently by the shoulders and turned her back towards his room. She swayed and looked as if she was about to fall. She didn't protest again when he steered her towards his room.

He was relieved when she lay down on the bed and closed her eyes. It reminded him of a child falling asleep. One minute she'd been looking at him with unfocused eyes as if she was about to say something, the next she was fast asleep. He took her shoes off and covered her with a blanket hoping it wouldn't rumple her dress too much. She didn't wake.

Stefano went downstairs, collected the airbed and sleeping bag and carried them up to his room. He settled down on the floor next to the bed. It was important to be there in case she woke in the night and needed him.

As he fell asleep he noticed that the sleeping bag carried a faint trace of Gemma's perfume and he remembered that she'd slept in it when her mother was here. He felt relieved that Pamela had gone and hoped she'd never come back.

He was glad Mike Bridges was no longer a threat and that the rest of his enforced stay in England should pass more peacefully. Why, then, did he feel so unsettled?

CHAPTER TWELVE

Gemma felt as if she was rising to the surface through deep, black water. She'd slept deeply and as she opened her eyes she tried to remember where she was and what had happened. The wallpaper was different – pale green patterned with leaves. There was a small red clock on the bedside table that she didn't recognise and the fragment of sky she could see through the curtains gave her a view of the church spire. The sheets smelled different – of spicy aftershave …

With a sense of shock she realised she was in Stefano's bed. What had happened last night? She couldn't remember. Had they …? Surely she'd have remembered if anything had happened between them – but then you heard of drugs being put in wine and food and girls being date-raped. Her clothing was undisturbed apart from her shoes being taken off. Gemma's mind spun with uncertainty as the bedroom door opened.

"Tea and toast," said Stefano. He was fully dressed and if anything romantic had happened he was giving no sign of it. "You are better this morning?"

"Yes," she said. "What happened last night?"

"You looked …" he mimed someone falling about unsteadily. "And your face was the colour of flour."

Gemma sat up and took the tray from him. "Thank you," she said. "Where did you sleep?"

"Here," he said. "On floor."

"Oh," said Gemma, feeling suddenly shy. She hoped she hadn't snored or dribbled or talked in her sleep.

She finished her tea and toast and then went to the bathroom. She had a long, deep bath, feeling the water ease away the stress and strain of the previous day. She inhaled the scent of the lime and ginger bath oil she'd bought in Dalesbury that was said to be good for giving energy and coping with difficult situations. She had a feeling that sorting out the desecration to Great Aunt Anna's room was going to be one of those.

She'd hung the dress she was wearing last night in the steam from the bath in the hope that the creases would drop out. She wished the creases and uncertainties in her life could be dealt with as easily.

She put on jogging bottoms and a sweatshirt, brushed her hair and cleaned the bathroom before going downstairs and washing up her breakfast things. Stefano was sitting out in the garden again. He was frowning at his mobile phone as if it had upset him.

She took a couple of phone calls for restaurant bookings and started fiddling with her laptop, checking Facebook and emails. *You're putting it off*, she told herself. *Just pitch in and do something. It will make a difference.*

She got some black bags and a duster and went upstairs determined to leave the room as Great Aunt Anna would've liked. Gemma began by re-folding the clothes that had been carelessly tossed from drawers and cupboards. Some of them, like the pink summer dress with white daisies on it that was her Great Aunt's favourite, brought back memories of picnics and days on the beach.

There was the blue velvet hat that she used to wear to church and the fur coat she'd had off the local greengrocer in exchange for some money he owed her.

"Where he got it from, heaven knows," she'd once said.

Gemma found all the cards and presents she'd made for her – some of the cards torn now in her mother's frenzy to find something. What had she been looking for? There wasn't a square inch of the raspberry pink carpet that wasn't covered in items that her mother had tossed about. Some of the ornaments had broken - like the little black china cat Gemma had won at a fairground.

She worked methodically, tidying a drawer at a time, the memories flooding back. Time passed quickly and with a shock Gemma realised it was lunchtime.

She went downstairs for lunch and to catch up with her emails. There was one from Allan and Molly wishing them good luck with the competition and a whole host of others offering them special advertising rates provided they signed up today.

"We go to Cash & Carry?" asked Stefano. "Or I take your car and go?"

"Come on," she said, "let's go now."

They loaded the boot with the things on Stefano's list and then they called at Diana's on the way back to collect the birthday cake she'd bought for him and kept there. She'd have preferred to make him one, knowing he was certain to pronounce a shop-bought one as "'orrible" but if she'd have made one at the café he'd have wanted to know what she was up to.

Diana showed them the almost-cleared shed and the brochures advertising summerhouses that she was currently looking at.

"My ex wouldn't recognise the place if he came back to it," she said. "Not that I'd let him in. Barnaby's the only male company I want."

Barnaby thumped his plumy tail on the ground as if applauding the comment.

The afternoon was slipping away by the time they got back to the café and unloaded everything. Gemma hid the cake in a cupboard in the Club Room hoping Stefano wouldn't go there in search of anything.

She laid the tables ready for the evening and made sure there were fresh flowers. The smell of roasting chicken – an ingredient for tonight's special of pollo alla cacciatora (Hunter's Chicken) drifted through from the kitchen together with the yeasty aroma of the pizza dough Stefano was experimenting with. Gemma's stomach growled with hunger but she had work to do. Earlier she'd started preparing English trifle (something Stefano called zuppa inglese – English soup). She finished these, adding whipped cream and grated chocolate to the tops, remembering how this used to be a really special dessert eaten mainly on Sundays when she was a child.

Before the customers started arriving, she went upstairs to check on her room. It still smelled strongly of 'Poison' despite the open window. She'd sleep downstairs tonight on the airbed, she decided. It would probably take the rest of the week to clear away the rest of the havoc her mother had caused. She'd sorted the scattered powder and tissues, used cotton wool and tights only worn once and discarded that were just left on the floor. There was a half-drunk cup of tea on the bedside table and an empty bottle of gin left amongst the rumpled bedclothes that Gemma knew for certain was not hers.

Her mother had been meticulous, if untidy, in her search. No drawer or cupboard had been left untouched.

"I would not like my grandfather's room to be treated like this," said Stefano from the doorway. "I am glad she has gone."

"So am I," said Gemma.

In Great Aunt Anna's room the scent of roses and violets rose from everything she touched as if she was still in the room. Gemma was surprised that her mother hadn't been aware of it, but then she never had been the most sensitive of women. She continued the tidying up she'd started that morning wanting to return the room to way it had been left.

She'd carried up the bag of things that her mother had tried to steal and spent some time putting these back where they belonged. The elaborate hat pins that lived in a violet patterned stand on the dressing table brought back special memories of watching Great Aunt Anna getting ready for church and securing her blue velvet hat with the big pearl pin.

"Does that go right into your head?" seven-year-old Gemma had asked.

"Thankfully, no," said Great Aunt Anna, "or I'd have given up using them long ago." Her lips had curved into a raspberry sorbet smile and she'd given Gemma a warm hug.

There were silver rings – one with an oval of rose quartz in the centre that Gemma had been told was meant for her. "It means love," she was told.

"Who do you love?" she'd asked her Great Aunt.

"I love Gemma," she'd said but there was a far-away look in her eyes as if she'd thought of something that made her sad.

Gemma slipped the ring on and it fitted perfectly, as if it was meant to be there. It felt as if her Great Aunt was giving her blessing, wishing her well.

Gemma noticed that she only had twenty minutes to get changed for the evening. She would have to finish the rest of the room tomorrow. It was as she was closing the door that she noticed a black tin under the chest of drawers, probably kicked there by her mother in her frenzy to find something of value.

Gemma pulled it out. It was about eight inches by six, with pink roses painted on the lid. Some of the paint was flaking off. It didn't weigh much. Something rattled inside it as she turned it in her hands. She lifted the lid. There was a sealed envelope addressed to Gemma. She recognised her Great Aunt's swooping writing – like black birds across the cream paper. Underneath the letter was an Italian coin and a small black and white picture of a man in dark trousers and white shirt.

She carried it downstairs.

"Look, Stefano!"

He picked up the coin. "We stopped using lire in Italy when I was a child."

His face went pale when he looked at the photograph. "This is my Nonno Riccardo. How did it get here? What does the letter say?"

"The first customers are arriving. We'll read it later."

The mystery nagged at Stefano as he prepared dish after dish, his mind not really on his work. He wished he'd paid more attention to the stories his grandfather had told him. He tried to think back to the times they'd had time together – working in the olive groves or going fishing in a small boat. There was the time he'd taken him to that special place and it seemed there was something he wanted to say but hadn't quite managed to do so. Stefano's mind spun back to a day of blue skies and lemon blossom and an old house near the sea.

CHAPTER THIRTEEN

After the café closed, Stefano made them a snack of warm ciabatta and Cheddar cheese – something he had developed a liking for. He poured them glasses of red wine and they sat, one on each side of the kitchen table where Gemma had once made cakes and biscuits with her Great Aunt.

She took the envelope out of the box and slit it carefully.

She read slowly, so that Stefano could understand, her eyes filling with tears as she discovered what her Great Aunt had suffered.

My darling girl, If you are reading this then I am dead and roaming at peace in an eternal springtime. My story begins in 1950 when I met and lost the love of my life.

When I was young I lived in the big house on the other side of the woodland that you can see from The Cockatoo. I loved the woodland and used to wander there as a young child, leaving offerings at the fairy tree and making dens. I felt I had a magical life until my mother died and my father remarried within the year to a woman with a cold heart.

From then on she treated me like some sort of Cinderella-like skivvy. My father believed her side of every story and used to beat me for the slightest thing. She never said a word in my defence.

My father had what they used to call 'champagne tastes and lemonade money.' He was addicted to gambling and used to drink heavily. They had wild parties at the house and I always hid whenever one of those was going on – too many lascivious eyes and groping hands.

"Ugh – poor Great Aunt Anna," said Gemma, taking a sip of her wine.

I was only sixteen and already one of the men – a doctor – had cornered me in the kitchen and said that he was determined to marry me. I said I didn't want to marry anyone – I was too young. He felt my breasts as if he was testing peaches for firmness and said with a sickly leer that it felt as if I was old enough. I knew it was no use asking my father for help – he'd take more notice of his friend than he would of me – particularly if there was money on the table.

From the time when my mother died, the person who showed me the most love and support was a lady called Dorothy who ran a tea-shop at The Cockatoo. Her mother had inherited it and she told me the old stories of the building and the people who had lived here. I came to love it more than I did my own home – which was a home no longer, more a place to be endured.

Gemma glanced at Stefano. He clearly didn't understand everything but his face looked sympathetic.

Dorothy taught me how to cook. Baking calmed me. When I kneaded bread I was taking the knots and problems out of my life, hitting back at the people who were hurting me. When I experimented with flavours for cakes and biscuits and had fun decorating them it took me out of myself and gave me a new purpose in life. When people came into the café and bought them, it gave me confidence that I could make a success of my life.

I was planning to leave and make a fresh start and it was then that I met someone in the bluebell wood.

I'd gone in there on my way back from Dorothy's to make a wish at my special tree. The bluebells were in full flower and the scent was intoxicating, reminding me of hyacinths. My special tree was an oak with what looked like a fairy door at its roots. It was in the part of the wood where the bluebells were thickest and I could sit amongst them and imagine myself drifting on an inland sea. I looked forward to finding some peace there. However, sitting beside it on the ground, jacket off and sleeves rolled up was a man with tanned skin and dark curly hair.

At first I was worried that he was one of the 'party animals' that used to invade our house, but when he spoke I knew he was a stranger here. His accent was unfamiliar, foreign and exotic but my experience with men up to that point made me wary. I spoke to him haughtily. "What are you doing here? This is private property."

"Mi dispiace. I am sorry. I did not mean to intrude. I came here before – a long time ago. It comforted me then and I hope it will do so again."

His eyes looked so sad that I felt sorry for being irritable with him. I wondered what his particular sorrow was.

"Please stay," I said.

"Grazie." His eyes were the colour of cream sherry or dark amber.

He told me then that he'd been a prisoner of war and had been held at the camp near here. I remembered walking near it with my mother and seeing the men inside the wire. Many of them, I heard, worked on the land and I wondered if he'd been one of the men I'd seen working in the fields helping to plant or harvest or pick apples and plums.

"The bluebell sea reminds me of the Mediterranean near my home," he said.

I'd seen the Mediterranean on the map, of course, but never expected to go anywhere like that.

"What is it like – your home?"

"It is – was – beautiful. Like paradise."

He looked upset.

"I would love to see it."

The church clock struck five, the sound carrying on the still air. I realised I should have been home half an hour ago, dreaded the thought that my father or step-mother might come looking for me.

"I must go," I said. "I hope I'll see you again."

I thought of the lost look in his eyes all evening while I was serving drinks to my father's guests and then trying to escape their unwanted advances.

He was there again the next day and I wondered where he slept.

His name was Riccardo Andrea …

Stefano gave a cry of shock when he recognised his grandfather's name.

His name was Riccardo Andrea and he'd married his Italian sweetheart when the war started. He got captured during the fighting and ended up in a prisoner of war camp not far from Charworth. It wasn't as bad as he'd expected. He was thankful to be alive and he was also glad to be surrounded by so much beautiful countryside. When he was sent to work in a local orchard he relished the contact with the earth and with growing things. He told me that most people talked about the apple tree being the one in the Garden of Eden that mattered. He'd always believed that it was the lemon tree that was the Tree of Life.

He returned to Naples after the war to find that there had been an earthquake that had killed almost as many people as the Germans had – including his beautiful wife Stella. He tried to settle back to life there but it had no meaning without her.

Stefano understood this last part. He couldn't begin to imagine what his much-loved grandfather had gone through as a young man but he knew what it was like to lose the love of your life. He'd wanted to die when he'd discovered Sofia with his stepbrother.

Gemma drank some of her wine and then she picked up the pages and continued reading.

Things were getting nastier at home. Riccardo was concerned about the bruises from rough handling on my skin. He threatened to go and speak to my father. I was afraid for him if he did. My father had a nasty temper. My father's gambling habit was now totally out of hand and there were rumours that he would become bankrupt. It was like being part of a Grimm's Fairy Tale when I overheard him and my stepmother talking about me one night.

"Our only chance is to let Leverson have his way and give permission for him to marry Anna."

It was just like Hansel and Gretel overhearing that they were about to be left in the dark forest – except if they married me to that lascivious Doctor Leverson there would be no way out of the darkness, ever.

There were two people I wanted to tell – Dorothy and Riccardo. However, when I went to find Dorothy, I was horrified to learn that she'd had a fall and broken her hip. Her daughter, hatchet faced and totally lacking in sympathy, had moved into The Cockatoo to look after her and I'd lost my release with the baking.

Riccardo held me as I cried. I could feel the beat of his heart through the thin fabric of his shirt. He took my face in his hands and kissed away my tears. "Do not be afraid," he said. "I am here. I will help you. You do not have to stay here. There is always a choice in life."

I believed him and I felt at that point, surrounded by the scent of bluebells, that anything was possible.

I went home determined to stand up for myself. I remember we had cauliflower cheese for tea. I've never liked cauliflower since. A peacock butterfly was trapped against the window. I knew how it felt, being able to see the outside world but not fly free. While we were eating I was told that my father was in debt and the only way we could keep this house and his reputation intact was for me to marry Doctor Leverson.

I refused, of course and was soundly beaten for it. My father was all for starving me into submission but my stepmother told him not to be so stupid. It was no use doing anything that would damage my looks. William Leverson was well-known for liking girls who were on the plump side. Instead, I was threatened with being put in a mental hospital if I didn't comply. William Leverson sat on my bed and told me about the last girl he'd signed the papers for as calmly as if he'd been talking about going out for afternoon tea. The girl wasn't mad – just pregnant and an embarrassment for the family.

"Will you let her out when she's had the child?"

"Maybe – but then maybe not," he said kissing my hand and pushing an ugly emerald ring onto my third finger before leaving me alone.

The following day, my stepmother contacted her dressmaker and she came to measure me for a dress that was not of my choosing. The stiff white net was itchy, the design too fussy and the stupid dressmaker kept on about my romantic whirlwind wedding.

Doctor Leverson visited me every day and took great delight in touching me, squeezing my breasts and putting his clammy hands under my skirt.

"I can do whatever I like with you once we're married, my dear," he said. His brown eyes were bloodshot and his breath sour.

I thought about running away. I thought about killing myself rather than submit to his unwanted embraces.

When I saw Riccardo in the woods I broke down in tears and told him everything. He was angry and wanted to take me away there and then but because I was so young I was afraid he might be prosecuted for abduction – Leverson had friends in high places. I didn't want Riccardo to get into trouble because of me. He kissed away my tears and I knew I would always remember the smell of him. Lemons and salt.

I gave him a photograph of me taken in the orchard when the blossom was out. He told me how beautiful the almond blossom was in Italy and about the smell of lemon blossom.

"Lemon trees fruit and flower all year round," he said. "They are the true tree of life and in one mosaic I have seen it is the tree in the Garden of Eden with Adam and Eve and the serpent."

Riccardo gave me a silver lire coin for luck and a photo of himself, standing in a grove of gnarled trees.

"Olives," he said. "They can live for hundreds of years – just as our love will."

I clung to him, wanting to believe what he was telling me, that this current nightmare would pass and that there was a brighter future waiting for me.

We sat amongst the bluebells inhaling their beautiful scent and planned a future away from here. I began to see new pathways and a clear sky where there had only been brambles and clouds. We sat close together, so close I could feel the warmth of his skin through his shirt. He kissed me and I felt my stomach flip over with desire. His kisses became deeper, his hands explored my body but I felt no shame. This was nothing like the unpleasant encounters I'd had with William Leverson.

I pulled his shirt from the waistband of his trousers, felt the smoothness of his skin, the scar on his chest where he'd been injured during the war.

We lay amongst the bluebells our embraces becoming more intimate until I was damp with desire for him. I felt a brief moment of fear as he entered me, a pain that made me pull away from him before we found a rhythm together and then it felt as if we were floating above the trees. My senses exploded with a rainbow of colours and I wished it could carry us far away from here. It felt as if we were the only people on the planet – as if nothing and nobody could harm us.

When I came back to earth it was with a greater sense of fear and dread of the future than I'd had before. I was also worried that we'd been so absorbed in our passion that we may have been observed. I dreaded to think how the doctor would treat me if he didn't get the virgin bride he was expecting.

Riccardo told me to be ready. He'd make the arrangements and we'd be away from here by tomorrow night. My father and stepmother were hosting a party for her birthday and if their usual ones were anything to go by it wouldn't be long before those attending were too drugged or inebriated to stand upright let alone give chase when I made my escape.

I should've known better. Nothing in my life up to that point had ever been simple. I should've guessed that my stepmother might be a little suspicious that I was too carefree and happy for a girl who was being forced into a marriage she didn't want.

I tried not to arouse suspicion, to be quiet and compliant as I had been up till now. I should've run there and then, hidden in the woods until Riccardo came for me. My life would've been so different if I had done so.

I spent the morning of the party visiting Dorothy, knowing it was probably the last time I would see her. I tried to imprint every detail of her and the kitchen that had been such a life-saver for me onto my mind. I hugged her when I said goodbye but I didn't say anything about going away. I didn't want any reprisals against her.

When I got home my stepmother seemed edgy and busy which was in complete contrast to her usual lethargy. She sent me upstairs to fetch something from my room and I noticed something on the bed. It was the photograph Riccardo had given me. I know I'd put it away safely in the tin that I kept at the back of my wardrobe where I keep all my special things. She knew. I felt a sense of complete panic as the bedroom door slammed behind me and I heard the key turn in the lock.

I opened the window but I was too high up to climb out – even if I hadn't been scared of heights. I thought of Riccardo waiting for me in vain and thinking I didn't care about him and my heart broke.

I was married by special licence the following day. I felt as if I was made of stone as I repeated my vows like a ventriloquist's doll. I'd been shown photographs of the mental hospital and some of the inmates and I had an unnatural fear of being driven through those gates. If I'd refused to comply then William Leverson would've signed the papers without hesitating. I may never have been released.

Suffice to say the marriage was every bit as miserable and degrading as I'd expected. The only spark of happiness was my daughter Stella, born nine months after the marriage. She had eyes like Riccardo and I'd felt a spark of joy that I still had part of him with me.

My joy was short-lived though. She died when she was two from a convulsion. My doctor husband was too drunk to save her. I buried her in the churchyard, and felt another piece of my heart die.

The house we lived in was in a bad state of repair – it always had been because my father and stepmother placed a higher level of importance on buying drink and drugs than they did on safety. The walls were mildewed and the wallpaper hanging off the walls. The house had once been the residence of the lord of the manor. He'd be spinning in his grave if he could see the state it was in. My father had electric shocks on several occasions because of the dodgy state of the wiring. My horrible husband laughed and ridiculed me when I suggested calling in an electrician because I'd noticed sparks flying from one of the sockets.

"I suppose you'd like the place redecorated like something out of the Ideal Home Exhibition," he said mockingly.

I turned away from him, knowing I'd suffer for the comments I'd made later. I knew by then that all he wanted was his meals on time, clean shirts and sex on demand – although even then he found fault. The food was too hot or too cold, his shirts not ironed well enough and my body not welcoming enough to his unwanted embraces.

The only bright patches in my life were the mornings when he was out seeing his patients. I used to go to the shops and then call in to see Dorothy who was now fully recovered and back to making her pies and cakes. I was with her on the morning the house caught fire and burned to the ground. I'd left my father, stepmother and husband sleeping off the excesses of the night before and walked the long way to town through the bluebell wood.

Dorothy and I stood in her kitchen watching as the blaze lit up the early morning sky and smoke and fragments of ash like black feathers drifted towards us on the breeze. The Fire Brigade said it was dodgy wiring. My father, stepmother and husband died. Everyone thought I'd be devastated but all I could feel was light.

The only darkness in my life was being without Riccardo and not knowing exactly where he was or if he still wanted me.

I travelled to Italy to try and find him. I knew it was a needle in a haystack task – he may not have gone back to Sorrento, the place he'd talked about so much and dreamed of us both living in. I felt I already knew it, he'd said so much about it during the short time we knew each other.

I travelled there in hope and returned in despair. Sorrento was every bit as magical as he had told me as we lay in each other's arms for those few brief hours. The sea was indeed the same colour as a bluebell wood and I could see how it would've comforted him, so far from home.

It was by now several years since I'd seen him. I'd felt an ache in my heart leaving England and Stella's tiny grave behind.

Now in Sorrento I resolved to put the past behind me and build new and better memories. I went around every café and trattoria asking if they knew Riccardo Andrea. Most people didn't understand what I was asking. My grasp of Italian was poor and I wasn't sure what sort of work he'd be doing.

He'd said that his parents ran a café in Naples (Napoli he called it with that charming accent of his). Finally, when I'd almost given up hope, a lady told me that he and his wife ran Trattoria Andrea up on the hill near the olive groves.

Wife. The word was like a knife in my heart.

I walked in the direction the lady had shown me – after all, it would have been awkward to do otherwise having asked the question. I knew she was watching my progress as I went up the street on shaking legs, longing to see him, dreading that I would and possibly cause an upset to what was probably now a settled life.

I stopped at the edge of the olive grove, standing between the blue of the Mediterranean on one side and the grey-green of the olive leaves on the other. In amongst the gnarled olive trees I saw him, even more handsome than the last time. He and a young woman were picking olives, shaking them into a net. She was small with hair the colour of Muscovado sugar. A little boy with dark curly hair who reminded me painfully of Stella played in the dust around their feet.

I turned away. There was no place for me here.

I cried all the way home to England. Wept until I had no more tears, until I was dried out inside.

Dorothy saved me. "Find other things in life to love," she said. "Be thankful for what you have been given."

I sat by Stella's grave and resolved to build a new life here and a place where others could be encouraged and rescued as I had been.

The following year, Dorothy sold The Cockatoo to me – her daughter had no interest in it and I was able to pay her off with the insurance money I received after the fire. I also kept the orchard next to the café and hired a young man to manage it.

My heart didn't thaw until my older sister Kate (who had long left home before the events of my story and never had to endure a wicked stepmother) had a baby late in life. When she died I took care of little Pamela – which brings me to you, Gemma, a true reincarnation of Stella.

Tears were pouring down Gemma's face by now and Stefano looked visibly distressed too.

"Do not read any more tonight," he said.

"I must," she said, dabbing at her face with a soggy tissue. "I need to know how their story ends – why they never found each other."

In case you and Stefano are wondering why you are together now, then this is the reason why."

"Riccardo gave me so much in the time we were together – he taught me how to love and to believe it was possible to change things and create a better future. I think we both had happy lives in different ways, even though we never found each other again. I was determined that you, Gemma, were going to be luckier in love than me.

Nice try Great Aunt Anna, thought Gemma, *but he's just not right for me.*

She took a deep breath and brushed away more tears before she carried on reading.

Now I knew where Riccardo lived, I found out as much about him and his family as I could. I rejoiced in my own way when his son Antonio got married to Lucia and their son Stefano was born. I grieved for everyone, especially Stefano, when Lucia died.

There was an abrupt sound as Stefano pushed his chair back and left the room. She heard his heavy footsteps on the stairs and then his bedroom door slammed.

Gemma rose to her feet to go after him just as her mobile rang.

"You're on the telly," squawked Laura's excited voice. "I missed it earlier. I've just seen the programme on the iPlayer. You both look absolutely brilliant and loads of people have voted for you already. "

"Great."

"You could sound more enthusiastic," said Laura who sounded as if she was bouncing off the walls. "What's up?"

"If you've got a spare few hours I'll tell you."

"That good eh? What's happened? You seem to be doing really well but you sound totally pissed off."

"My mother paid us a visit."

"That explains a lot. What did she do?"

"She was a total pain in the backside, then she tried to nick a load of stuff and she ransacked Great Aunt Anna's room before she left."

"And what about the lovely Mr Chips?"

"He's dead."

"Seriously?"

"Seriously – it's been more dramatic than an episode of Eastenders here."

"First chance I get I'm coming to stay again," said Laura. "Particularly if you win the next round of the competition. You'll need some help fighting off the fans."

Tears poured down Stefano's face. He remembered so clearly the day his mother died. It was spring – nearly his birthday – and he was almost thirteen, no longer a boy but not quite a man.

He was getting ready for school – had drunk caffe latte and eaten two cornetti filled with apricots for breakfast while his mother toyed with an espresso coffee that she didn't appear to want. Her dark shoulder-length hair was bundled into a loose knot at the back of her head and he noticed there were a few threads of silver.

The kitchen smelled of vanilla – he would never forget that as long as he lived. She'd made ice cream the day before and the scent of the vanilla pods combined with the smell of lavender and washing powder. The sheets were on the line, pure white and cracking with the wind that had started blowing the almond blossom from the trees.

Stefano had got up late and was now hurrying to get to school on time. He'd lost his maths book, had wasted valuable minutes finding it and now his friend was waiting for him at the door.

"Fetch the washing in for me, Stefano caro, it's raining."

The wind had whipped up the rain clouds and a heavy shower had come across the Bay.

Stefano's friend was smirking at him – a challenge.

"Fetch it yourself," he said. "That's women's work."

He'd gone to school regretting speaking to her so unkindly, despite the admiration of his friend. His mother hadn't said anything but she'd got wearily to her feet and gone to fetch the washing herself. He remembered later how pale her face was and that she was holding her side as if she was in pain.

When he got home from school, the doctor's car was outside and he hurried inside, a sick feeling of dread clutching at his heart. He headed for her bedroom but was stopped by his Nonna Maria. Her eyes were red with weeping. His mother was dead and he never got the chance to say goodbye to her. From that time on he associated the smell of vanilla with a sense of loss.

His father shut himself away, emerging only to do his work in the Trattoria. The following year he married a big blousy woman called Clara who had two older boys. She had money and was prepared to sink it into Trattoria Andrea provided her two boys had an equal stake in the business. His father agreed and Stefano felt increasingly that he was the outsider.

He spent more time with his Nonno Riccardo, tending the olive groves and learning about how to grow lemons and how to make limoncello – that special drink that was sold as an aperitif at the Trattoria and that also tasted so good over gelato al limone. Every family had their own special recipe and the label on the Trattoria Andrea bottles read: *'Drink and close your eyes. You will hear the rustle of leaves in lemon trees as the breeze comes in from the Bay of Naples …'*

Nonno Riccardo had told him the story of the origins of limoncello.

"Many liqueurs were developed in convents," he said with a smile. "It must have provided some excitement for the nuns. In the 1600s the nuns of the Santa Rosa convent in Conca dei Marini were using it to flavour sfogiatella Santa Rosa – their famous lemon pastry. But to my mind no one can beat your Nonna Maria's torta di limone."

Once, just before Nonno Riccardo had his first heart attack, they went for a walk to a place bordered by a crumbling stone wall and secured by a gate. To Stefano's surprise his grandfather produced a large wrought iron key and unlocked the gate. Inside it looked like something out of a fairy-tale. The place was overgrown and neglected. A small villa, once white as a sugar cube but now with flaking paint, stood amongst gnarled olive trees, their fruit unpicked. The smell of lemon blossom and salt drifted on the soft breeze. Through a small crack in the wall, Stefano could see the indigo blue sea beyond. He wondered why they had come here.

Nonno Riccardo sat on a wooden bench silvered with age and closed his eyes. Stefano went to explore. The front door of the villa was locked but he went round the back where there was a sort of kitchen garden. Bees and butterflies drifted lazily among rosemary flowers and lavender.

Stefano looked in through the windows. The villa looked as if it was waiting for someone to arrive, although everything was covered in cobwebs.

He returned to his grandfather who opened his eyes and looked almost surprised to see Stefano there, as if he'd been in his own private dream world and expected to see someone else.

"Who lives here?" asked Stefano.

"Nobody. It will be yours one day Stefano but you will please say nothing to anyone about our visit here today. Will you promise me that – on your honour?"

"Yes," said Stefano.

"Not even your Nonna Maria knows of this place – it is the only secret I have kept from her."

"I promise," said Stefano, "on my honour."

"We must go home," said Nonno Riccardo. "I am tired."

That night he suffered a heart attack and nobody knew if he would still be alive when the sun rose. It was to be the first of three that he suffered and the last one killed him.

Stefano had kept his word and said nothing to anyone. In time the place he'd at first called Villa Limone faded from his mind. He wondered if it had even been real or whether it had been one of his grandfather's vivid stories that really made you feel as if you could feel and see and hear what he was talking about.

Now, when he thought about it, the images came flooding back with the scent of lemon blossom and the salt tang of the sea. He saw the large wrought iron key in his grandfather's veined hand and the Sleeping Beauty neglect of the garden beyond. Stefano wished he'd asked more questions but he had a feeling his grandfather wouldn't have told him anything if he had.

Nonno Riccardo had said little about his early life – apart from the fact that he'd grown up in Naples before the war. Stefano's Nonna Maria, who adored him, had told him stories about how they'd met but there were large gaps of time that Stefano now realised he had no idea about.

Stefano lay on his bed, eyes focused on the cracks in the ceiling as he tried to remember what his grandmother had told him. She was beautiful but there was an air of mystery about her and he remembered the day he'd teased her about her blue eyes that were so different from anyone else in the family.

"I never thought anyone would marry me," she said. "I lived in the north and I was the daughter of an Italian mother and a German officer – that's why I have the dark hair and the light eyes. After the war, my mother was shunned by the local people – but what happened wasn't her fault. She had no choice in the matter. She didn't blame me. She loved me unconditionally but she died young, leaving me alone and grieving.

I met Riccardo when I was trying to sell the last of my mother's jewellery – her wedding ring and rosary. I didn't want to sell them. They were the last things of her that I had but everything else had to be sold in order to clear our debts. The money I would raise from the sale of those precious things would keep me for only a few weeks unless I managed to find work. I was reluctant to move. My mother's grave was a place of security. I even slept there once.

So I stood in the market square with my meagre offerings and Riccardo came and spoke to me. He was gentle and kind, brought me bread and coffee without the usual suggestiveness that comes with such offerings. He talked to me, asked what I intended to do. He bought the items from me – said he couldn't bear to see anyone else lose their heart.

He didn't look as if he could afford to do so.

I walked away from the market with him. There was no reason to stay now that the goods I had were sold. We sat by a fountain and drank red wine and he told me he'd recently returned from England. He looked so sad when he said this that I didn't press him any further.

He was travelling back to Sorrento – the place he'd always dreamed of living. I knew from what he'd said that his wife had died after the war in the earthquake that had devastated Napoli. I had no idea what had happened to him back in England. He clearly wanted to close the door on that. I had no reason to stay where I was. The next morning, after leaving flowers on my mother's grave for the last time, I picked up my bundle and followed him south."

Stefano was surprised to hear his grandfather had been to England. It was something he'd dreamed of doing when he was younger – visiting London and having fun seeing all the famous landmarks. As he grew older, he'd felt less sure he wanted to go – the English people who visited the Trattoria did nothing but complain about the weather there and he certainly didn't fancy the food if what they served in an 'English bar' he'd visited in Naples was anything to go by.

He'd never thought of England having beautiful countryside – although he had to admit that there were lovely things here like the apple orchard next door erupting into a riot of pink blossom.

Nonno Riccardo's last words were about a bluebell wood – whatever that was – as if long-held memories were growing in his mind and squeezing out through the cracks.

Stefano felt guilty for feeling bad about his own problems when his grandfather had clearly suffered so much more. He'd lost two women he'd loved and had gone on to live a happy and useful life. If he and Gemma were lucky enough to get to the end of the challenge they had been set then he would go back to Sorrento and buy his own lemon grove. He hoped he'd be luckier in love than Riccardo and that Sofia would come back to him.

Gemma read on to the end of the pages, glad that Stefano wasn't there to witness how upset she was.

I decided that, whatever happened between me and Riccardo in this lifetime, I would do my best to create happy lives for you, Gemma and for Stefano. There was no way I would ever have broken up what appeared to be a happy marriage. I am assuming it was because I don't believe Riccardo came looking for me.

May you both be happy and make the most of what life gives you.

Gemma smoothed and folded the pages. Her tears had fallen, smudging some of the ink. She put them back in the envelope and then into the box, closing the lid as carefully as if she was tucking in a sleeping child.

She poured two glasses of brandy, tucked her laptop under her arm and carried everything upstairs. She set the glasses down on the small table on the landing that held a night light and tapped on Stefano's door.

He opened it. His eyes looked red as if he'd been crying.

"I thought you could do with one of these." She handed him one of the glasses.

"Si, grazie."

He held the door open for her to come in.

"We should celebrate," she said, "we've been on the telly."

"Cosa?"

"Laura rang. She's seen us on the iPlayer on the Dining Hotspots programme."

"You have seen it?"

"No."

Gemma plugged the laptop in and waited for it to power up. She pressed a few keys and Stefano watched over her shoulder.

Dining Hotspots were clearly looking for a romance as well as great food and it was almost embarrassing to see the closeness of some of the shots.

The Inheritance looked good and the viewing public were on their side judging by the way the voting was going. "Voting closes at midnight," said a syrupy voice, "be sure to let us have your vote."

It was after midnight now and with fizzy feeling in her stomach, Gemma pressed the button that said 'results.'

Seamus McGinty's face appeared on the screen, looking like a kid who'd just been let loose in a sweet shop. He chuntered on for what seemed like half an hour but was probably only five minutes about how difficult the choice between the contestants was. The contenders varied from two Indian brothers who were creating meals based on Indian fairy-tales to a hippy couple enthusing about their new range of vegetarian dishes and the courses they ran teaching people to make cosmetics from garden flowers. The unfortunately named 'Sam and Ella' had the spaced out look that goats have and Gemma wondered what else had gone into the food to get them through to the next round.

Lucinda Stockton-Smith's clipped tones cut across Seamus's enthusiastic Irish babbling. "Come along sweetie, some people are trying to get to bed tonight. Put them out of their misery and tell them who's through to the next round."

Seamus pulled a face like a child being told off.

"I'd better do as she says," he said, making a great show out of taking an envelope out of his pocket.

"The voting public have chosen as follows. In third place are the lovely 'Sam and Ella' – wish you'd do something about the name darlings – it could put some people off. In second place are Magnus and Matilda and the Steampunk Café and our winners are the fabulous Gemma and Stefano and their fusion of English and Italian dining at The Inheritance."

He made a show of being overcome and the last view Gemma had of him before she switched off her laptop was of him having his brow mopped by Lucinda.

Gemma looked at Stefano. "I can't believe it," she said. Great Aunt Anna would've loved this.

She burst into tears and before either of them knew what was happening she was in Stefano's arms and he was rocking her gently like a child.

"There is nothing to cry about," he said.

"No," she said, "we are both lucky to have had people who have loved us so much."

CHAPTER FOURTEEN

Stefano woke to a view of blue sky with white fluffy clouds racing across it. He felt unsettled by the memories that had been aroused last night by the letter Gemma had found and by the way his body had reacted to Gemma's, instinctively seeking to comfort her as she wept.

They had broken apart only because the phone had rung downstairs. Gemma's mobile was switched off and Laura had phoned to offer her congratulations. Stefano was relieved about the interruption. He was bothered about the 'romance' element of the competition – the mention of which had led to some nudging and winking from the people who had attended the storytelling night. Stefano's fists clenched under the bedclothes. If they or the organisers of the competition thought they were getting a love story about him and Gemma then they could think again. It wasn't going to happen – ever.

As he awoke a little more, he thought he could smell something cooking – a spicy aroma of something that reminded him of Trattoria Andrea was drifting up the stairs and he wondered what it was.

He'd noticed that Gemma was spending more time in the kitchen. Experimenting, she called it. He wasn't sure if he liked it. He'd become used to it as his space – but when he thought about it, she had more right to be there than he did.

When he'd first seen her working in the kitchen she'd looked awkward and nervous. From comments that had flown between her and Laura he gathered they'd had a nasty cookery teacher at school. How could someone be unpleasant and teach children to cook well? Stefano didn't understand.

He knew he'd not been the easiest person to live with since he arrived in England but coming here had felt very much like being treated as second best which is what he felt he had been since his mother died and his father remarried. Gemma's letter had made Stefano think about his mother and finally face up to the guilt he'd carried with him since the day she died. He knew this weight of guilt made him behave unreasonably – like the time he'd shouted at Gemma because she was using vanilla in a recipe.

He'd told her she was holding the spoon wrong, that the consistency of the mixture was too stiff, that it would taste disgusting like most English food. She'd looked as if she was about to cry and had shrunk into herself reminding him of a dog he'd once owned who'd cowered in the corner when he'd shouted at it for wetting the floor when he'd been late back to let him out. That had been his fault for being late, just as Gemma had done nothing wrong. Stefano's reaction had been because the smell of vanilla had reminded him so forcibly of his mother and the last time he saw her.

He knew that since then she got up early so she could try things out when he wasn't there. Apart from her scones and what was now known as *Torta Inheritance* she had not given him anything else to try. She tested them on the ladies who came once a week to sew, knit and chatter – or Dan and his pregnant sister.

Stefano felt irritated by that. They had six months to show a profit and claim their joint inheritance. They wouldn't do that by giving food away to people who had more than enough to start with.

Stefano wondered what would've happened if he and Sofia were running the café together. She'd done waitressing for Trattoria Andrea but had no real interest in the work. She liked posh restaurants but didn't really take much interest in the food.

"They are places to be seen," she told Stefano when he protested at the price he'd paid for a salad that she'd barely picked at. "Important people go there. That's why I need to look my best."

Stefano noticed that Gemma appreciated good food. She had overcome her dislike of pasta which, as she admitted, had come from eating those disgusting pre-packaged meals they'd seen in supermarkets. Stefano hadn't tasted one but they looked like something he wouldn't give to a dog.

Gemma watched fascinated when Stefano made fresh pasta, rolling out the sheets of dough thinly and passing them through the machine he'd been lucky enough to find, unused, in Diana's garage.

"I've seen someone doing it in one of the Jamie Oliver restaurants," she said, "and I could've stood there all day watching."

He'd noticed when he held her the previous night that she was all softness and curves, unlike Sofia's elegant slimness. She'd joked to Laura about her "muffin top" indicating the small roll of fat around her middle.

"Better than a cake shelf," Laura said, pointing to her own non-existent stomach.

"That'll come with time if I stay here much longer," said Gemma.

As he thought about the cheerful banter between the two girls, Stefano felt homesick for his own friends. His spirits plummeted when he remembered it was his birthday – usually a time for celebration with presents and a cake. This time it looked like business as usual. He rolled over and pulled the duvet over his head.

He didn't have many minutes peace before Gemma knocked on his door.

"I'm making coffee downstairs," she said. "We're going out in half an hour."

"What's going on?" he asked, but she'd gone. He could hear her footsteps fading away down the stairs.

He checked his phone. Nothing. No messages. No voicemail. He got out of bed reluctantly and headed for the bathroom, hoping that a shave and a wash would make him feel more like facing the day.

When he got downstairs, his cup of espresso was already poured and there was a present wrapped in red paper and tied with silver string waiting for him.

"You remembered," he said.

Gemma turned a smiling face towards him. Her eyes shone, reminding him of the colour and texture of a pigeon's feathers.

"Open your present," she said, pointing to it.

Stefano untied the string and folded back the paper to find a wooden box, a block of art paper and some brushes. The box contained watercolour paints.

"What is this?"

"You remember our pledge? I promised to read some poems in front of an audience, now you must paint a picture."

"Capito," said Stefano. He had a feeling he wouldn't do as well with his side of the bargain as she had with hers. He'd give it a try if only he could remember what to do.

Gemma finished her tea and toast and fetched the wicker picnic basket from the cupboard under the stairs. She could remember the last time she and Great Aunt Anna had used it. It was on a picnic several years ago when they went to collect blackberries and damsons from the fields beyond the wood. Shortly after that time they'd lost touch – Gemma had moved several times from one flat to another and Great Aunt Anna had gone travelling. Pamela, always jealous of the relationship between the pair of them, had neglected to pass on any post until it was too late. Gemma never saw her Great Aunt again.

"What are you doing?" Stefano asked.

Gemma was packing an old basket with a handle with food, napkins and glasses. The spicy smell he'd noticed earlier was stronger as she got a tray out of the oven. She packed several items in a thermal box and put it in the basket. In went a bottle of wine and a cardboard box that she fetched from the Club Room.

"I'm packing a picnic," she said. "I'm going to show you the bluebell wood."

They left the café and headed through the orchard where the blossom was fading slightly and in one or two places tiny fruit buds were setting. Stefano took the basket from her, the touch of his fingers as they brushed hers making her jump as if she'd had an electric shock. He didn't appear to notice. The proximity of him and his spicy aftershave made her feel nervous and she wondered if she'd done the right thing inviting him for a picnic. It had seemed a good idea when she planned it yesterday but now it was happening she wasn't so sure.

The silence between them vibrated like a wire under tension as they walked between the lines of trees. Gemma's stomach churned with nerves, bubbled up into a fizzy feeling in her chest and poured out as a torrent of memories that Stefano probably wouldn't understand and it would only serve to add fuel to what he thought about English girls – that they were empty-headed flirts who dressed badly. She'd heard him say as much to whoever he'd been talking to that time she'd heard him on his mobile in the kitchen.

She took a deep breath, tried to slow down and focus on the blossom and the newly-arrived swallows diving and swooping for insects.

"I used to love sitting under the trees and letting the blossom fall on me," said Gemma. "It was like being in a pink snowstorm or amongst a group of ballerinas in tutus."

"I thought of dancers when I saw it," said Stefano, "but in Italy the blossom happens all the year round, not just in the spring. The lemon blossom is white and it smells ..." He kissed his fingers to show how perfect it was.

Stefano was surprised. He hadn't realised how beautiful the English countryside could be as Gemma pointed out flowers on the way to the woods – primroses, violets and wood anemones that had delicate veins almost the colour of her eyes. He'd been so focused since he'd arrived here on what he'd lost that he'd forgotten to do what his Nonna Maria used to tell him to do – count his blessings.

"Stop right now," she used to say to him when he ran to her with minor upsets as a child – a lost toy that seemed like the biggest tragedy or not being picked for a team at school, "be thankful for what you have. Close your eyes and think of three things you are grateful for. If all else fails go outside at night and look at the stars and you will see how little your problem matters."

Stefano felt lighter now that he'd begun to shed the guilt he'd carried over his mother's death. He was beginning to see how his grandfather could've become entranced by the English countryside – especially if there was a woman involved. Stefano's memories of Sofia were mostly linked to the places they'd gone together – sitting at a table at the beach bar at Marina Grande and listening to the soft sound of the waves lapping the shore, smelling salt and seaweed and drinking iced lager.

The weather was cool here. In Sorrento he'd have been in a t-shirt. In England he needed a fleece. Gemma was wearing a purple top and black jeans. Her hair was loose and he was captivated by the colour of it – blonde didn't really do it justice. It implied something that came out of a bottle or packet, like the time Sofia had turned up clearly proud of her peroxided hair and he'd gone moody on her and said he didn't like it.

No – Gemma's wasn't like that. He struggled to find a good description. It was the colour of ripe corn he decided. Ripe corn with pale sunlight on it like the dappled light filtering through the trees as they reached the edge of the woodland. He'd not noticed how beautiful it was before. Usually she scraped it back from her face into a ponytail or a loose knot for the evening. Today it was loose and rippled around her shoulders as she moved.

"Who owns this woodland?" he asked.

"My Great Aunt," she said, "at least she did! I suppose we will if – when – we complete our challenge."

"What will happen to it when we go?"

"I don't know."

Gemma hadn't thought that far ahead. She'd been looking at writing courses that she could do *'when this is over'* in between sending poems to various publishers. She didn't dare count her chickens before they'd got through the six months and she knew whether they'd succeeded or not.

She'd given no thought to what would happen to *The Inheritance* once she and Stefano had completed their tasks. With a jolt that made her feel as if something cold and heavy had landed in her solar plexus, she realised that Stefano would obviously want to take his share and go back to Italy and that she may not have enough money to buy him out. Without a 'proper job' she may not get a mortgage and she would have to stand by and watch the café being sold.

Even if she ended up with enough money to do what she wanted, she would still be faced with saying goodbye to the only place where she'd felt truly happy.

Nothing could have prepared Stefano for his first sight of the bluebells. It was, as his grandfather had said, just like standing by an inland sea. Silver trunks of trees rose ghost-like from the endless stretch of indigo blue. The scent was overpowering, intoxicating. He bent down and touched one of the flowers. It felt waxy, like a candle, each small bell curving from the stem a perfect replica of the one next to it. He could imagine how Nonno Riccardo would've been transfixed and why he would have wanted to spend time here. He wondered how he'd first discovered it because it wasn't exactly easy to find. Maybe he'd never know now. He wished once again that he'd asked more questions and paid attention to the stories he was told.

For the first time in a long time he felt the urge to paint something and he busied himself taking photos to build into a collage of ideas as a teacher had once suggested.

Gemma was sat on a mossy tree trunk scribbling in a notebook, picking one of the tiny flowers and pressing it carefully between the pages. He noticed the sap oozing from the flower and how intense the colour was against the white paper. In her top that matched the colour of the clump of violets at her feet, she looked part of the woodland.

They moved on through the woodland, every so often catching glimpses of sky and clouds. The path ahead of them looked as if it was splashed with gold leaf as the sunlight grew stronger and filtered through the fresh green leaves.

"Where are we going?" he asked.

"I want to show you where the house was – the one Great Aunt Anna wrote about. The one she was living in when she met your grandfather. It's a long time since I've been there. She didn't like being near it, for obvious reasons. She said she found it spooky."

Stefano felt an icy shiver down his spine when he stood amongst the ruins of the house. It had once stood in a large clearing and a narrow lane led up to it from the road that led to Dalesbury but now the woodland was swallowing it. Brambles and ivy reached higher than the brickwork that was left standing. White convolvulus trumpets and bryony filled in the blank spaces where the windows had been.

The nail-studded wooden front door hung off its hinges shielding the dark space beyond. Fragments of curtains hung from what had once been windows, the fabric too old to discover what colour it had been. The remains of wooden chairs now had festoons of last year's old man's beard. In a small space outside the house was the remains of a bonfire and a few empty beer cans.

"It looks like a setting for a horror film," said Stefano.

"That's what a group of lads thought a few years ago," said Gemma. "They came here looking for a place to drink and do drugs and by all accounts ended up leaving a bit quicker than they arrived – according to the local policeman."

"It is haunted?"

"They thought so – although they were probably so out of their heads that they mistook the birch trunks or a blowing curtain for someone lurking in the undergrowth."

Gemma walked slowly around the ruins, remembering how the place had both enchanted and scared her when she was a small child. It was like being in the middle of a fairy-tale – one where the wicked witch was waiting to pounce. Having read her Great Aunt's letter, she tried to imagine what it would've been like to have to go through that front door knowing that the man she loved was out in the woodland waiting for her, and then the cruel twist of fate that separated them forever.

Stefano had put the picnic basket down and stood, arms folded, leaning against a birch trunk watching her. Gemma felt nervous under his gaze.

"What are you thinking?" he asked.

"I found this place by accident when I was about seven," she said. "We'd come to the woods for a picnic and to collect conkers and autumn leaves. I wanted to play hide and seek and Great Aunt Anna agreed to count and then come and find me." She paused, remembering what the dried leaves had felt like under her boots as she raced along the pathways. "I went the opposite way to where we usually went and I ran and ran. I could no longer hear her counting. I got scared. The woodland is thicker here and the paths narrower as if the trees were living creatures closing in on me. Then I saw the house – or the remains of it. Great Aunt Anna had never told me about it. We never came here. As far as I knew, she'd always lived at The Cockatoo as we called the café then.

I crept in through the door and it was like being in a wicked fairy's house. Everything was scorched or broken. The only thing I did find was a gaudy looking necklace of orange beads.

It was dark when Great Aunt Anna found me. It was the first and only time she was ever angry with me. She snatched the necklace off me and hurled it into the undergrowth and then she marched me home to bed. I got no tea that night and no bedtime story. I remember thinking bad things about her and crying myself to sleep. Having read her letter, I'm not surprised she didn't want me to go there, but she never said anything."

"Perhaps she couldn't," said Stefano. "Sometimes when something hurts us very much we just want to hurt other people."

"Yes," said Gemma, noticing the slight flush on his cheeks, wondering what memories this had aroused for him. She felt guilty. This was meant to be a birthday picnic for him, not a day for dredging up sad memories.

"Come along," she said, "it's time we had our picnic."

They headed back the way they'd come, past the crossroads where it was said the highwayman who'd sheltered at The Cockatoo had been hanged a couple of hundred years ago. They turned left and arrived at the place where the bluebells were the thickest.

"This is my favourite bit of the wood," said Gemma, "by the scrying pool."

"Che?"

"The water in the pond is very dark and a group of local witches used to meet here to tell fortunes."

"Was your mother one of them?"

Gemma laughed. "It was a long time ago."

The water was edged with rushes and purple loosestrife. The canopy of trees was less dense here and she could see clouds reflected in the water.

Dragonflies hovered, their wings shimmering like rainbows where the sunlight caught them.

They sat side by side on a mossy tree-trunk and Gemma opened the picnic basket. She gave the bottle of wine and the corkscrew to Stefano and he opened it.

"The bottle has stayed cold."

She held up the thermal jacket she had for it and got out the glasses. He poured wine into them and handed her one.

"Cheers. Happy birthday."

"Salute."

Gemma unwrapped the pasties from their box, wrapped one in a napkin and gave it to Stefano.

He bit into it.

"What is it?" He supposed this was what she was making early this morning. He tasted his spicy Bolognese sauce mixture, thin buttery pastry and a hint of Cheddar cheese.

She looked at him uncertainly.

"Is good," he said.

"It's an idea for the next round of the competition," she said, "a sort of Anglo-Italian pasty."

"Pasty?"

"We have Cornish pasties," she said. "Originally they were made from meat, potatoes and turnips. Now they have lots of different fillings."

"Yes," he said, "I have seen. The pastry is very thick – not like this. You make good pastry."

"I have cold hands most of the time."

He reached out and touched the hand nearest to him.

"It is very cold," he said, rubbing it gently between his.

Gemma's first instinct was to snatch her hand back but her body wanted him to go on touching her.

His eyes looked soft as velvet as he gazed at her and it felt as if they were the only people on the planet. It was only another small movement for his other arm to go round her shoulders and draw her closer to him.

"I wonder if they ever sat here," he said.

Gemma sipped her wine, feeling in a daydream. There was a timeless quality to the day and it was impossible to tell whether she was Gemma or Anna or whether this was now or sixty years ago.

Stefano felt as if he was in a dream world. In a few minutes he'd wake up and find himself in his bed upstairs at the café. He'd wake to another day of preparing meals and experimenting with recipes and wishing he was back in Sorrento when another part of him was firmly anchored here among the bluebells and the girl with golden hair sitting by his side.

He turned Gemma's face towards him and he kissed her. Her lips were soft against his and he felt his stomach flip as if he was going down too fast in a lift. She smelled of coconut shampoo and a perfume that blended perfectly with the bluebells.

Gemma's first instinct was to pull away when he tried to kiss her, but her body wouldn't obey her. Instead she kissed him back, feeling safe and protected in his arms, inhaling the spicy smell of his aftershave and the salty tang of his sweat. She felt as if she was on one of those fairground rides that makes your stomach feel as if it's turning somersaults.

A strange noise – a cracking of twigs under heavy boots – roused them from their romantic interlude. They pulled away from each other like magnets repelling and looked at the source of the noise. Three men in yellow high visibility jackets were walking through the woodland as if they owned it.

"What are they doing here?"

"I don't know," said Gemma, running her fingers through her hair.

"I will go and speak to them?"

"No," said Gemma. There were three of them and it didn't do to make a fuss if you were outnumbered. "They're probably taking a shortcut from somewhere."

It sounded a flimsy excuse even to her.

"Birthday cake," she said, getting the box out and undoing it. "I'm sorry it's only a bought one."

"I never expected to get one," he said. "Thank you."

They ate slices of cake and finished the wine, still sitting close together. He didn't attempt to kiss her again and she felt disappointed. She told herself it had only happened because of the emotion of yesterday with the letter and the fact that it was his birthday today.

"I wonder where they used to sit together – my grandfather and your aunt."

"There was a tree she used to call her magic place," said Gemma. "We always used to leave an offering there when we came like flowers or feathers or coins. I often wondered why she called it that, but now it makes sense."

She headed towards the edge of the pond and threw a coin in.

"What are you doing?"

"Making a wish. When I was a little girl I used to believe that mermaids lived in the pond. Every time I came I left them an offering and made a wish."

"What did you wish for?"

"I can't say, it's unlucky to tell anyone."

They packed up the picnic stuff, putting the empty wine bottle and the wrappings back in the basket.

"It's much lighter now," said Stefano as they headed towards the centre of the wood again where the cross-roads was and took one of the other turnings.

"This is her tree," said Gemma pointing to a large oak tree with mossy roots and what looked like a door at the base of it. "Great Aunt Anna used to tell me stories about the door opening at special times and of a staircase leading to fairyland lit by a golden lantern."

"My grandmother used to tell me stories like that," said Stefano. "I stopped believing them when my mother died."

He put the basket down and touched the rough bark.

What happened?" asked Gemma.

Stefano noticed how her eyes looked the colour of rain-washed slate when she was upset.

"I was horrible to her," he said. "She asked me to fetch the washing in because it was raining and I showed off because my friend was there. I told her it was women's work and she should do it herself. She didn't say anything, just looked so terribly pale and sad. I went with my friend and I looked back at her. She was holding her side as if she was in pain. I wanted to go back but was more worried about what my so-called friends would say if I did. It was the last time I saw her."

Stefano watched Gemma's face, wondering how she would react. When he'd told Sofia she'd only shrugged and said: "Why are you still bothered about that? It was a long time ago." She'd gone back to examining her nails as if bored by the subject.

He noticed how Gemma's eyes filled with tears. "That's so sad," she said. "But it wasn't your fault. You were only doing what most kids would've done. I feel bad when I think about poor Great Aunt Anna being ill and dying without any of her family with her. If I'd known she needed me I'd have been there like a shot, but they contacted Mum instead and she didn't bother to tell me until after the funeral."

"So we both have things we regret," said Stefano taking her in his arms and kissing away the tears that were rolling down her cheeks. "Maybe we should make a wish at this special tree that all the hurt from the past is healed and we have a better future."

"I didn't mean for your birthday to be a sad occasion," said Gemma not wanting to move from the circle of his arms. She could feel the beat of his heart against her cheek and feel the warmth of his body and the firmness of the arms that held her. His lips brushed her hair, travelled softly down her cheek and found her lips again.

They stood fused together, the scent and sounds of the woodland ebbing and flowing around them until Gemma's phone beeped – a harsh alien sound amongst so much beauty.

They sprang apart, staring at each other in shock when they realised the time and that Guy and Hilda were waiting for them at the café for the meeting about the next Storytellers event.

Gemma's lips felt bruised from being kissed and she knew she must look a sight with her untidy hair and dishevelled clothing. Now that they'd left the enchantment of the woodland, she was sure people must be looking at them and making assumptions, speculating. Hilda's inquisitive green eyes certainly missed nothing as she watched them walking back through the orchard together. She was wearing an unusual assortment of clothing and colours today – a blue dress teamed with orange tights and a foxglove pink cardigan – as if she'd got dressed in the dark.

She was photographing the blossom in the orchard and put the camera away into her capacious green leather bag.

"Everything alright, Gemma?" she asked.

"Fine," said Gemma, feeling a flush stain her cheeks. She felt like a hermit crab that was between shells, fragile and vulnerable as if she wanted to go to her room and hide there until the strange feelings inside her subsided. "Sorry we're late. We had a walk in the woods to celebrate Stefano's birthday."

"I see," said Hilda with a world of feeling loaded into those two words.

"There is cake left," said Stefano. He looked as if he also felt out of place. "I will make coffee." He strode ahead, unlocked the café door and went in. He didn't look back at Gemma.

Guy arrived late and full of enthusiasm as usual. Gemma was thankful that he didn't notice she was a little distracted. She could still feel the sensation of Stefano's arms around her and smell his aftershave on her clothes and hair. She couldn't believe he didn't feel the same but he gave no indication that he did as he poured coffee into the cups, got plates and napkins and cut the remains of the cake into slices.

"So have you heard all the rumpus about the compulsory purchase of land to do with the new road scheme? I'd guess you must've done because it probably affects you more than anybody." Hilda got out a stripy piece of knitting and started clicking her needles while she drank her coffee.

"No, we hadn't heard anything." Gemma felt sick. "How long has this been going on?"

"Since for ever," said Guy looking up from a sheaf of papers he'd taken out of a battered leather briefcase. "It's what your friend Mike Bridges was involved in – he hoped to get a spin-off with building some starter homes on a plot of land he owned on the other side of the wood."

"Where do they want to put the road?"

"Through the wood," said Hilda. "That's why Mike was so keen to buy this place from you. He thought the new road would make access to his land easier and that he could make a fast buck with his houses."

"Will it definitely happen?" asked Gemma.

"Not if we've got anything to do with it," said Guy, "we've got a good protest group going. What we need now is a bit of luck on our side and some extra money. That's what the next Storytellers is about."

"Do they have to put the road there? Can't they put it somewhere else?" Gemma felt like bursting into tears again and she felt like running into Stefano's arms for comfort again, except that he was sitting with his arms folded looking stern and forbidding.

"There is an alternative," said Guy, "but it would pass right by the local MP's back yard. Needless to say, he prefers the alternative."

"We need to plan for the third round of the Dining Hotspots competition," said Gemma, "if we're lucky enough to get that far! I – we – need to do something that involves the community. We've got a few ideas," she glanced at Stefano, "but would welcome your help."

"What have you thought of?" Hilda finished another row of yellow wool, joined on some dark blue and resumed her clicking of needles. "Is there anything I can help with?"

Sorting out my scrambled heart, thought Gemma.

"I'd thought of doing a recipe book that involved the community and their favourite food plus any holiday memories about Italy. We'll add any special recipes from *The Inheritance* and we could hold some baking competitions or demonstrations that might draw in a few people."

"Great idea," said Guy.

"I'd also thought about a play or singing event that could involve the local people but I don't think I've got the time to write a play and I don't know what sort of singing we could do that would appeal to everyone."

"What about the Morris Men? They do a Mummers Play don't they?" asked Hilda.

"It's not quite the right time of year for it, but yes they do. Or at least we could adapt it to the situation."

"What is this?" asked Stefano.

Guy searched the photos on his phone until he found some shots of the local Morris Men. Stefano looked bemused as he stared at the men in white shirts crossed with coloured braid that Guy told him were called 'baldricks.' One of them wore a horse's head and the rest had flowery straw hats that looked like the sort of thing old women wore to church.

"They wear bells as well," he said. "You can hear them before you see them."

Stefano laughed out loud.

"You are having fun, yes?"

"No, this is serious. They dance and bash sticks around and it's all to do with fertility and making the crops grow. "

He searched his phone again and found some photos of the Mummers Play that seemed to Stefano to involve men dressing as women, a knight in armour, a dragon, the devil and a doctor who administered a life-restoring dose of something when the knight got killed.

The English were certainly strange if they spent their time watching stuff like this.

"I'm wondering if we could adapt it to include an Italian flavour or two. Any ideas?"

"Limoncello," said Gemma. "You could use limoncello as the life-restoring dose."

"What is it?"

"My grandfather told me it was first made by the nuns of the Santa Rosa convent in Conca dei Marini," said Stefano.

"Great," said Guy. "So we could have an Italian nun and a bottle of limoncello instead of the doctor and a bottle of brandy."

He and Hilda left, promising to keep them updated with any news.

"I'll do all I can to stop them getting their hands on our woodland," said Gemma.

Stefano was about to second that opinion. He'd been blown away by the visit there today and for the first time since he'd arrived he could see why the last words his grandfather spoke were about the bluebell wood. His mobile vibrated with an incoming message. His heart leapt when he saw it was from Sofia.

Ciao Stefano. Buon compleanno. Ti amo. Sofia xxx

She loved him.

CHAPTER FIFTEEN

Stefano's senses were still in turmoil from having Gemma in his arms. He hadn't meant for that to happen. He felt as if he'd been unfaithful to Sofia, although she'd been the one who'd betrayed him and gone off with Theo.

He didn't know how to respond to Sofia so he didn't say anything. He'd sleep on it and reply tomorrow. It would all be clearer in the morning.

However, his dreams were full of heart-stopping kisses and passionate embraces in the dark, the feel of arms and legs wrapped around him and the scent of bluebells. He'd assumed the girl he was with was Sofia but when a shaft of dream-light illuminated her, he saw it was Gemma with her corn coloured hair and dove grey eyes.

Gemma dreamed of searching for Great Aunt Anna in the woodland. A white mist filled the gaps between the silver birch trunks, hovering above the bluebells. She could see her just ahead, her velvet hat almost the same colour as the flowers. In a few more strides she would've caught up with her.

But something was wrong. She could hear a sound that was like thunder. It vibrated the ground and she could hear loud crashes and splintering wood. The wood was full of demolition equipment, churning up trees and bluebells. She shouted for Stefano to help her but he was far away growing lemons and didn't care about her or England any more.

Stefano thought the Bay of Naples was the only place that had spectacular thunder storms. He used to hang out of his bedroom window watching the silver threads of lightning split the plum coloured sky again and again. He loved the rumble of thunder and the drumbeat of the rain on the corrugated iron roof of the shed where his grandfather kept the equipment used to tend the olive trees.

"Stefano, close the window. You may be struck by lightning," his Nonna Maria used to say and he remembered how he'd turn to her laughing, his face and hair wet from the rain where he'd been leaning out to watch the storm flashes over Capri.

Nonna was scared of storms and used to hide in the cupboard under the stairs. Stefano expected Nonno Riccardo to tease her but he didn't. "If you're ever unfortunate enough to have to fight in a war and suffer an artillery barrage then you may not be so keen on the sound of thunder in the future," he told Stefano, his eyes taking on a far-away look.

It was one of the few references he made to the war or his earlier life as if it existed behind a door that he wanted to keep shut.

Stefano lay for a few moments absorbing the sound of the storm. The rain lashed the windows and drummed on the roof of the small shed in the café garden. He thought he could detect a faint smell of the sea but was sure this was probably a figment of his imagination. The sea was so many miles away and it was the first time in his life that he'd not lived within the sight and sound of it. That was another thing he was looking forward to when this was over, being able to swim in the sea and feel the power of the waves or go out in a little boat fishing with his friends and notice how the sunlight on the water made the colours dance.

He was deep in his waking dream floating on an indigo tide. Pale light from the landing filtered under his door from the night-light that Gemma always had on the landing. On one occasion he'd switched it off and she'd told him to leave it on. The stairs were steep and it would be easy to fall down them if you missed your footing on the way to the bathroom.

Stefano hadn't agreed, the bathroom door was miles away from the top of the stairs but he'd merely grunted and complied. It was no big deal.

The torrential rain eased momentarily as if the storm was drawing its breath. It then came back full force and overhead with a deafening clap of thunder and bolt of lightning that lit up his room. There was a loud bang and then total darkness.

Gemma was deep in her dream world. One of the diggers had changed to a black car that was pursuing her through pathways that were getting narrower. Twigs caught in her hair and snagged at her clothes. She'd lost sight of Great Aunt Anna, the bluebells were churned into the mud and all that was left was the ruins of the house that seemed to be growing in power. The green tendrils that had filled the windows were now reaching out to grab anything within range, gaining strength from what they devoured.

A man was chasing her, forcing her through the doorway, trapping her against the rough wood. She could feel it grazing her back as he placed his hand over her mouth to silence her screams.

145

Gemma awoke in the room that still held a hint of her mother's presence with the faint smell of 'Poison' that still lingered. She could feel the softness of her dressing gown that she always spread on top of her duvet like a comfort blanket, but fragments of the dream still lingered. Her heart thudded and she sat bolt upright. Then she realised what was wrong. It was pitch dark. Gemma was afraid of the dark. She had been ever since she was a child and that time during a storm when she heard footsteps coming to her door and then sound of the door opening and the creak of the bedsprings as someone sat beside her, someone with rough hands …

He'd come up with some half-baked story about coming to see whether she was alright. Her mother had backed him of course. He was the new man in her life. He had money.

"Gemma has always been attention-seeking," she said.

Gemma had gone to a public call box the next day and through her tears had told Great Aunt Anna what had happened. She'd reacted calmly, told her to go and wait in the Library in town.

Gemma never knew exactly what her Great Aunt had said to her mother, but she'd driven down in her battered green Mini, collected Gemma and her stuff and driven her out of danger.

"She's lying," Pamela had spat while Great Aunt Anna waited for Gemma to pack her bag. "Cedric never laid a finger on her. He was worried because he thought she might be frightened of the storm."

"Gemma's not a liar. And if Cedric's such a good sort, why did he threaten the child with what he would do if she told anyone what would happen?"

Pamela had shut her red lips mutinously and hadn't kissed Gemma goodbye when she left.

Although Cedric hadn't actually harmed her – Gemma had lashed out in panic, landing him a wallop in the testicles that had made him lose his grip on her long enough for her to break free and lock herself in the bathroom, only emerging when Pamela hammered on the door in the morning demanding that she let her in. She needed the loo.

Cedric was glowering in the background and when Pamela disappeared into the bathroom, he hissed: "You got away with it this time – but you won't escape for ever. And don't even think of telling your mother or anyone else. They won't believe you."

Now the past was replaying itself. It was pitch dark and Gemma thought she could hear footsteps. It may only have been the drip-drip of rain from the guttering, she couldn't be sure. She had to get out, move to the light. If she'd had her mobile phone upstairs, she could've used that but it was downstairs in her bag. She huddled into her dressing gown, sobbing in her haste to escape the unnamed terror.

The door opened and strong arms gripped her. She screamed and struggled and tried to fight him off.

"Shhh, it's OK. It is just the storm."

Stefano's calm voice repeating the same words. His arms held her tight. He smelled of soap and toothpaste and his body was warm against hers. He gathered her into his arms, sat with her on his lap in the armchair, rocking her as he would a child.

The last time Stefano had experienced a creature in this state was when he was coming home from school and noticed a ginger kitten stuck in a large tree. Some other boys had been treating it badly, pelting it with sticks and stones. He'd arrived in time to see the kitten race up the trunk of the tree and then not be able to get forwards or backwards.

He'd taken pity on it, knew what it was like to get stuck like that. His step-brothers had led him into similar situations and then abandoned him. The kitten's piteous cries wrung his heart and he whispered gently to it as he hauled himself upwards, grazing his hands and knees on the rough bark.

The kitten was holding on with needle-like claws, its blue eyes looked wild and its tail stood on end like a bottle-brush. It clearly wasn't sure whether Stefano was a friend or enemy and it arched its back and spat. *At this rate*, Stefano thought, *we will both fall and break our necks*.

Bracing himself, he took off his shirt so that he could form a make-shift net to catch the kitten in. The kitten scratched his bare arms as he did so, but ceased to struggle as he cradled it against his chest, transferred it into his school bag and climbed down the tree.

He'd carried it home and sat with it on his lap feeding it morsels of cooked chicken. It purred, tried to wash itself and then fell asleep against him and he'd felt honoured to be trusted after the pain that the kitten had obviously suffered.

Now, cradling Gemma in the darkness he was reminded of the same sense of panic of the kitten stuck in the tree. She was mumbling incoherently about someone coming after her, trying to take her nightdress off.

"It wasn't my fault, Auntie," she was saying. "I didn't ask him to come to my room. He tried to get in my bed. He threw my teddy out, he ..."

The last words ended with sobs that tore at her chest and Stefano wondered who had tried to get into her bed. He gathered from the way she said it that she'd only been a child.

Whoever it was, he wanted to kill the bastard for trying to hurt her.

He rocked her gently as if she was still a child to be soothed from a nightmare.

"Who was coming after you?" he whispered.

"Cedric. He wanted to ..."

"He's gone. He won't be back."

She gave a sigh and her body relaxed against him, reminding him of the way the kitten had clung to him.

When Gemma awoke, the power had come back on. It was full daylight. She was in her dressing gown, lying in Stefano's arms in the big red armchair in her room. She pieced together the events of the previous night – the storm and the power cut and the bad dreams that had flooded in with the darkness.

Stefano was fast asleep, his head leaning against the high back of the chair, his thick dark eyelashes fanning his cheeks. His arms were still around her and she felt a flush of anxiety wondering what she'd said last night. Mark had often complained that she talked in her sleep. She hoped she hadn't said anything inappropriate.

She had a feeling he might feel embarrassed to wake up and find them in this position so, moving slowly, she wriggled free, relieved that he slept on, and headed to the bathroom to get dressed.

Stefano, waking in an unfamiliar place, tried to remember what had happened. He hoped he hadn't said or done anything that he shouldn't. It was difficult to sort out truth from dream. His body stirred with the sensations aroused by the memory of a woman's skin touching his and of arms and legs wrapped around him in the darkness. He knew it was Sofia that he loved so why did Gemma disturb his dreams?

CHAPTER SIXTEEN

Stefano went to the bathroom, shaved, washed and got dressed. He was in no hurry to go downstairs and face Gemma. He didn't know what he would say to her – or what she would say to him. Dreams and nightmares all seemed to be part of the storm which had now passed leaving a sky that looked like faded denim.

He didn't know why he'd gone to her last night, apart from the fact that in the darkness she sounded like a wounded animal that needed comfort. She was downstairs now, he could hear her in the kitchen talking to somebody on the phone.

"See you later," he heard her say.

He watched from the top of the stairs as she headed towards the door, car keys in hand and her handbag over her shoulder. She was wearing a skirt today that showed off her shapely calves and a chocolate brown velvet jacket that reminded him of the colour and texture of the mousse his mother used to make. Her hair was loose again and he could smell her delicate floral perfume. He wondered who she was meeting, feeling a shaft of jealousy at being left out of something that she'd clearly taken trouble dressing for.

She is entitled to her own life, he told himself. *In a few weeks from now she will have her own life – and so will you.*

He watched from the window above the door as she walked across to her car, unlocked it, got in, started the engine and drove off, not in the direction of Dalesbury but towards the top end of the High Street.

Stefano wanted to go after her, to tell her she shouldn't waste time and energy on someone like Dan Bridges, which was more than likely where she was going. He stood staring at the place where her car had been as if willing her to return. It remained stubbornly empty and he was getting cramp in his right leg.

He went down to the kitchen to make coffee, but traces of her perfume lingered and he didn't want to be there. He sat outside watching the swoop and dive of swallows across the pale blue sky toying with a pen and paper. Gemma had asked him to write down some of the recipes he used for the book that was being produced for the last part of the competition, but he found this almost impossible to do. So much of what he did was instinctive and he rarely measured ingredients.

He gave up the task, went back up to his room and fetched the box of art materials Gemma had given him for his birthday. He fetched a jam-jar full of water and sat outside. Even here there were reminders of Gemma in the top she'd worn yesterday and had rinsed out this morning. It was hanging on the small washing line dripping onto the tub of mint, the scent of that reminding him of holding her last night and the smell of her toothpaste.

He couldn't remember how to begin a painting. It was a long time since he'd left school and given up hope of being an artist.

"It is a hard way to earn a living," his grandfather had said.

To be fair, he hadn't said 'don't do it' but Stefano had taken it as that and given up.

All thoughts of continuing to paint and trying to sell his work faded as work in the Trattoria increased. Space was a problem. There was nowhere for him to work. His bedroom above the Trattoria was small and cramped and the light was poor. Then he'd met Sofia and tried to pretend he was joking when he said he wanted to paint.

"So you're going to turn into one of those men in funny hats who set up easels by the square and try to persuade tourists to buy their pictures." She'd wrinkled her pretty nose and laughed and he'd laughed with her trying to pretend he didn't mind.

As he ran through the list of excuses in his mind, he realised they were just that. Excuses. If he'd really wanted to paint then he could've asked his grandfather if he could use his guest room provided nobody was staying with him. Or he could've concentrated on smaller pictures and made the best of the space in his room. He could've bought a lamp with a daylight bulb. At the very least he should've enrolled on a part-time art course and continued to develop his craft.

It was ironic that it had taken a visit to a bluebell wood in England to remind him of his love of colour – especially when he'd lived beside the Mediterranean all his life.

Stefano closed his eyes and tried to recapture the sight of the ultramarine carpet of bluebells splashed with patches of golden sun. He decided to create a painting in memory of his grandfather who was responsible for bringing him here.

He picked up a large brush, took a piece of paper and soaked it with water. Then he mixed ultramarine paint and did a wash of blue across the paper. Yesterday it had been difficult to tell the difference between the colour of inland sea and sky.

The small garden was a sun-trap and it helped to dry the paint.

Stefano added several more washes, adding a new one as each layer was nearly dry creating a translucent quality that almost captured the magic of being there.

He made himself a snack of focaccia bread, cheese and tomatoes and ate that outside with a bottle of lager. The phone rang several times while he was indoors – Allan to say that he and Molly were coming to the next Storytellers event, a lady wanting to run meditation classes and someone making a booking for the café.

When he came out and looked at his painting again, he felt disheartened. He'd decided before lunch to go for the mixed media effect and had added some slashes of silver to indicate the silver birch trunks with the light on them. He'd added more blue to the spaces in between but had a feeling he'd gone wrong and he didn't know how to put it right.

He left his art equipment where it was, took his lunch things in and washed them up and then collected his keys, left the café and headed up through the orchard towards the wood in search of fresh inspiration.

The paths were muddy after so much rain and after looking at his trainers – they were the only ones he had – he headed back to the café where he'd noticed a store of wellington boots under the stairs. Gemma had told him that they were kept there so that any visitors didn't have to miss out on a walk in the woods because the weather was bad.

He sorted through them until he found a pair that fitted, cleaned the dust and dirt off them, and then retraced his steps through the orchard to the gate that led into the woods. He could smell damp earth and leaf mould before the scent of the bluebells reached him on the breeze.

The storm had blown down some tree branches and created puddles along the paths that reflected patches of sky. Sunlight was filtering through showing up the diamond droplets on the leaves and making the rainbows dance.

Stefano went back to the tree that Gemma said was the place to make wishes. He stood there, surrounded by bluebells, breathing in the scent feeling that there was something he couldn't quite grasp at the edges of his vision – a vague idea for a series of paintings that he wasn't even sure he was capable of creating. Feeling rather foolish, despite the fact that he was on his own, he made a wish.

Then he went back to the ruins of the old house, noticing its creepy atmosphere and took photos, knowing that this would probably have upset Gemma if he'd done it yesterday. Well, she didn't need to know. By the time he started this painting he would be back in Sorrento, no doubt finding it hard to imagine that he was ever standing here in this woodland near an English village.

He'd taken a detour round to the place where he and Gemma had their picnic yesterday. The water in the pool looked darker than ever and the atmosphere was as mysterious as before. That must have accounted for them ending up as they did.

Stefano wondered what would've happened if Gemma's phone had been switched off. He felt himself growing hot as he remembered the sensations that kiss had aroused.

He heard the warning cry of a magpie and caught a flash of movement through the trees. Dan Bridges was walking through the woods as if he owned them. He was carrying a rucksack on his back and wearing boots caked in mud.

Stefano was confused. He was sure Gemma had got dressed up to go out with Dan this morning so what was he doing here, prowling through the woods? He didn't know whether to challenge him or not. As far as he knew, these woods were private, but if the men tramping through it yesterday were anything to go by, it seemed that people in England just did what they liked.

He shrank back into the shelter of the trees. He didn't particularly want to talk to Dan. He didn't like or trust him any more than he had his father. He didn't know whether to tell Gemma he'd seen Dan in the woods – it struck him as being a bit like telling tales.

Gemma had had a busy day. She'd taken Sarah for her antenatal appointment in Dalesbury. Dan had contacted her yesterday, saying he was worried because his sister seemed a bit withdrawn.

"I think she needs another woman to talk to," he said. "I don't know anything about pregnancy and birth. I've tried to help her but I keep saying the wrong thing and then she goes all quiet on me."

"I'll try," Gemma promised, "but I don't exactly know much about it either."

"You're a girl though."

"Very observant of you," said Gemma, making him laugh. "I'll see what I can do."

She'd taken Sarah for her appointment. The girl looked pale and she had dark circles under her eyes as if she hadn't slept well.

"You're not worried about the birth are you?" Gemma asked as they moved from one set of chairs to another as Sarah was weighed, measured and had her blood pressure taken.

Sarah shook her head. "No," she said. "I know it's going to be horrible. Auntie Pat told me."

"You don't want to believe everything people tell you," said Gemma. "They're not always right."

Sarah sat looking down at the floor, her hands clasped protectively over her small bump.

"Then what's the matter?"

"It's him," she said. "My Dad. He's still around."

"Let's go for a coffee," said Gemma. "I think we could both do with one."

They walked to the café where Gemma had met Hilda, sat outside and ordered coffee and slices of carrot cake.

"What's been happening?" Gemma asked.

Sarah's eyes filled with tears. "He's still there. In the chippy. I know he's dead because I saw him, but I keep noticing things."

"What sort of things?"

"The smell of the tobacco he used, his aftershave and the sound of his feet on the stairs."

Gemma took a deep breath. She didn't know what to say to comfort Sarah.

"What does Dan say?"

"He just laughs it off and says I'm imagining it, which makes me feel like I'm being neurotic."

"That's typical of how most blokes are," said Gemma feeling as if she wanted to shake Dan for not being a bit more sensitive.

Her mobile bleeped with an incoming message.

R u getting anywhere? Dan.

Gemma waited until Sarah went to the loo and then rang him back.

"She thinks your Dad is still around – and she's upset because you don't believe her."

Dan went quiet.

"Dan?"

"It's no good us both being like gibbering wrecks. We've got to carry on living there."

"There are things you can do about it."

"Like what?"

"I don't know, I'll think of something."

Gemma noticed Sarah coming back so she ended the call abruptly.

She was relieved to see Hilda on the other side of the street and waved to her.

"Who's that?" asked Sarah, eyeing her curiously.

"That's Hilda. Don't be fooled by the strange colour-schemes. She does all sorts of amazing things even if she does look a bit weird."

Gemma introduced Hilda to Sarah and noticed how the older woman's eyes flicked over the girl, missing nothing. She could easily be spooked by Hilda's ability to turn up whenever she was needed if she hadn't been so down-to-earth. Some people were quick to be dismissive of Hilda and her partner Charlie, describing them as looking like those dolls knitted from random scraps of wool.

"I didn't expect to be in Dalesbury today," said Hilda, "but then a friend's cat was taken ill so I came to give it some reiki."

"How does that work?" asked Gemma. "I've seen it advertised but never knew anyone that had it."

"It's to do with energies and healing," said Hilda, "and you can do it from a distance as well."

"Can you make places better too?" asked Sarah.

"What sort of places?" asked Hilda.

It was the most animated Gemma had seen Sarah since Dan had rescued her.

"There's been weird things happening," she said, pushing her straggly fringe out of her eyes. "The power keeps going on and off and Dan's had it checked and they say there's nothing wrong with it. The lights keep flickering and there's a funny smell. Dan laughs at me when I tell him about it and says he hasn't noticed anything."

"Maybe you're a bit more sensitive than usual with being pregnant," suggested Gemma, not wanting to say anything about her recent phone call to Dan.

"You're not crazy at all," said Hilda reaching for her green leather bag. The smell of patchouli rose from it as she rummaged, disrupting knitting wool, rescue remedy and a notebook with strange symbols scribbled on it.

"Charlie calls my bag 'the Tardis'," she said as she found the diary she'd been searching for. "Now, when is a good time for me to come and see what I can do about your house guest? Is it possible to come when your brother is out? What I have in mind may not work unless we all believe it's going to."

Sarah looked uncertain again and fiddled with her teaspoon.

"I could take him to the pub tomorrow lunchtime," said Gemma. "After all, I've got a legitimate excuse – he's been collecting recipes and stories from customers."

The other reason she didn't tell Hilda and Sarah was that she wanted to see if there was any change in the chemistry between them since Mike had died. She'd expected to feel a surge of passion when she was out with him, but had been surprised to find that she regarded him more like a brother – whereas being close to Stefano was causing sparks and she didn't know why.

When she got back to the café she was surprised to find that Stefano had gone out. There was no reason why he shouldn't but it was a bit out of character as he'd not shown much interest in places since he'd arrived. She was pleased to see that he'd already made use of the art materials she'd bought him and was amazed at what he'd achieved so far.

The painting was clearly the bluebell wood but a dramatic version of it with white mist hovering above the inland sea around the towering silver birch trunks.

"It is not very good."

She hadn't heard Stefano approaching because she'd been so transfixed looking at the picture.

"I love it," she said.

His fleece had a streak of mud on it and he was carrying some twigs with new oak leaves on them.

"From the magic tree," he said.

"You've been back to the wood?" asked Gemma.

"Si, I need to look again for more pictures."

Gemma nodded. She understood. When she was thinking about a poem, she sometimes needed to be alone, to have space in her head to think. Mark had never understood this and had interrupted every five minutes especially if she told him what she was doing. If she'd spoken to him when the football was on or he was checking his bank statement then it was a different story.

She wasn't surprised to get up the following day to find Stefano had gone again. Part of her thought of following him to see if the same magic existed between them in the woods. After all, she had as much right to be there as he did. She thought of texting him and seeing if he wanted to come to the pub with her and Dan at lunchtime but in the end decided against it as the pair of them clearly didn't get on.

Hilda was going to Sarah's so she made sure Dan was out of the way in good time.

"What did you mean about being nervous at home?" she asked as they walked along the road towards The Green Man.

Dan had a folder with recipes in it that people had given him.

"I didn't say that," he protested. "Sarah makes me nervous – it's like she's scared of her own shadow."

"And you're not, I suppose?" she said.

He waited until they'd got their drinks and took a long drink of cider before replying.

"I'm shit scared of the place, but if I panic then so will Sarah and where can we go? The place is ours now and I'm going to try and hang on to it until after Sarah has the baby and then think about doing something else."

"What's happened, Dan? Tell me."

"It's the store room mainly – where Dad fell down the stairs. I went up there to get some cooking oil and when I started to go down them, it was as if someone was trying to push me and I nearly lost my footing. I've got nowhere else to store the stuff but I really don't like going up there."

"Have you thought of having the place exorcised?"

He laughed.

"Yeah – they'll be carting me off to the funny farm next if I start talking like that."

Gemma sent up a silent prayer that Hilda wasn't getting the same reaction from Sarah. She pushed the menu towards Dan but he wasn't really looking at it.

"Mum believed in all that stuff about crystals and colour healing. Dad told her it was a load of rubbish and that the people doing it were a load of charlatans. If she'd not kept on maybe things wouldn't have ended like they did."

"You mean if she'd just kept quiet and put up with what he dished out?" said Gemma, feeling that she couldn't quite believe what Dan was saying. She wished she hadn't suggested lunch. She didn't want to be anywhere near a bloke that was expressing views like that. He was really no better than Mark.

Dan sat quietly fiddling with his beer mat.

"So you're going to put up with living in a place you don't like with a creepy atmosphere that you're trying to blame on dodgy electrics except that everyone knows they're not, rather than admit that there's more to life than the blindingly obvious?"

Dan looked startled.

Gemma drained her glass of cider, stood up, put her bag over her shoulder and headed for the door.

"Gemma – wait."

Dan caught up with her a bit further down the street.

"Where are you going?"

"Back to your place to see how Hilda and Sarah are getting on."

"You mean you set me up for lunch just to get me out of the way?"

"Yes," said Gemma, "although we did have the recipes to sort out too."

"Why didn't you say?"

"Because of the way you reacted just now. You'd have just ridiculed the whole thing and then it might not have worked."

Gemma paused outside the chip shop door. Hilda and Sarah were in there, standing hand in hand, looking up towards the top of the stairs where the store room was.

Dan went to open the door.

"Don't," said Gemma. "Let them finish."

Dan ignored her and barged in.

Hilda's eyes snapped open. "He was there," she said.

"Who?"

"Your father. You want him gone from here don't you?" She held Dan in an ice-green gaze.

He nodded.

Hilda got a phial of what smelled like rose water out of her bag and sprinkled it round the four corners of the room. She went round again swinging a crystal pendulum and saying a short incantation. She went to the top of the stairs.

"No." Dan was following Hilda up the stairs. His voice had taken on a hint of Birmingham accent. He sounded like his father.

Hilda swayed at the top of the stairs, stood firm as the lights flickered, an overpowering smell of whisky filled the room and with a huge bang everything went dark.

Dan stumbled back down the stairs and collapsed in a heap on the floor.

"He's gone." Hilda sat down on the top step, her face pale. "Mike's gone."

She put her pendulum back in her handbag.

"What's happened to Dan?" yelled Sarah rushing forward.

"Give him some air," said Hilda. "Gemma, call an ambulance."

"I don't want an ambulance," said Dan, waking up. "I'm fine, just a bit tired."

"It feels different here now," said Sarah. "It's not creepy any more. I've always wanted to go to a séance but I suppose this is the nearest I'll get."

"You sound just like our Mum," said Dan giving her a hug.

"Do I?"

"Yes, you do," said Hilda. "I did readings for her on more than one occasion. I'll do yours one day."

Gemma looked at Dan to see how he'd react to this but he looked as if he'd just had a great weight removed. They'd gone into the shabby sitting room behind the shop and he sat back in an armchair and closed his eyes.

"I felt as if I was being taken over," he said. "Does that sound stupid?"

"No," said Hilda. "I'd say you've had a lucky escape. Things should improve for you now."

"I think this calls for tea," said Dan.

"There's no milk," said Sarah. "I meant to buy some yesterday."

"Don't worry, come along to the café. We can have a mini celebration." Gemma hoped Stefano was still out.

Stefano felt irritated when he saw Dan and his pale-faced sister heading towards the café. They were with that strange woman who was dressed in what looked like a collection from his grandmother's rag bag. They'd clearly been up to something and Stefano didn't like being left out.

He didn't know why Gemma bothered with someone like Dan. Stefano didn't trust him. He was willing to bet that Dan hadn't said anything about being in the woods yesterday. He wondered what he was up to and whether it was anything to do with that new road scheme everyone was talking about. Dan's father apparently owned a field on the other side of the wood where he'd wanted to build houses. He was now dead so it potentially made Dan a rich man if the scheme went ahead.

Stefano went up to his room and stayed there while Gemma made tea for everyone. He could hear them downstairs in the café, the chink of cups against saucers and the smell of buttered toast. What was the English obsession with toast? Gemma said she found it comforting, he didn't see why anyone would.

The low buzz of chatter was getting on his nerves. Stefano found some music on his phone and put his headphones on. He looked critically at the new painting he'd started as part of the series he'd planned using the woodland for inspiration.

Earlier he'd found a large piece of board and had positioned it over the top of the chest of drawers in his room. It made it just the right height for painting on and he'd set up that corner of the room as a make-shift art studio, shifting the lamps around and hitching back the net curtains to give the best possible light. He'd damped another piece of paper and taped it to the board so it didn't wrinkle. He'd given this a series of washes, building up the ghostly quality as he wondered whether he dare risk upsetting Gemma by painting the derelict house. He reasoned that it was her Great Aunt's bad memories that needed to be laid to rest and that this was all part of the story he was trying to tell with his pictures.

He'd gone back today and taken more photos of the house with his digital camera this time. Stefano created a few preliminary sketches from these. There was a gothic fairy-tale quality to the pictures in the combination of images and the way that nature was reclaiming the house and hiding the furniture.

His new picture included a chair that he'd seen encased in ivy tendrils, an old cooker and a shoe abandoned in the mud like Cinderella's slipper. There was a dream-like quality to the picture and he was soon absorbed in his new creation.

He paused when he heard the sound of the door downstairs and watched as Dan, Sarah and Hilda headed along the road. When he looked at Dan, feelings of frustration bubbled to the surface. Having seen the bluebell wood, he now felt a connection to it. He hated the thought of bulldozers coming in and uprooting any of it for their new road scheme. It was part of his heritage and he wanted it to stay that way.

CHAPTER SEVENTEEN

The next Storytellers night was a great opportunity for Guy's group to practise the Mummers Play. The only dissenting voice was a sour-faced woman who complained about a nun appearing in the story.

"You're making fun of religion," she shouted from the back. "Some of us take it seriously."

The young man with the ginger stubble who was playing the nun rolled his eyes.

"Why do these people turn up to events like this when they've got no sense of humour?" Guy muttered to Gemma.

The play proceeded with St George being revived by a shot of limoncello.

The food was served and the sour-faced woman was again the only person who was determined not to enjoy herself.

"The menu's limited to say the least," she said.

Gemma took a deep breath and walked across to speak to her. "This is a special evening," she said with a polite smile. "If you'd like to experience more of a range of dishes then please come on another night. We'd very much like to see you." This last bit wasn't true but Gemma knew she needed to be diplomatic.

Thankfully the woman's opinion wasn't shared by everyone else in the audience who demolished the pizzas and plates of lasagne that were put out for them followed by tiramisu and Gemma's chocolate brownies.

Guy introduced the second half which included the open mic.

Gemma read some poems and then, feeling very nervous, she told everyone about the progress of the café and how they were doing the recipe book, the Mummers Play and some cookery demonstrations as a way of involving the local community for the next part of the Dining Hotspots television programme.

"We hope to set up more permanent links between England and Italy," she said, then blushed as she realised how this might come across to the audience. She could see Stefano's face as he stood, arms folded at the back of the room. He looked furious.

Laura always said "If you've got yourself into a hole, then back off and stop digging."

Gemma knew she should've shut up then and just thanked everyone for coming and let them get on with the open mic, but nerves and the fact that she'd just read for the second time and the poems had been well-received got the better of her and she gabbled on.

"Lemons and apples have been a theme of ours from the beginning," she said. "Watch this space."

She stepped down to a chorus of cat-calls and applause and noticed a few people slapping Stefano on the back. He glared at her and stomped off in the direction of the kitchen.

"Do I deduce that congratulations may be in order?" asked Diana.

"No," said Gemma. "I don't know why I said that."

"Perhaps it was your heart talking."

Gemma thought back to the kisses she and Stefano had shared in the woods and felt herself going hot again. She wasn't attracted to him, she wasn't. Reading Great Aunt Anna's letter had fuelled that – there was no other reason.

Allan had been in the audience – he was on his way to cover a bigger event in Bristol and Gemma noticed him scribbling away with an amused glint in his eye.

"You two have done so well," he said. "I'd like to think that this will carry on in some way once you and Stefano complete the six months. You've given me loads of material to put in my blog as always. Good luck with the next round of the competition – my whole office is rooting for you."

He hadn't said 'go your separate ways' and Gemma was a bit worried as to what he was going to put in his blog.

The sour-faced woman came up to her at the end of the evening. "You might think you're riding high at the moment young lady, but you'll come crashing down with a bump when the compulsory purchase order comes in and they put that road through. Nobody will bother stopping here then."

"Surely they can't just move in with the bulldozers and dig up the wood?" Gemma asked the solicitor when she and Stefano had their next meeting.

"That depends," he said, "on whether there's a viable alternative. In this case there is – but it if they take things further then other factors might come into play."

"Non ho capito. I don't understand," said Stefano.

"There may be other reasons why a route is not taken," said the solicitor. "As far as I can see, a lot of this so far has been hot air and rumour and may never happen – or at least not in our lifetime. Anyway – let's look at the matter in hand and see how your joint business venture is faring."

Gemma handed over the monthly figures and watched as he scrutinised them, a smile spreading like sunshine across his round face.

"Anna would've been proud of you both," he said.

Stefano left the solicitor's office wishing he'd said something about seeing Dan in the woods – but what would he say? He may have only been taking a short-cut, he wasn't doing any harm and however he tried to phrase something it just sounded like he was being petty.

The secretary at the solicitors who he'd met on his first day here – the one who'd made him feel welcome by greeting him in Italian – was on her lunch break. If she'd been around he might have had a try at voicing his concerns. There was probably an innocent explanation but Stefano still didn't trust Dan Bridges.

He didn't get a chance to brood about Dan for too long. When they got back to the café, the morning paper had been delivered. Gemma had never had a daily paper before now, preferring to catch up on the news on the BBC website, but since Allan had taken them under his wing, she'd made a point of having *The Telegraph* delivered. Stefano set himself the task of trying to read small sections of it as a way of improving his English – mainly the sports pages and anything related to Italy.

He scowled when he saw the photograph on Allan's page of *The Telegraph*. Why was there this obsession with people wanting to create a romance between him and Gemma? The photograph showed the two of them watching the Mummers Play. It was the bit where the nun was giving a glass of limoncello to the armour-clad St George. Gemma had been laughing at the bemused expression on Stefano's face when Allan took the photo.

The caption read: *Limoncello sparks a love affair.*

Gemma felt embarrassed by the tone of the article – and she could tell from Stefano's frosty reaction that he wasn't pleased either. She wondered what had happened. It wasn't Allan's usual style and she wondered why he'd taken a provocative approach. It was only when she read down to the bottom that she noticed the by-line. 'Sadie Richards standing in for Allan who is currently not well.'

She pushed all feelings of indignation aside and dialled Molly's landline.

"He's in hospital having his gall-bladder out," said Molly. "Silly old devil had been suffering from stomach pains for nearly two weeks and trying to pass it off as a bug. He was literally busy with work one minute and then in the operating theatre the next. He passed a few of his nearly completed articles to his assistant and, at the new editor's suggestion, she gave them a make-over. I hope she's done a good job?"

Gemma didn't like to say anything further in case she caused Allan additional worry.

"It just didn't sound like his usual style," she said tactfully.

"We're both so hoping you win the competition," said Molly.

"Thank you," said Gemma, ignoring Stefano's sour look as she finished the call and went back to the work she was doing on her laptop.

Dan called in with a few more recipes and they spent some time going through them, weeding out some and seeing what fitted together.

"Are you coming to the meeting about the road?" he asked.

"I didn't know anything about it," said Gemma.

"It's this afternoon at two fifteen. You should've had some information about it."

"We've not received any information – but we'll be there."

Stefano had his suspicions that Dan had something to do with them not getting the information. He knew he was being unjust, but the fair-haired Englishman was more irritating than a mosquito buzzing round at night.

"Why did our letter not come?" he asked Gemma.

"I don't know. We can ask them this afternoon."

The council chamber was crowded by the time they arrived. There was a stir of interest amongst a group of people at the back of the room when they walked in. They'd clearly not expected them to turn up. The sour-faced woman was part of the group. The room was hot and stuffy. There was a table at the top of the room with three men in grey suits sitting behind it. The buzz of conversation was louder than the maroon and grey pattern on the carpet and the cocktail of perfumes and after-shaves made Gemma's head spin.

Before the meeting started, she made herself known to the lady in metallic red glasses who was in charge of the list of speakers.

"You should've had a letter," she said, running a finger down the list. "It was sent to you over a fortnight ago, inviting you to speak at the meeting if you wanted to. Each person has three minutes."

"I would have liked the chance to say something," said Gemma, "and so would my business partner.

"I'll have a word with the secretary who sent the letters out," said the lady in glasses. "She may be able to shed some light on the mystery."

Gemma was not at all surprised when she went to speak to the sour-faced woman who'd complained about everything at the Storytellers evening. She was willing to bet an iced fruit cake against a stale rock bun that the woman deliberately hadn't sent the letter, especially when she glared across at Gemma.

The lady in the glasses went to the three men at the top table and there was a brief consultation of a list and some notes made. She came back and spoke to Gemma.

"There appears to be some irregularity here," she said, "so the Chairman is happy to give you three minutes. We realise of course that you've had no time to prepare any notes, so if you'd rather not bother we would quite understand."

"I'll do it," said Gemma, anger and frustration driving her forward.

Stefano had no idea what was going on. The place looked totally disorganised and reminded him of brief shots he'd seen of the English Prime Minister's question time, with the same farmyard-like babble of sound in the background. He could see Gemma was angry and that they'd been missed out of something. Dan was sitting on the far side of the room. Stefano was sure he was mixed up in something underhand. He was sat looking at some papers and Stefano didn't trust him an inch.

He could sense Gemma's nerves as the meeting started and the Chairman did his introduction and then various people got up and spoke about why the woodland didn't really matter and how important it was that they had the new road that would link the site that was proposed for new houses on land that had been owned by Michael Bridges and that had now been left to his son Daniel.

Dan's head came up when his name was read out. Stefano thought he looked smug and he wanted to wipe that look off his face.

Gemma tried to stick to the facts and not let her emotions rush in when she stood up to speak. Three minutes seemed a long time when every pair of eyes in the room was focused on her. She felt betrayed by Dan, especially after the way she'd tried to help his sister. He was sat on the far side of the room looking smug, on the side of the people who wanted the new road to go through the woodland. He'd always said he liked the countryside and now it seemed he'd been lying. Those times when she'd seen him, he must've been doing his research for his own ends.

Stefano gave a brief nod when Gemma sat back down. She wasn't sure that their views would be of much importance in the overall scheme of things, especially as they wouldn't be there for much longer. The thought made her feel as if a cold stone had lodged itself somewhere in her solar plexus.

It all seemed like a foregone conclusion when Dan got to his feet. Some people were already gathering their papers together and preparing to leave.

"I see him in the wood," whispered Stefano, his breath warm against her ear.

"Why didn't you say?" she said.

He shrugged. "You like him."

She shot him a glance. He didn't look back at her.

Dan gathered his papers and got to his feet looking as if he had all the time in the world.

"My father had a vision of creating a housing estate on the land where my grandfather grazed sheep." He paused and looked around the room. "It is not my vision."

There was an audible intake of breath from some people behind him.

"That land has been left to me in my father's will. I have other plans for it. There is no way my land will be built on – and the woodland linked to the Cockatoo café – I mean *The Inheritance* - should not be either. I have done extensive research and there are environmental factors that should be taken into account."

There were whispers of 'traitor' that caused the Chairman to raise his head and glare towards the corner of the room where the sour-faced woman and her husband sat.

"I have evidence to prove that there are Natterjack toads on my land and in the woodland. The derelict house in the woods has a colony of rare bats and there are noble chafers in the apple orchard. I have suggested that the

Department of Food and Rural Affairs does a survey before any further action is taken. I have applied for Countryside Stewardship for my own land and intend to create a nature reserve there."

Dan received a mixed response to his announcement. Gemma was on her feet and clapping as were a number of other people, including Hilda who'd arrived late to the meeting.

The sour-faced woman had leapt forward and grabbed Dan by the sleeve of his jacket. "You'll be sorry," she hissed. "You might think you're being very clever but you'll be laughing on the other side of your face before too long – you and that trollop of a sister of yours."

"Don't speak about my sister like that."

"It's disgusting, that's what it is, girls having babies out of wedlock." She still had hold of Dan's arm and her face was mottled red and twisted in anger.

A girl sitting quietly in the opposite corner got to her feet and started taking photos.

"What do you think you're doing?" asked the woman.

"I'm from the Charworth Gazette," she said, "and I've been sent to do a report of the meeting."

The sour-faced woman subsided like a deflating balloon.

"It's a lot livelier than I expected," said the young journalist to Gemma. "And it sounds like it might be a happier outcome for you and your husband." She nodded towards Stefano as she made for the door, obviously eager to write up her piece for the editor.

"He's not my husband," said Gemma as she went to congratulate Dan.

"I'm pretty sure I can get the *DEFRA* people on side," said Dan. "They've done some preliminary searches on my ground and seemed to be in agreement with me. My dream would be to create a nature trail that goes up through the woods and around my land – provided the people who take on the café after you are happy."

The sour-faced woman came back for another salvo now that the journalist had gone. "You're not honouring your father's wishes then?" she snapped.

"He never honoured mine or treated me with respect," said Dan. "I think I've suffered long enough. It's time to do what I want."

"What about us?" she went on. "My husband and I had agreed to buy some of your father's houses."

"They aren't being built now, so it's no longer an issue is it, Mrs Robinson?" said Dan pleasantly. "When I finally settle my father's affairs, I'll make sure you get your money back."

"Your sister won't be able to stay in the fish and chip shop with you when she has her baby."

"Why not?" he asked, his eyes taking on a steely glint.

"She's not married is she? You'll lose all your customers. Nobody will want to buy from you if she's staying there."

"It strikes me," said Dan, "that you should practise a little more of the Christian charity that you preach to others on Sundays."

The sour-faced woman gathered up her coat and bag and hurried off. "I've never been so insulted," she said as she left the room.

"Is she something to do with the church?" asked Gemma.

"She used to be my Sunday School teacher – and a more miserable piece of work I've yet to find. She actively supported Dad when he sent Sarah to stay with our Auntie Pat after Mum died."

"Let's hope all the problems are out of the way now," said Gemma, but she had a nasty feeling they hadn't seen the last of Mrs Robinson.

CHAPTER EIGHTEEN

By the time the filming for stage three of the competition had been set for the middle of June, Gemma realised it would only be a matter of weeks before she and Stefano went their separate ways and carried on with their lives. The problem was that now she was within grasp of having the money to do whatever she wanted, Gemma wasn't sure what that was any more. She was relieved that Dan appeared to have the problem with the woodland and the orchard sorted out and that it wouldn't disappear under new housing.

She made a mental note to ask Hilda and Charlie if they'd continue to watch over the orchard, gather the apples after they'd gone and make apple juice as before.

Stefano was focused on his paintings. He'd done a full series of pictures of the woodland before the bluebells faded. It felt significant to him that his birthday was when they were in flower. He was sorry that they were finished now but he enjoyed the plants and flowers that replaced them. He liked the butterflies that flittered around in the sunshine and tried to learn their names – comma, speckled wood, peacock and fritillary. He especially loved the blue butterflies that looked like fragments of sky fallen to earth. He didn't know what he'd do with the pictures other than take them home and keep them in memory of his grandfather and his time in England.

Diana had been captivated by one of the pictures when she called in one morning. Stefano had propped it on the dresser in the kitchen intending to take it to his room and forgotten about it.

"I've often seen misty mornings like that," Diana said, "and I like the way you can see what looks like two ghosts walking hand in hand through the wood."

She stepped back to take a proper look at the painting from a distance.

"Yes," she said. "It's really good and it's given me an idea."

"What?"

"Has he got any more?"

"Yes – why?"

"Where are they?"

"He's put them in the Club Room for now."

"Perfect – at least we won't have to break into his room."

"What are you up to?"

"A community project with a difference. You did say you needed to do at least one?"

"What are you up to?"

"They love anything that includes children don't they? I'm never sure why – but we're not all the same are we? It just seems if you want to get the 'ahh factor' then that's an important ingredient. Anyway, looking at these pictures, it occurs to me that you could invite school groups to come and have a tour of the building, write stories and draw pictures."

"So where does Stefano's artwork fit in?"

"Well – as your friend Laura said at the outset, these walls need some pictures. I know Francine and her friends put some of theirs in but they need to take them away because they're part of their college portfolios. What if we put Stefano's in their place? The advantages would be they're local and they fit with the theme of what you're doing for the telly."

"He'd need to agree to it," said Gemma doubtfully. "And they'd need to be framed."

Of the two aspects, convincing Stefano was the most difficult, particularly with the mood he was in at the moment.

"Leave both of those things to me. I'll talk him round," said Diana giving Gemma a flirtatious look. "I was quite a girl in my younger days. Where is he?"

Stefano found it impossible to refuse the Englishwoman with the wild hair and long red nails. She was as unstoppable as a runaway horse once she started to talk about his paintings.

He tried to push her idea aside, claiming that he had work to do, but she wouldn't let him escape.

"We need paintings on the walls," she said with a smile that matched her scarlet nails.

"Get them from somewhere else." He knew he was scowling.

"We want your paintings."

They faced each other like two chess masters, unwilling to break the deadlock.

"You are afraid?" she said, her face teasing.

"I am never afraid," he said, getting up and putting on his apron as if to indicate that the meeting was over.

"Well then – that's settled," she said with a big smile. "I'll get the pictures framed and tell Gemma to put them in the order that looks best."

"I didn't say I agreed."

"You didn't say you didn't either."

Stefano got out his marble chopping board and a large saucepan. The woman was impossible. He'd speak to Gemma about it and tell her they couldn't display his paintings. They weren't good enough. He picked up a knife and began to slice an onion with vicious strokes.

"One more thing." Diana was back in the kitchen, invading his space. The light caught her wild hair turning it into a silver halo. Her smile was angelic. "You need to give the pictures names," she said sweetly.

Much to Gemma's surprise, Stefano had named his paintings, some of which she didn't understand because they were in Italian, and had put them in the order he wanted them, going round the walls from the left hand side of the entrance and finishing on the opposite wall. They told the story of the romance between Anna and Riccardo and the layers of paint hinted at events that happened before their story began and what would happen in the future as if the artist had a crystal ball or a scrying mirror.

As she did what amounted to a walking meditation around the café, Gemma reached for her notebook. Each painting produced a flood of memories that led to an idea for a sequence of poems that could accompany the paintings. If the Dining Hotspots people were so keen on the idea of threes, then here was another one – Stefano's paintings, her poems and then poems or stories from the local community when the school children came to visit.

The head-teacher of the village school was bubbling with enthusiasm when Gemma suggested her idea.

"What fun," she said. "I'm sure they'll love it – and so will the teachers especially if you're offering biscuits and home-made lemonade."

Charworth School wasn't the only place to be happy about the new developments. When Gemma emailed the Dining Hotspots team with an update on what they were doing you could feel the excitement fizzing along the airwaves when the response came back.

'*Great stuff! Really looking forward to the next round.*' Lucinda, Seamus and the team.

CHAPTER NINETEEN

There was an electric-storm feel of excitement on the day the television crew were due to arrive. Gemma and Stefano had been up early preparing food for the evening. Gemma had made her, now famous, Bolognese and Cheddar Pasties. There were also going to be pizza, bowls of salad and Torta Inheritance with amaretto cream. Everyone attending would be given a glass of Prosecco or apple juice.

Gemma had created an eye-catching centre-piece of apples and lemons. A display board held the stories and poems written by the local school children and on a table near the till was a stack of *Inheritance Recipes* – the book that many of the local people had contributed to.

Laura had insisted on coming up to help and she was interested in everything that had happened since her last visit.

She noticed how things were still a little prickly between Stefano and Dan, despite the fact that Dan's hard work had brought about a change in circumstances where the road was concerned.

"Stefano doesn't like many people though does he," Laura said. "I'm surprised you've managed to stay here as long as you have."

"He's alright when you get to know him," said Gemma, "and he's more sensitive than you realise."

"Oo oh!!"

"Don't go getting any ideas, Laura. It's not like that."

"Like what?" Laura looked at her innocently.

"You know."

The Morris Dancers arrived slightly the worse for drink. They'd been taking part in midsummer celebrations since early morning and one or two looked decidedly pale. Thankfully the ones taking part in the Mummers Play looked reasonably alert considering they'd been up so early that morning. They spread themselves over the Club Room and Gemma passed around mugs of strong coffee.

The film crew arrived and began setting up their equipment.

Gemma and Laura had just finished setting the tables and laying out trays with glasses for the Prosecco when Lucinda and Seamus arrived.

"It looks as if you've got all bases covered," said Seamus looking round appreciatively.

Gemma crossed her fingers behind her back, hoping that Francine and her friends would be here soon. Thankfully Laura and Dan were there and could help out if needed. Gemma was pleased to see that the chemistry that was lacking between her and Dan was there full force between him and Laura.

The first guests arrived and the atmosphere grew warmer as the heat from the kitchen spread.

Dan got a message on his mobile and his face went pale.

"What is it?" Laura asked.

"It's my sister – she's just called an ambulance and they're taking her to Dalesbury hospital. She thinks she's starting with the baby, but she can't be. It's much too early." His hair looked wild where he'd run his fingers through it in his agitation.

"Go and be with her Dan," said Gemma. "We'll manage here."

"I'll drive you," said Laura. "I can't let you loose on the road in that state."

Francine and her two friends arrived full of apologies for being late and blaming the poor time-keeping of their last lecturer.

The evening began. Lucinda did a brief introduction, interrupted by Seamus who did a recap of the story of Gemma and Stefano and how they'd done in the competition so far.

"We'll add clips of what happened in the previous rounds and what the people are like – and how the viewers voted," he'd explained earlier. "You're definitely favourites so far – I think everyone seems to be rooting for you two getting together."

Gemma blushed when she remembered what it had been like being in Stefano's arms."

"Ooh, do tell me dear! Do I detect a softening of attitudes?" Seamus stared at her avidly.

She shook her head. "No," she said. "Nothing like that."

"Come on, you can tell Uncle Seamus. I promise it'll go no further than the next film clip." He smiled encouragingly.

"That's what I'm afraid of." Gemma smiled and tried to move him on to looking at the cookery book but he was like a dog with a bone.

Lucinda was talking enthusiastically about the paintings. Gemma had created poems to go alongside some of them and told Lucinda about how she intended to do some more.

"You'll have to get a wiggle on," said Lucinda in her cut-glass accent, "he'll be back in Italy before you know it."

Her words made Gemma feel as if a cold stone had landed where her heart should be.

They did an open mic session while the customers were served their food and the film crew set to and did their work. The plates were cleared and the Mummers Play began. It had got to the part where St George had collapsed with his injuries and someone had gone in search of something to revive him. The nun had arrived with her bottle of limoncello, causing a great deal of laughter about her habit that showed more than a bit of hairy leg

Stefano and Gemma were standing together near the kitchen door laughing at the reaction of their visitors to this new variation of the play.

There was a commotion at the door and a girl burst in. She had raven black hair and glittering dark eyes with so much mascara and false eyelashes on them it was a miracle she could open them. She was wearing a tight-fitting red dress and black high heels and, ignoring everything else in the room, she hurtled across and threw herself into Stefano's arms.

The camera-man's attention switched abruptly to follow the latest interruption eliciting cries of "I could be dying here" from the Morris Man who was playing St George and: "Some people think a short skirt gets you everywhere," from the nun.

"You should be taking notice of me, I am Stefano's girl," spat the new arrival holding tight to a stunned-looking Stefano.

"Have the directors of Corrie heard about you lot?" asked Seamus. "I've never known a place like it."

"I am Sofia." The girl had broken away from Stefano and cornered Lucinda who, for once, looked ruffled from her usual composure. "I am Stefano's girl. I want to be model. When Stefano is TV star we will both be famous."

"This programme is about Stefano and Gemma. They are running this café together," said Lucinda.

"I do not care about *her*," said Sofia. "I am here now. She is nothing." She turned her back on Gemma.

Stefano came to life then, as if he'd woken from a dream, and led Sofia away from everyone and up the stairs. By now the café was pin-drop quiet and everyone must've heard the twin sets of footsteps going up the stairs, the shutting of a door and then silence.

Sensing that the drama was at an end, the customers melted away like ice cream in a heatwave. The Morris Men gathered their equipment and Guy got on the microphone and thanked the remaining customers for coming. Gemma was in a state of shock. All the work they'd done for this round of the competition was likely to be wasted because this girl from Stefano's past had shown up.

Gemma couldn't say how bad she felt seeing him with his arms around another woman. She hadn't realised until that point how much he'd worked his way into her life and into her heart. Now it was too late to tell him – not that he'd have cared anyway if he'd had a girl back home all along.

Laura returned with Dan in tow. They had their arms round each other and both looked shattered but happy.

"It's a girl," they chorused. "Very tiny but perfectly formed."

Seamus sat with his head in hands. "I don't believe this place – it's like Paddy's Market."

"What's been happening?" asked Laura. "I didn't think the party would break up just yet." She looked at Gemma's stricken face. "What's wrong?"

"Everything," said Gemma and burst into tears. She didn't know what had upset her most – the disruption to the filming or seeing Stefano with his arms around Sofia. The thought of what they were doing behind the closed door of his bedroom brought back all the insecurities and jealousy of discovering Mark's infidelity.

"I think this calls for wine – for everyone," said Guy taking charge and going out to the kitchen and coming back with two bottles of chilled white wine and some glasses. "We all look a bit shell-shocked."

"I'm so sorry it's made a mess of the filming," said Gemma. She'd dried her tears and was fiddling nervously with her wine glass. "I suppose this means we're out of the competition?"

"Hard to say, dear," said Seamus. "It'll be up to the viewers."

"We've got one more team to interview," said Lucinda crisply, "then the programme will go live next week and we'll wait for the viewers' ratings."

Lucinda, Seamus and the film crew packed their equipment up and disappeared in their people-carrier with the blacked out windows.

"I'll go back with Dan for a bit," said Laura, "just in case we need to get to the hospital again."

Gemma noticed how Laura slipped her hand into Dan's as they reached the café door and felt a stab of envy that her friend had found what she'd had under her nose all the time and not realised. She gathered the glasses together and carried them out to the kitchen. Most of the clearing up still needed to be done and the uneaten food put away in the fridges.

Her heart sank. She felt just like the bit in Cinderella when everyone except her was going to the ball.

"Come on," said Guy. "This won't take long. I'll wash. You dry and put away."

"You'd do all that for me?" Gemma burst into tears again. His arms went round her and she smelled tobacco and coconut. "I'm sorry," she sniffed against his shirt, "I don't usually get emotional like this."

He didn't say anything, just stood and held her in the middle of the kitchen until there was the sound of footsteps clattering down the stairs and Stefano burst in. His hair looked wild and his clothing dishevelled as he grabbed two bottles of chilled beer from the fridge and a basket of left over bread and headed back towards the stairs.

He looked as if he was about to say something – his lips started to frame the words – but then thought better of it and left the room.

Gemma broke away from the shelter of Guy's arms. "Let's get this done," she said and then we can all get some sleep."

This last was a forlorn hope. After Guy had finished helping her with the clearing up, Gemma went upstairs to bed. There were traces of Sofia in the bathroom – a diamante hair clip, used make-up remover pads in the bin and the sickly smell of her perfume.

She lay in bed wide awake, her eyes feeling gritty with tiredness but unable to sleep, her senses alert to every creak of the bedsprings in Stefano's room indicating that Sofia was reclaiming what she saw as her property.

CHAPTER TWENTY

While Sofia was in the bathroom doing her hair and make-up, Stefano stared moodily out of the window. The sky was a perfect blue, even if it did have grey clouds in it, he'd got Sofia back in his life which was what he thought he wanted all the time he'd been in England – so why did he feel that life had turned sour.

Last night when he'd come down to the kitchen, he'd felt eaten up with jealousy when he saw Gemma in Guy's arms. He felt even worse when he saw her tear-stained face. If only Sofia had arrived today and not yesterday it might all have been different. They'd have completed the filming at least and all the hard work they'd put in wouldn't have been wasted.

He wanted to go downstairs this morning and talk to Gemma, tell her that Sofia's arrival was a complete surprise to him. He hadn't invited her and he didn't know why she'd come. She'd barged back into his life in much the same way as she'd left it – because she spotted a better opportunity for herself.

"Why didn't you tell me you were coming to England?" he asked when he could disentangle himself from her arms last night.

"I wanted to surprise you."

Well, she'd certainly done that. And wrecked the filming, not to mention all the hard work that they'd put into the community projects. Stefano had gained a lot of confidence in his artwork from people saying they'd like to buy prints of the paintings when they were available. He'd particularly liked seeing the school children copying his pictures and writing stories about them. He'd missed that, being in England, the parents bringing their children to the Trattoria and the funny things they said. They'd enjoyed the English gingerbread and Italian biscotti made with almonds.

"Why did you come now and not before if you wanted to be with me?"

"You weren't famous then."

So that was it. Sofia had always been obsessed with fame and getting noticed. She'd dumped him for Theo when the Trattoria got a special award.

Theo. His half-brother. He had a fiery temper and might think that Stefano had encouraged Sofia to come to England.

"Does Theo know you're here?"

"Not yet. He was away on a golfing holiday with his friends. He will find out when he gets back. I left him a note."

"Why didn't you wait and tell him?"

"The filming was yesterday."

To her it was perfectly logical that she'd do that – just as she was sure that Stefano still wanted her in his life.

Except that Stefano had changed. He hadn't realised until last night when Sofia was in his arms again that she wasn't the one he wanted. He wished he'd had the courage to say, on camera, how he felt but he'd been so stunned by Sofia's arrival that the words had dried in his mouth.

Sofia came back from the bathroom, dressed, perfumed and elegantly made up as if she was going to a film premiere. She was wearing the same shoes as last night, totally impractical and unsuitable for what he had in mind.

"We are going out?" she asked. "In your car."

"It's not my car – it belongs to Gemma and she's out in it. We're going for a walk."

"Walk?" Sofia couldn't have looked more disgusted if Stefano had suggested mud-wrestling.

"A walk – where?"

"To somewhere that was very important to my grandfather."

"Family again! Is that all you think of?"

"Love matters."

Sofia tossed her head and followed him down the stairs.

He made coffee for them while he packed the wicker basket with some provisions.

"Picnics are for children," said Sofia.

"Stay here then."

She followed him out of the café, up through the orchard where the apples were growing on the branches. Hilda and her husband had grazed sheep in here until a couple of weeks before so they needed to be careful where they put their feet in order to avoid treading in what they'd left behind.

In the woodland, the bluebells were over but a few clumps of late primroses survived as did violets. The air was full of the smell of elderflowers and wild roses. Gemma had made elderflower champagne and they'd drunk it one lunchtime when Diana, Francine and Guy had visited to discuss the various community projects.

"Why have we come here?" asked Sofia.

"This is a very special place. It's where my grandfather met Gemma's great aunt."

"Oh, her." Sofia tossed her dark hair and set her red lipsticked mouth in a sulky pout.

Gemma went to see Hilda. She was in her untidy kitchen sorting a diverse variety of projects as usual. Charlie was in his tool-shed carving love spoons for a craft fair they were going to in a few weeks' time.

"It's the Welsh connection, he can't help it," Hilda said as she dried the feathers of a toffee-coloured hen. "Mabel here took it into her head to try and swim like the ducks. I thought she was dead when I picked her up. I never thought when I did my first aid course that I'd need to do CPR on a hen."

She cleared a pile of half-finished cushions and a bagful of crocheted granny squares off the high-backed settle and sat Gemma down with a mug of coffee and a slice of her famous tea-bread that was made from dried fruit soaked in strong tea.

"Now, I take it you've escaped from the café because of the latest developments? I must admit I thought you'd be along sometime today."

"Don't take any notice of her," said Charlie coming into the kitchen with a box of finished love spoons and a ginger cat at his heels who jumped onto his lap when he sat in his rocking chair.

Gemma was reminded of the night of the storm when Stefano had held her on his lap and how she wished she could put the clock back and tell him how she felt. How could she have let Sofia march in and take him from her?

What if it's what he wants? The voice in her head nagged at her. *You were there and any bloke will take what's on offer.*

"Be clear about what you want and don't be afraid to say," said Hilda cutting across her thoughts. "Fate works in surprising ways. Now – looking at that sky I'd better get that washing in before it gets another soaking."

Gemma took it as her cue to leave. She felt the usual sense of peace as a result of being with Hilda. Great Aunt Anna always said you should never give up hope, there was always a chance your luck would turn.

Except hers never did, did it? And maybe yours won't either. The aggravating voice in her head prodded at her all the way back to the café.

She parked the car in her usual spot, got out her key and went back into the café.

Stefano and Sofia had obviously had breakfast together and hadn't bothered to wash up after themselves. Gemma moved the dishes into the sink, noticing the red lipstick marks on Sofia's cup. Well, they could clear up their own mess. She had better things to do.

Laura called in on her way back from the hospital where she and Dan had gone to see Sarah and the new arrival.

"She's so lovely," she said.

"I thought you were going home today," said Gemma.

"There's not much to go back for." Laura took a piece of gingerbread from the tin Gemma had made for the school children. "My job finishes at the end of the month and I'd planned to go and live back at Mum's for a while until I found something else. Thankfully she's great, but it's not really what you want when you think you've gained your independence is it?"

She finished the piece of gingerbread and took another one. "These are good. Besides, I was worried about you."

"I thought Dan had crept up the list a bit from what I saw yesterday."

Laura blushed. "There is that too."

"I'm pleased for you," said Gemma swallowing the lump of tears in her throat.

"So where are they?"

"Where are who?"

"Stefano and the Red Queen."

"No idea. Why should I care where they are?"

"Because you do. Come on Gemma Lawrence. I've known you since primary school. This is like that episode with Stuart Baxter when he chose that girl with red hair to be his wife when we were playing 'Farmer's in his den.' You pretended like mad that you didn't care a fig about it and then didn't eat your school dinner because you were too upset. Of course you care."

Gemma got up and started pacing up and down the kitchen. "OK – so what if I do? What can I do about it?"

"Stop pacing up and down the kitchen for a start. You're making me giddy. When they get back you need to tell him at the first opportunity and then he can make his own mind up. Don't give in to the Red Queen without a fight."

"What if he tells me to piss off?"

"Then at least you'll have had the truth straight from the horse's mouth." She got up, wrapping another two pieces of gingerbread into a napkin. "These are good. OK if I take another one for Dan? Must go now – see you later, Gem. Text me if anything happens."

Gemma switched on her laptop and checked her emails. There were three from the Enchanted Dining team and one from Allan. She ignored them, feeling she couldn't face anything to do with last night. There was a missed call on her mobile from Lucinda. *"We've sent you three emails and would like to talk to you urgently."*

Lucinda sounded polite as usual and her posh voice with its clipped vowels gave nothing away but Gemma sensed it was to let them know in advance that they'd blown it. There was no way forward from here.

The time was getting on and the weather outside was getting worse. Gemma was reminded of the night of the storm. She didn't know where Stefano was, not that it was her place to care anymore but customers would be arriving soon and expecting something to eat.

Her phone rang. She answered it.

"I've got hold of you at last," said Lucinda. "I need to talk to you about last night."

"I thought you would," said Gemma. "I'm sorry to have let you and the viewers down after everyone saying such nice things about us."

"They're still saying nice things," said Lucinda. "Even after last night's upset."

"How do they know?"

"Various clips have appeared on You Tube and Facebook and have attracted a large number of followers."

Gemma was too stunned to speak for a moment.

"Gemma, the viewers are still rooting for you and Stefano."

"But there isn't a 'me and Stefano' any more. I don't even know where he is."

"The viewing public don't give up easily. All I rang for is to say we're going to include the various extra clips we've been sent in the next programme and let them make their own minds up. So ignore the first two emails I sent you. Our producer has had a change of heart."

Stefano's visit to the woods with Sofia hadn't been a success. She started complaining about her feet hurting and her shoes getting messed up before they'd even got to the wood.

"Why didn't you wear trainers?" he asked before he remembered she wouldn't wear anything like that in a million years. She was all for show rather than common sense.

"We could go back for wellington boots," he suggested. Again she gave an exaggerated shudder.

"So why are we going here?" she asked.

"Because I want you to see it," he said, knowing at the outset it wasn't going to mean anything to her in the way it did to Gemma.

Why should it? said the voice in his head. *She's not from here and there is no family connection.*

Sofia picked at the food he brought and wouldn't sit down to eat until he'd taken off his fleece and spread it on the mossy stump where he'd sat with Gemma that magical day. Sofia wasn't interested in butterflies, dragonflies or wild flowers. She picked the filling out of the prosciutto rolls he'd made and left the bread.

"If I'm going to be a model I have to think about my figure."

Stefano remembered how Gemma had tucked into a Bolognese and Cheddar Pasty sitting on that stump when they'd come here to celebrate his birthday. He realised how he liked to see a woman enjoying her food and remembered how irritated he'd been in the past when he'd taken Sofia to posh restaurants and she'd sent most of her food back untouched.

"You don't know that you're going to be a model yet."

"That's why I've come to England. You're not going to say in this little place for much longer. We can go to London or Paris or New York."

"I don't want to go to those places. I hate cities. I want to go back to Sorrento and paint pictures and grow lemons."

"Lemons! Pictures! You and Theo sound exactly the same. All he wants is to stay in that blasted Trattoria making his speciality pizzas. He wants us to get married, have children and for them to grow up doing exactly the same." She flung her untouched glass of wine at him.

The glass shattered against a stone and Stefano bent down to pick the bits up. He cursed as he cut his finger on a fragment of glass.

"Why do you bother with that?"

"Because an animal could hurt itself. It's called having consideration for others."

Stefano finished picking up the glass and wrapped it in a napkin. He found a tissue to put round his injured finger. Sofia was standing almost pawing the ground like some dangerous animal. In her exotic clothes with their vibrant colours she looked out of place here. He thought of Gemma with her eyes that reminded him of the colour of a dove's wing and wished she was here with him.

The sky had grown darker and Stefano felt sure he felt a spot of rain on his cheek. This was followed by a soft tattoo of rain-drops landing on the leaves and a low growl of thunder.

"We need to find shelter," he said.

Gemma was horrified to get a text message from Mark. The last she'd seen of him was when Stefano had rescued her. She hadn't expected to hear from him again.

Not sorry to hear you've finished with the moody Italian. Maybe we can give things another try. I know I behaved badly but I will make it up to you. Love Mark x

Gemma didn't hesitate to send a reply.

Mark - You are the last man on earth I want to be with. Please don't bother getting in touch again. Gemma. She pressed 'send', a feeling of anger spurring her on to keep going.

The rain was battering the windows and she pitied any customers who were on their way out in weather like this. The kitchen was dark as midnight and as she switched on the lights, there was a funny click and the power went off. That was all she needed!

As she turned, it was to see a dark figure in the doorway. All her fears of the darkness surfaced in a wave of hurt and anger. It was typical of Mark not to take no for an answer and come back to claim what he thought was his. Well, he could think again.

"Get away from me you bastard," she yelled, picking up the heavy marble rolling pin from the kitchen surround.

"Mi scusi," said a voice she didn't recognise. "I look for Sofia?"

At that moment the power came back on and Gemma found herself gazing at a startled looking man who was the same colouring as Stefano but who looked more like a modern-day pirate with his close-cropped beard.

"If you're who I think you are," she said, "you'd better put that apron on and see what you can find to cook for our customers. The café opens in less than two hours."

The rain had eased now, but water was streaming from the guttering and, looking outside the café door, Charworth High Street had a mini river running along each side of it.

To Gemma's surprise the man did as he was told.

"I'm sorry," she said, pouring him a glass of wine, "I don't know who you are."

He looked at her with a blank expression. "Cosa?"

His English clearly wasn't as good as Stefano's, even if he did understand food.

"What is your name?"

"Si. Capito. My name is Theo."

"Stefano's half-brother?"

"Cosa?"

"Fratello."

"Si."

Gemma was spared from any more of this monosyllabic conversation by the arrival of the camera-man from last night.

"I left some of my equipment here yesterday," he said. "It must've been all the excitement."

"I think Guy put it in the Club Room last night," said Gemma.

"Forget my head if it wasn't switched on," he said. "I'll just text Seamus to tell him I've got it. We're only just down the road in a little place not far from Stroud."

"I'll make you a coffee," said Gemma.

"Ooh, change of staff is it?" he asked, noticing Theo in the kitchen instead of Stefano. Gemma remembered how his freckled, boyish face had lit up last night when the drama started.

"Not exactly," she said. "Stefano's – busy – right now."

"Yeah, right," he said. "I've heard it called some things."

He looked out at the weather. "At least the rain's stopped. That storm really was something else."

His mobile bleeped with an incoming text.

"Seamus has told me to stick around for a while and film the aftermath. Is that OK with you?"

"Whatever." Gemma was determined that nobody was going to see how much she cared. Her chat with Hilda this morning had got her focused again on what she wanted. In a few weeks from now she'd be able to go off and follow her dreams of taking her writing more seriously. She tried, without success, to feel enthusiastic.

The camera-man had just finished sorting out his equipment when the sound of raised voices heralded the arrival of Stefano and Sofia. The first customers were arriving, shaking out their umbrellas and putting them in the stand by the door. They stared open-mouthed at the spectacle Stefano and Sofia created. They were both soaked to the skin. Sofia's hair hung in rat's tails and her mascara was streaked down her face. She'd broken one of her heels and her shoes were caked in mud.

The camera-man was having a field day filming her and she was doing her best to stop him.

"Bastardo !"

She looked even angrier when Theo emerged from the kitchen carrying baskets of bread for the tables. "What are you doing here?"

"I came looking for you to tell you something."

"What? I am not going back to that horrible little Trattoria. I am going to stay here with Stefano and be a model."

The customers in the café had given up any pretence of looking at their menus.

Several of them had been in the café last night and had clearly not taken to Sofia from the looks they were giving her.

"You can stay in England if you want to Sofia," said Stefano. "But you will not be with me."

She opened her mouth to protest, looking like a creature from the swamp in her wet and muddy clothes.

"I have been trying to tell you about the life I want. It is not the sort of life you want." He turned to the camera-man. "I want to say this on film," he said, "so that everyone will see I mean it."

Gemma stood looking at him and he wanted to sweep her into his arms but he was afraid of her telling him to go away. He didn't know what he'd do if she did. If he thought losing Sofia had broken his heart it wouldn't in any way compare with how he'd feel if Gemma said she wasn't interested.

"Get on with it, mate," shouted one of the diners.

Stefano smiled. He was soaking wet, his hair was plastered to his head and his trainers left wet marks across the wooden floor. He got down on one knee next to Gemma. The camera panned in close.

"Gemma, I want to tell you that I love you. That I didn't know until I saw you with someone else last night. Please tell me there is hope for us?"

Stefano got to his feet. His heart felt frozen in his chest. Gemma hadn't moved. Then with a yelp she was in his arms and he felt her warmth against him.

"That's what you call a kiss," shouted the vociferous diner and the whole restaurant burst into a round of applause.

There was the sound of footsteps going up the stairs and the slam of a door as Sofia headed for the bathroom.

Theo was doing a great job bringing in plates of risotto from the kitchen as Stefano and Gemma were reluctant to let go of each other.

"I've just sent Seamus a text to fill him in on what's been happening," said the camera-man. "He's really excited and will be along soon."

"Grazie," Stefano said to Theo as they shared a bottle of wine later.

"Non c'e problema!" He searched in the rucksack he brought with him. "This came for you from the lawyer just after you left. We didn't know where to send it." He handed Stefano an envelope. Inside was another envelope with Stefano's name on it in his grandfather's handwriting and something that felt like a key.

Seamus had duly turned up to join in the party. He was excited about Stefano's announcement to Gemma on camera. "I knew it from the start, dear," he told her.

He looked at Theo and Sofia staring stonily across at each other from opposite sides of the kitchen table.

"What's the story here?"

"Sofia thought she could get back with Stefano and be famous – you know, famous chef, famous model. She'd already left him for Theo, Stefano's step-brother. Theo followed her to England to tell her he'd found someone else ..."

"But she still wants to be a model – right?"

"Yes," said Gemma.

"As it happens," said Seamus, his face lighting up with enthusiasm, "we're running a series on wannabe models. I can put her in touch with the guy that's organising it. He's just left his wife and is looking for a significant other with very little brain. It sounds like they'll be perfect for each other."

Later, he took Sofia and Theo to a Travel Lodge ready for their separate journeys the next day. Theo was eager to get back to Sorrento to be with his new love and Sofia was bubbling with excitement at the thought of living in London and being a famous model.

That night, lying in each other's arms, Stefano read Gemma his grandfather's letter.

Dear Stefano

By the time you read this, I will be dead.

I want you to know that I have always loved you and valued the time we spent together.

By now you will know why I loved England so much – and one woman in particular. I am sorry she and I spent so little time together, but I hope we will find each other again in God's bluebell wood.

Your grandmother Maria was a wonderful woman and I loved her dearly, but not with the same intensity as Anna, the woman I found in England. I tried many times to rescue her from her loveless marriage and each time ended in failure. I was worried that she'd end up being incarcerated in the mental hospital she so feared, so I returned to Italy to prepare a place for her.

You already know the place! I took you there once when you were young. I was going to tell you the full story then, but I feared my secret was too much of a burden for one so young. I think from your reaction that you loved the place as much as I did, although I never lived there.

Anna was on her way to me when she died. She'd come to Italy before, many years ago and had seen me with Maria and Antonio. She was a woman of honour and went away rather than break up a union that appeared to be happy. I don't, in truth, know what I would have done if she'd come to me that day.

Fate robbed us yet again of the chance to spend our last days together. I know the terms of Anna's will and hope that you and Gemma find the happiness that we failed to do.

We will both be with you in spirit.

Much love.

Nonno Riccardo

Stefano kissed Gemma's tears away. She wrapped her arms around him and kissed him back.

"Don't cry," he whispered, stroking her skin under her dark blue top. "There is nothing to cry about."

He told her about the house he remembered as the Villa Limone and how it would be a wonderful place to write and paint and grow lemons.

His kisses grew deeper and without knowing how, their clothes were like sloughed skins on the floor and they were touching each other, until the heat of desire brought him on top of her and she pulled him, clasping her legs round him so that it felt like they were travelling together through a night sky sprinkled with stars that suddenly exploded into a rainbow of colours that gradually fell to earth as they collapsed against each other.

CHAPTER TWENTY ONE

The sun was setting over the Bay of Naples when they finally broke away from the party at Trattoria Andrea. Stefano and Gemma got into his battered white Fiat and headed out of the town towards the place where Stefano had walked with his grandfather so long ago.

He parked the car under an oleander tree and they got out. Gemma was still wearing her simple white wedding dress – the one she'd worn for the ceremony in England. On her head was a garland of orange blossom. Her face looked peaceful, like a Madonna, and he wanted to remember exactly what she looked like at this moment so that he could tell their grandchildren in years to come.

They stood wrapped in each other's arms looking across the water towards Capri. A small red boat was making its way towards Sorrento, churning a v-shaped wake behind it. The first stars were emerging forming a pathway of light across the darkening sky above Mount Vesuvius.

Earlier this morning, they'd visited the place where his grandfather was buried and scattered some of her great aunt's ashes onto the soil there. She'd planted some bluebell bulbs for both of them and read a special poem that had made them both cry.

"Nonno Riccardo would've loved you," he said turning her to face him.

She looked up at him and smiled – a world of love in her dove grey eyes.

"The Tree of Life is the perfect name for our new venture." she said, "Our visitors couldn't fail to be inspired by being in paradise." She paused. "It's funny, I used to hate pasta but I love it now. The way you make it."

"I am also devoted to your English scones – the way you make them." He turned her face to his. "Now is time for love, not food," he said as their lips met in a loving kiss. "It is time to go home."

Stefano took the large wrought iron key from his pocket and unlocked the gate to the place his grandfather had taken him so long ago.

They walked together up the shady path between gnarled olives. Patches of late sunlight dappled the path like gold leaf. This time Stefano had a key to the front door. He opened it and then scooped Gemma into his arms and carried her over the threshold. She felt warm and soft in his arms. Her garland fell off but he could still smell orange blossom on her skin.

"You can put me down now," she said as he pretended to drop her.

"I never want to let you go, you are more precious than all the lemons in Sorrento."

"High praise indeed," she said, wrapping her arms round his neck and drawing his lips towards hers.

He placed her down gently on the ground, holding her in his arms, her head fitting comfortably against his collar bone.

The scent of lemons and salt drifted through the open windows as they made love to the sound of the sea and a crescent moon rose over the Bay of Naples.

EPILOGUE
TWO YEARS LATER

Stefano and Gemma made a springtime journey back to Charworth for two special reasons. The first was the fairy-tale wedding of Dan and Laura in the little village church where their own wedding had taken place.

Dan had sold the chip shop, feeling that a new start was needed. He and Laura had been the joint owners of *The Inheritance* since Stefano and Gemma moved to Italy. Much to Gemma's delight they'd gone back to the original name of *The Cockatoo*.

When they were having some renovations done, the builders found some papers in a secret recess that gave more information about the man who'd originally built the place. There were also a few artefacts, including a pistol that could have belonged to a highwayman. These were now displayed in a glass case.

Laura, who loved stories as much as Gemma did, was all set to create a new theme to the café but that, as everyone said was another story. For now, the day was about her wedding to Dan.

"I hope you'll be as happy as we are," she said as they set off for the church.

Gemma was matron-of-honour and the other bridesmaid was Dan's sister Sarah. She and her baby Charlotte had lived at the café temporarily but now Sarah had moved to a cottage in Dalesbury and was training to be a florist. She blushed when Gemma asked her about her love life.

"There is somebody," she said. "He came into the florists to buy something for his mother's birthday."

"And then came back the next day to buy something for his aunt," said Dan to a chorus of happy laughter.

Best of all, it was Stefano and Gemma's baby daughter Stella's first visit to England and they were glad she'd experience it at the best time when the bluebells were in flower and the woodland was like an inland sea. On the day after the wedding, they'd gone to the woods for a picnic, carrying the baby in her carrycot and settling her beside the wishing tree. While Stella slept, they drank wine and made love among the bluebells, in memory of Riccardo and Anna.

If you enjoyed *Apple Orchard, Lemon Grove*, please share your thoughts on Amazon by leaving a review.

For more free and discounted eBooks every week, sign up to our newsletter.

Follow us on Twitter and Instagram.

Printed in Poland
by Amazon Fulfillment
Poland Sp. z o.o., Wrocław